P9-CNH-700

PRAISE FOR *CHOOSE YOUR OWN MISERY: THE OFFICE*

"In their rip-roaringly funny book, *Choose Your Own Misery: The Office*, the two *Onion* alums make a dark and decidedly adult play on beloved childhood "choose your own adventure" novels …[*Choose Your Own Misery*] may be the funniest book released this year."—**Newsweek**

"*Choose Your Own Misery: The Office* is a bittersweet, brutal, and frequently hilarious twist on the childhood classics." —**Nerdist.com**

"[F]or former Choose Your Own Adventure fans and devotees of dark, dark humor." —**Publishers Weekly**

"[*Choose Your Own Misery: The Office*] is one of the few books I've made sure to bring with me to show others when going out…even though filled with miserable and sometimes darker choices, [it] is definitely one of the funniest books I've read lately." —**Techaeris**

"Hell, the only reason for going to work is to goof-off reading Jilly Gagnon's and Mike MacDonald's book, *Choose Your Own Misery: The Office*!" —**E. Jean Carroll, former writer for** *SNL*

"*Choose Your Own Misery: The Office* [is] the most addictive, clever, and honestly hilarious decision tree you've ever read." —**Zack Bornstein, segment director at** *Jimmy Kimmel Live!*

"Sorry, I've been spending every waking hour lost in your maddening madcap narrative labyrinth. I'll try to send a blurb for the book by the deadline!" —**Jamie Brew, Associate Editor at Clickhole**

"It's time for you to choose your own miserable adventure, just like you do every day of your miserable life, but now in hilarious book form!" —**Nate Dern, Head Writer for Funny or Die**

"Oh, how I laughed at this droll little book. Then, slowly but irreversibly, it filled me up with dread." —**Jesse Andrews,** *New York Times* **bestselling author of** *Me and Earl and the Dying Girl*

"Hilarious...perhaps my former career in office work drudgery wouldn't have been so horrible (and apparently scarring) had Mike MacDonald and Jilly Gagnon's humor/guide book, *Choose Your Own Misery: The Office* been available to me during those long days in a cubicle where I prayed for death." —**Forces of Geek**

"If you enjoyed the irreverent film *Office Space* or can relate to the weird situations created by the modern day office environment, then you'll definitely enjoy this book. It's a R-rated, first-person journey of tough decisions that will make you ponder if the well-being of your job is truly worth having to deal with those weird coworkers." —**Rediscover the 80s**

"Hilariously written by a duo of talented authors, *Choose Your Own Misery: The Office* will make anyone who's having a hard day at work feel better about his or her job. Or, if you don't work in an office, you'll get a behind-the-scenes look at what could go horribly wrong if you did have to go to an office after a hangover! Such a fun read— you can literally start over and over to choose your own misery if you don't wanna go where it's taking you! Note: It's a bit raunchy but hilariously so! Read/Laugh at your own risk! Or...go to a freaking job you hate! LOL!" —**SE Reviews and Reads**

"[*Choose Your Own Misery:*] *The Office* cleverly puts a sadly sarcastic, grown-up spin on what was always a childish diversion." —**Beauty in Ruins**

"The best part about this book is the humor. As I was reading this book I found myself laughing several times and getting sideways looks from the people around me...A quick and easy read through many different adventures, *Choose Your Own Misery: The Office* would make a fantastic gift for someone you know who's running the rat race, or maybe bring it to that office holiday party (as long as your coworkers have a sense of humor)." —**Project Nerd**

CHOOSE YOUR
OWN MISERY

THE
HOLIDAYS

BY MIKE MACDONALD & JILLY GAGNON

DIVERSIONBOOKS

Diversion Books
A Division of Diversion Publishing Corp.
443 Park Avenue South, Suite 1008
New York, New York 10016
www.DiversionBooks.com

Copyright © 2016 by Mike MacDonald & Jilly Gagnon
All rights reserved, including the right to reproduce this book or portions thereof
in any form whatsoever.

This is a work of fiction. Names, characters, places and incidents either are the
product of the author's imagination or are used fictitiously. Any resemblance to
actual persons, living or dead, events or locales is entirely coincidental.

This book is a parody. It was not authorized by Chooseco, the publisher of
Choose Your Own Adventure. Choose Your Own Adventure is a registered
trademark of Chooseco LLC.

For more information, email info@diversionbooks.com

First Diversion Books edition November 2016.
Print ISBN: 978-1-68230-319-1
eBook ISBN: 978-1-68230-318-4

To eggnog,
a shining beacon of creamy joy in an
otherwise dark and miserable season.

WARNING!!!!

Do not read this book straight through from beginning to end! These pages contain too many different forms of misery for any one person to experience end to end. And it will feel like all your choices are meaningless if you do it that way, since they'll lead, inexorably, to existential absurdity, and while that's basically true of both life and this book, that's a pretty grim way to read.

The shit that happens to you in this tome of endless, unavoidable misery is still your choice, on some fundamentally meaningless level. You are responsible because you choose, and frankly, you're too old to keep blaming how things turned out on your parents. After you make your choice, live with your shit. The rest of us have to.

Think carefully before you make a move...or don't. Frankly, it won't make much of a difference. None of what we do makes much of a difference. We're all just programmed to die.

"THAT'LL BE $18.37," THE CASHIER SAYS, SNAPPING HER GUM AND looking supremely bored.

Jesus, all you ordered was a Chicken Ranch-a-Palooza and a soda. And the salad the cashier is passing across the counter looks like something reduced-to-sell. Is there anything worse than airport food? Besides every other part of the airport, that is?

But you're not going to let that bring you down. Not when you're about to head off to the best Christmas ever.

Your older brother's family is with his wife's parents in Seattle, your sister and her pretentious bore of a husband insisted on having "Christmas at home" for the kids, and you haven't been dating your girlfriend Lindsi long enough to be expected to attend her family's holidays. Since none of you will be in the same city, your parents decided they'd take a "freedom cruise," the title of which made their offer—that you could join "if you insist"—feel even more halfhearted. They were probably as excited as you were when you said no.

But you have a better plan. A plan that totally avoids the special hell that is the holiday season. You and your Jewish friend from college are heading off to an all-inclusive, child-free, tropical resort vacation.

You weren't sure he'd be okay with missing Hanukkah, but he reminded you it happened weeks ago, and that "none of us actually give a fuck about Hanukkah. You know that, right?"

Totally. You know Jewish stuff.

You wander toward the gate, digging your fingers into your painful lower back. A few days of daiquiris and white sand are gonna fix that right up.

You glance at the TV monitors. A reporter is being blown sideways by gale-force winds, sheets of rain whipping her face. Fallen palm trees litter the sand behind her.

"Tropical Storm Menudo made landfall last night, and while no deaths have been reported yet, the infrastructure in this developing nation was no match for its hundred-mile-per-hour winds..."

A map comes up, showing the path of Menudo.

It's centered on your island. Your magical, avoid-Christmas-for-once island.

You look over at the gate, starting to panic.

It's okay; the screen says the flight is still set to board in fifteen...

CANCELED.

Fuck.

You text your college friend but he isn't responding. Frustrated and unsure what else to do, you call your girlfriend, Lindsi.

"Ohmygod, *hey*, sweetie! Merry Christmas! Are you on a beach yet?"

"No, actually, I'm still at the airport." The line in front of your gate is already past the Hudson News. Double fuck. "They just canceled my flight. Apparently that tropical storm landed... on the island."

"Oh NO! That's terrible."

Lindsi completely gets you. Things are still pretty new, but she seems like a keeper.

"You should come here. My family would be thrilled to have you!"

You hear her whispering excitedly with her mother about you coming for the holidays.

Okay, "completely" might have been too strong a word.

If you want to take Lindsi up on the offer of a family Christmas,
turn to page 3.
If you're still holding out hope that you can find your way onto some *beach,*
turn to page 5.

Still, what choice do you have? If Menudo made landfall, there's no way you'll be getting to paradise before your vacation time runs out. And the prospect of spending Christmas alone in your apartment is about as appealing as the salad you're holding.

"Wow, what a great idea," you say, trying to force some enthusiasm into your voice. "It'll be a great chance to get to know your family."

Lindsi lets out a squeaky squeal, like a fairy's fart, and starts talking rapidly to someone on her end. You can't hear much, but the words "Told you he was marriage material" drive a shard of ice into your heart.

She better not expect a drawer at your place when you get back.

"I should go," you say. If you stay on this call longer, you might change your mind, and it sucks to break up with someone in winter. The bed gets so cold. "I want to get a jump at the rental car counters."

"Ohmygod, totally," she says. "I can't wait to see you, sweetie-kins! Drive safe, okay? Love you!"

"Mmmmm," you mumble before hanging up. *Sweetie-kins? Love?* In mere minutes this has gone from "best Christmas ever" to a horror movie.

Too late now, though. You head to the rental car counter and get in line. An hour later, you make it to the front. The man standing there looks like some reality competition reject, with his nerd-chic glasses, straw fedora, and "ironic" T-shirt.

"Hi there," you say in your cheeriest holiday voice. Airport employees are probably used to being shat on by customers; this will definitely get you better treatment.

"Hi." He rolls his eyes extravagantly.

So much for that idea.

"I wanted to rent a car?"

"We have compacts and conversion vans left," he says, typing in a way that's somehow simultaneously bored and judgy.

"Which is cheaper?"

"Our smallest vehicle will run you $255 a day plus gas, and..."

Oh, Jesus.

"Okay, umm, I'll get back to you."

You head to the next counter and wait in line for another forty-five minutes.

"You can do a one-door for as low as $325 a day, without insurance or gas."

Fuck.

The woman at the next counter looks nice, though. Her face is doughy in a favorite-aunt kind of way, and she's wearing a cat sweater. Surely she won't try to gouge you.

"Oh, I'm sorry there, hon, that nice gentleman in front of you just rented our very last vehicle! But I can offer shuttle service back to terminal C, dontcha know."

If you want to go back to the first rental car counter and bite the exorbitantly expensive bullet, turn to page 6.

If you'd rather take your chances at the bus depot, turn to page 8.

"THAT'S REALLY KIND OF YOU TO INVITE ME…" How can you get out of this with the least effort? "But I don't want to impose."

You hear whispers in the background: "*Will we get to meet him?*"

"Don't be silly, silly-billy!"

You cringe.

"I know, I know, but I should catch up on work while the office…is quiet." Jesus, even a girlfriend as new as Lindsi will see through that bullshit excuse.

For a second it's silent.

"Um, you still there?" you ask.

"Yup."

"Cool. I thought the call dropped."

"Nope."

"Anyhow, thanks again. I appreciate the offer. I just have so much to do. Here."

"K." You hear a voice say, "*Wait, really?*"

"Well…awesome. Cool. Talk soon."

You hang up. That went well. Right?

On the bright side, you have the entire holiday to yourself. You can do anything you want. Anything at all.

Alone.

If you want to be "wild" and try to rebook your flight to somewhere else, turn to page 10.

If you want to call your sister, who still lives in your hometown, and see if you can crash her Christmas, turn to page 11.

6

YOU CAN'T PUT A PRICE ON NOT SPENDING HOURS ON A BUS. AT LEAST you got a Christmas bonus...which will go entirely toward this rental.

You finally make it back to the first counter. The man there sneers in...recognition?

"That's going to be $315 a day, plus a $200 security deposit, and you'll have to sign here to indicate you'll be bringing it back with a full tank."

"Wait, I thought you said it was $255 a day."

He wrinkles his nose in disdain. Like he can afford that on a Speedy Rentals paycheck. Wait, what do they pay? Is it more than your office?

"That was for our sub-sub-compact. We ran out of that model."

You splutter.

"I can show you the vehicle if it will help you decide."

"What about the other customers?"

He shrugs and walks through a side door. You follow.

The car he shows you is so small you're not sure it's legal on highways. Inside, the fabrics are stained, there's a multicolored array of crumbs on every surface, and a strange smell lingers, like old cheese and queefs.

"We can clean it for $75," the counter attendant sighs.

"Seriously? Is that legal?"

"It's the last car on the lot. I could get a kidney for it if I asked." You frown. Whose mind goes right to organ harvesting? "So, you know. Take it or leave it."

You take it.

With traffic, it takes you an hour to reach the interstate. You've barely made it out of town when you realize the tank is empty.

Awesome.

At least gassing up will give you a chance to move around. The driver's seat is shaped in a way that's making your back shoot lightning-like pain pulses to all your limbs. You can't feel your left foot anymore. But it's only another...128 miles, according to the

GPS. In traffic, that won't take more than…Jesus, you don't even want to think about that.

You pull off at the next exit.

"Excuse me, sir," someone whispers in your ear as you're pumping gas. What the fuck? You turn to see a man out of a fifties sitcom, hair perfectly parted, slight paunch filling out his patterned sweater vest, smile eerily wide.

You look around, hoping he's talking to anyone else, but you're the only person there. Where'd this guy come from? Also, he's inches away from your face.

"Ummm, yes?"

"Can I ask where you're headed?"

You can't think of a lie fast enough.

"Little Hampshireton," you say.

"It's a Christmas miracle!" He looks up at the gas station roof, smile growing wider. You must have to spend years developing the facial muscles for that. Or just have schizophrenia. "That's exactly where I'm headed, and my vehicle has unfortunately broken down. Would you be willing to convey me as far as the outskirts of town? I'd be ever so appreciative."

Bah, humbug! You don't have time for hitchhikers! Turn to page 12.
Earn yourself some Christmas karma and help this weirdo out on page 14.

THERE'S NO WAY YOU'RE GOING TO DROP A MONTH'S RENT ON A CAR rental. You head outside to catch the shuttle to the Greyhound station. It'll take longer, sure, but how bad can it be?

Oh, it can be very, *very* bad.

You've never been to the station before, so you're shocked at how gray everything is, like they coated the entire place in a fine layer of sticky-dust in order to keep the atmosphere on-brand.

You examine the torn, fading schedule taped to a wall near the main entrance. From what you can tell, there's an express bus that goes directly to Greater Bentneck, Little Hampshireton's more cosmopolitan neighbor. Surely someone can pick you up there.

You head to the ticket window. The plastic is so dingy with fingerprints you can't actually tell if anyone's inside. After a few minutes you call out.

"Hello? Can I buy a ticket?"

You hear a stirring from deep within the bowels of the bus station. Several minutes later, a wet, hacking cough announces a mystery Greyhound worker's presence.

"Can I help you?" It sounds like something from under a rock. You're not even sure if it's a man or a woman.

"Yes…please. I'd like a ticket for the Greater Bentneck express?"

"That bus left two minutes ago."

God DAMMIT. You should've known that dough-faced rental car employee was a waste of fucking time.

"Okay, well, I'm trying to get to Little Hampshireton. Is there another option?"

"Little Hampshireton?" The employee hacks thoughtfully. "If you take the 232 into Dinkeltown, you can pick up the Farminghamlet express until Wiggleswam, then grab the Ruralton local to Little Hampshireton."

It sounds complicated. Though painfully charming.

"How long would that take?"

"Oh, I'd say it'll run…about twenty, twenty-two hours? Assuming you catch the 9:02." You look over at the clock. It's only 6:38.

"Let me make a couple calls."

You're starving, and you can't decide which misery would hurt more—losing a day of your life to a bus schedule out of *Deliverance* or taking out a new loan to finance a rental car—until you eat.

You head to the vending machine outside.

The only options are a single box of spearmint Tic-Tacs and five rows of Combos. You buy two of each flavor. It's amazing how accurately cracker filling can replicate "omelet" flavors.

A car pulls into the depot as you're eating the second bag. It slows down, coming to a stop across from you. The window lowers, and a too-round, aggressively smiling man pops out. His hair is so smooth it looks like a Mr. Potato Head attachment.

"Hello, friend!" he says, smiling wider. How can cheeks move that way? "You look like you could use a ride. Where you headed?"

"Uh, Little Hampshireton?" You're too confused by that immobile grin to lie.

"What a coincidence. I'm headed to Little Hampshireton myself. Can I give you a lift?"

Hell no, that's how skin suits get started. You'll stick with the bus.
Turn to page 15.
What's so wrong with being extremely, painfully happy and offering rides to total strangers? Hop in! Turn to page 16.

10

It takes an eternity to make it to the harried agent manning your gate. She doesn't even look up at you.

"Um, hello?"

"What do you want?" she asks flatly.

"I was wondering about switching my flight."

She rolls her eyes. Jesus, it's not *that* strange of a request. What have all these other people been asking for, vouchers to the BeerXPress in the terminal?

"Where do you wanna go?"

You glance over at the board.

Vegas? Ugh.

Palm Springs? Meh.

Jamaica? Hmmmmm.

Part of you remembers reading somewhere that Jamaica is a mixed bag at best, but it would so perfectly match what you've already packed. Plus, you don't know anyone who's actually gone there; you'd have a social-media-worthy travel story.

The agent taps her fingers on the desk impatiently.

"Maybe, um, Jamaica?"

"The flight leaves in two hours and lands at Norman Manley Airport in Kingston."

Ohhh, *Kingston*. Sounds fancy.

If you want to just go for it and fly to Jamaica, turn to page 18.
If you want to get a flight voucher and head home for a "restful" Christmas, turn to page 19.

YOU CALL YOUR SISTER. YOU'RE NOT EXACTLY THRILLED ABOUT spending the holidays with her, but what are you going to do instead, sit home alone? She picks up, voice irritable. You decide to cut right to the chase.

"I was thinking of coming to your place for Christmas."

A long pause follows.

"Fine. We'll see you when you arrive."

She hangs up. Apparently she's as enthused about this as you are.

At least she still lives in your hometown. If she's not excited to see you, there will be plenty of other people who will be.

Like your nephews. They must be at least what…three and six by now? They'll be thrilled you're coming. You're the "cool" uncle.

You grab a rental car at the airport and head back to your place to throw a few things inside. Luckily, your hometown isn't far.

A few hours later, you pull into a parking spot in the town center to check your sister's address. Man, was this place always so quaint?

It's getting late. If all of the stores haven't closed yet, they will soon. You should probably bring *something* to your sister's, even though—or rather, because—she was bitchy on the phone.

If you want to grab toys for your nephews, turn to page 20.
If you want to go to the specialty foods store and pick something out for your sister, turn to page 22.

"OH, YEAH, I'D, UH, LOVE TO HELP, BUT I ACTUALLY HAVE TO MAKE some stops along the way…"

"That's all right with me!" His smile is so wide now you're seeing parts of the human mouth you've never actually seen. "I love learning about the things other people find interesting or necessary to complete."

What? Are there any mental institutions around these parts? With lax security?

"I also think I'm coming down with something." You cough feebly.

"Mother always told me my constitution was so strong I made the pigs healthier!" He laughs cheerily, his mouth opening like a terrifyingly bland theater mask.

"And I have personal space issues." Thank god, the tank is finally full. You put the nozzle back. "I'm sorry, I just can't help you tonight."

"Oh. Well…okay," he says, his smile dimming slightly. "I'm sure another kind individual on his or her way to Little Hampshireton will pull off at this specific gas station soon."

"Definitely." You avoid eye contact as you walk around the vehicle, but you can feel him staring, grin still firmly in place, eyes lifeless and glassy. That stare follows you for miles down the highway. Should you have taken him? No, nobody picks up hitchhikers anymore. *Especially* when they look and act like youth pastors. Those are always the ones that carry shivs.

As you pull off at the Little Hampshireton exit, you realize you don't have anything to bring the family, not even a bottle of wine. You hadn't planned on celebrating Christmas, after all, especially not with strangers.

Your phone died a few miles back. You frantically memorized the turns (exit 247, left, fourteen winding miles on Old Road, right on Big Elm Parkway/New Tree Road) just before it shut off, but you have no idea what's nearby. Plus, even if you could find something, you might never manage to get from there to Lindsi's parents'.

Still, they've invited you into their home with almost no warning. Surely you should bring *something*?

At the bottom of the exit you see a McDonald's, a fertilizer store that's closed, and a Git 'er Gassed station with an attached gift shop.

If you want to just show up empty-handed, turn to page 23.
If you want to try to cobble together a gas station gift platter, turn to page 25.

YOU DON'T WANT TO—HE'LL PROBABLY TRY TO CONVERT YOU TO some religion that involves spaceships—but it *is* Christmas, and you could use the karma.

"Sure." You force a smile. It can't be half as wide as his. "Hop in."

He grabs a huge, lumpy duffel, face-stretching grin never faltering, and gets into the front seat, stuffing the bag at his feet.

Huh. What's that shiny, metallic-looking object poking out at the corner?

It's almost certainly not a knife. Stop worrying about the hitchhiker's knife. This isn't a horror movie, right?

Though they always say that kind of thing in horror movies…

You clear your throat.

"So what's taking you to Little Hampshireton?"

"Oh, all kinds of things. Some people I need to see." He giggles, the sound girlishly high.

You stare at the bag. It's not even a duffel, just a huge drawstring sack. Who carries one of those? Is he a serial murderer with a Christmas fetish?

"What happened to your car? Are you just leaving it there?"

"I trust the kindness of strangers."

"Has that ever come around to bite you in the…" It seems weird to say "ass" to this man, like saying it to a psychotic child, or a senile grandmother. "Behind?"

"Sometimes, I suppose. But I don't let it bother me. What goes around comes around." He turns to you, head tilted slightly to one side, smile eerie in the semidarkness of the car.

Is this a veiled reference to murdering anyone who wrongs him?

"So what's in the bag?" You force a laugh. It comes out croaky.

"Maybe something for you…if you're nice."

The sound of his laugh echoes around the tiny vehicle. You feel your heart beating in your throat. You've always assumed you'd die violently…is this it?

If you want to try to force him out of the car somehow, turn to page 27.
If you need to settle the fuck down; it's all in your head, turn to page 29.

"THANKS," YOU SAY, BACKING A FEW STEPS CLOSER TO THE VENDING machines, "but I already have a ticket."

"All right, then! You have a beautiful day!" The man drives off into the night, grinning maniacally.

Oh yeah, you definitely made the smart call.

You head back to the depot, buy a ticket, and wait until the bus finally shows up.

The moment you board, your ears are assaulted by the piercing shrieks of an infant. You take a seat as far away from the noise as possible, but unfortunately it's in front of a six-year-old with a snub nose and grubby hands, who's clearly under the impression that your seat is a piñata. Kids are such assholes.

A homeless-smelling man is sprawled across an entire row toward the center, so you move to a sagging row up front. A spring—or something else you don't want to consider—pokes your back. You're just about to move again when an old lady with ear hair takes the last safe row. Fucking olds.

A sallow, overweight man in a strained uniform waddles on and turns to face the passengers. In a supremely bored voice he starts droning at you.

"This Dinkeltown-bound bus, with continuing service on the Farminghamlet express line, will be departing in five minutes. Please note that the restroom on this bus is out of order. Should you anticipate needing a restroom, large coffee cans can be purchased inside the bus depot for $12.99 each."

You laugh—good one, bus guy. He stares at you, obviously confused. Fuck, is he serious?

"Also, route delays are expected due to traffic. Please enjoy the ride."

He wheeze-sighs, sags into his seat, and starts doing a word search.

Can you really do this?

Can you afford not to?

If you want to go back to the rental car counter, turn to page 31.
If you want to tough it out on the bus, turn to page 32.

He's definitely too happy, like someone who's just converted to Mormonism, but still, he *will* get you to Little Hampshireton fast and free.

"Sure! So nice of you to offer." You open the back door to stick your duffel inside. A huge, almost man-sized bag is taking up the entire seat. The end is open; a thick rope dribbles out. You also see something shiny, like black patent leather.

Are Mormons really into S&M?

Whatever, none of your business. You hop up front, wedge your duffel at your feet, and you head off.

After a few minutes, the man turns the radio to a station playing "all Celine Dion's greatest Christmas hits!" Of course.

An announcer with a voice like a dental hygienist on Valium comes on. "Remember, folks, we're nearing the end of our Twelve Days of Christmas Clues Scavenger Hunt! Whoever follows the clues to our secret location will find $50,000! Every day we make it easier to unravel this Christmas cash mystery!"

She then starts listing the clues they've revealed so far, vague stuff like "Christmas is all about *bridging* differences and *covering* over problems."

"I know where it is."

"Excuse me?" You turn to the man, who's smiling as hard as ever at the windshield. Doesn't that hurt his face?

"The Christmas cash. I know this area like the back of my hand—grew up hunting around here with my Pip-Pop. If we turn off at the county road five miles up, then down a few gravel back roads, then take a little walk through the woods, I'm sure we'll find it."

"Oh. Sounds…isolated."

"It is. No one around for miles!" He laughs manically. "That's why no one's found it yet. But if we do, we can split it down the middle. Whaddya say?"

His smile is terrifying in the shadows of the car, garish and toothy and wet. What was that rope in the back really for? What kind of man wants to take a stranger deep into the woods?

"What would you even do with that money?" you say, trying not to let your fear into your voice.

"Give it to the cancer kids at the hospital, of course."

No one's that altruistic. It's certain now: this guy is definitely planning to rape and/or murder you.

"I can tell you're up for an adventure," he says, pulling over to the side of the road. "Let me just get my GPS out so we don't miss a turn in the dark."

He leans into the backseat. You see a flash of metal. Could it be a knife?

If you want to get out and run, turn to page 33.
If you want to hit him over the head first, so he can't follow you,
turn to page 34.

18

YOU LAND IN KINGSTON.

The airport seems…dingy.

There's a fleet of hotel representatives handing out cocktails in coconuts with comically long straws to the booked vacationers. You seem to be the only one who doesn't get to partake.

Oh well. You head to the tourism counter. A solitary employee is leaning on his elbow, staring at the coconuts longingly.

"Hey…mon?" Whoa, nope. Definitely no. You're not even close to pulling that off. "I'd like to book a hotel."

"Sandals Royal Plantation?"

You can't understand his accent, but you think you heard the word plantation? Is that right? It feels too racist to ask.

He hands you a thick brochure. Oh, it *was* plantation. Look at you, already understanding the locals.

Whoa, though, that "listed prices" section. That must be more than your entire net worth, even if you factor in your rare Pokémon card collection.

"What else do you have?"

"Not much."

"Really? Everything else is booked?"

He strokes his chin thoughtfully.

"Well there's always 'On the Beach.' It's for…locals."

He rummages around for several minutes before producing another brochure. Actually, it's more like a piece of cheap copier paper with what looks like…is that a drop of human blood in the corner? That can't be right. It must be barbeque sauce. Jamaica must be known for barbeque.

"Ten dollars a night?" You have to have read that wrong.

"Yeah."

That's worryingly cheap.

If you want the cheap "local" place, turn to page 35.
If you want to book the extremely expensive resort, turn to page 37.

KINGSTON, JAMAICA.

It sounds wonderful...

But not very practical. You don't even know whether you can drink the water in Kingston. Getting a flight voucher makes much more sense.

The bus home is almost entirely empty. A man wearing a Santa suit is passed out nearby, smelling like booze and sweat. Even though his sprawling, squelching body is taking up three seats, nobody is hassling him. For the first time since you've moved here, no one seems to be around to care.

You stare out the window: the streets are empty, the snow is gray and slushy, and by now most of the stores are closed.

You arrive home to what seems like a completely empty apartment building. You can't be the only one still here, can you?

"Hello?"

Your voice echoes off the walls: "Helloooooooooo."

You ate all of your perishables before leaving for the airport, so it's either the family-sized pack of Combos in the pantry or take-out. Then again, isn't Debby, your friend from a couple jobs ago, also home alone?

Sure, she can be pretty annoying even at the best of times: she has a terrible snort when she laughs, she wears velour skirts a size too small, and she constantly drones on about presidential history.

But she could save you from a whole lot of loneliness.

If you want to order Chinese food and endlessly stream videos on your laptop, turn to page 39.
If you want to give Debby a ring, turn to page 40.

You've entered the fourth circle of hell: the toy store, two days before Christmas.

There are so many people you're unable to see your own feet.

You start scanning the aisles, hoping something good will jump out at you.

You spot an Avengers costume for a five-to-seven-year-old. That'll fit Harrison, your older nephew, perfectly!

What about for little Otto? You need something easy for a kid that young to manage, but not one of those boring reclaimed-wood puzzles.

At the end of an aisle, you see an unattended shopping cart with two Super Soakers in it.

It's probably the cart the stock boys use to restock the shelves, right?

Sure, that's plausible. You grab one and head to the checkout.

• • •

DING-DONG.

"Merry Christmas!" you say, stepping inside your sister Lauren's house, unwrapped presents in hand.

"You made it." She checks her watch, sighing. "Come in. Be sure to take your boots off on the mat."

You do as you're told.

"Where can I put these bad boys?" you ask, proudly displaying the toys.

"That costume is too small for Harrison—you know he's nine, right? And it's too big for Otto. And you'll have to destroy the gun…"

"Destroy?"

"We have a strict no-guns policy in this house."

"This isn't a gun, it's a toy. A *water* toy…"

"Either way, it's plastic. We also have a very strict no-plastics policy in this house."

"No plastics?"

"That's what I said, didn't I?"

If you want to go back and exchange the gifts, turn to page 42.
If you want to tell your sister these gifts were for the boys to give to Toys for Tots, so they can learn the true meaning of Christmas, turn to page 44.

22

You weave between the idling SUVs in the specialty foods store parking lot until you find a space. You walk in, trying to imagine what your sister and her husband, Gregory, would like. He's a Europhile, right?

You grab some truffle oil, a wheel of brie, foie gras, and some crackers.

How much will this cost? Actually, forget that, they'll *love* it.

You head over to the drinks.

You pick out a bottle of expensive bourbon and some tequila, for an inside joke. Your sister will remember when you guys infused that watermelon on spring break, right?

Yeah. It will be hilarious.

"That will be $250," says the cashier.

Oof. But it's family. You pull out your card.

• • •

DING-DONG.

"Merry Christmas!" you say, stepping into your sister Lauren's house, tequila in hand.

"What time is it?" She checks her watch, yawning.

"Tequila-infused watermelon, round two?"

"What? What are you talking about?" She looks annoyed. "Just…take your boots off on the mat."

You do as you're told, then proudly display your groceries.

"Where can I put all this?"

She examines the food closely.

"Well, we don't eat dairy. Or drink *liquor.*"

"Oh…"

"And we cut out carbs five years ago. You knew that, right? As for the liver, maybe the freezer?" She scrunches up her nose.

"The freezer?"

"Did I stutter?"

Jesus, when did Lauren become such a bitch?

If you want to tell your sister she's being rude, turn to page 45.
Oh man, already this isn't worth it. If you want to tell her you're going to a hotel, turn to page 46.

You know what? They'll understand. They were so welcoming, and they know your holiday plans fell through mere hours ago. Better to show up with a big smile on your face than some half-assed assortment of every flavor of Combos.

A half hour later, you pull up to the house. It's just like Lindsi described: the one with Christmas sweaters on all the bushes. How they persuaded bushes to grow into human shapes is beyond you.

You tap on the door softly, assuming only Lindsi will be up, but the woman who opens it is unfamiliar. No, that's not true; you can see Lindsi looking like this in another thirty years. This woman has the same wide brown eyes, and the same rosebud mouth, but it's much more pinched. She's also at least fifty pounds heavier, with short, carefully permed hair, a Christmas sweater on which a cat is wearing its own Christmas sweater, and librarian glasses that were never, under any circumstances, "sexy."

"You can call me Mom," she says.

It makes that one late-night booty call—when you and Lindsi had just started dating and she hadn't told you her mom was visiting for the weekend—even more awkward to recall.

"I made it!" you say, smiling broadly. Maybe if you're cheery enough, her memory of that conversation will just disappear.

"So glad to see that; there are so many *drunks* on the road this time of year." Mom stares at you, eyes narrowed. Fuck, she totally remembers the call. Well, don't pick up your daughter's cell if you don't want to hear about ass-play.

"I see you didn't have time to pick anything up for the house. But that's all right." Mom purses her lips in something approximating a smile. "You were probably distracted."

"Mmm." You knew you should have stopped at that gas station.

You head inside, awkwardly carrying your bag. A man with a white beard, smiling eyes, and the exact amount of belly that makes you trust him emerges. This must be Lindsi's father. God, you hope Mom didn't tell him about that phone call.

"I'm Dad! Lindsi will be right down," he says, smiling warmly.

"She's just making herself *decent*."

"I know it's late, and I don't want to keep you up," you say. "If you just point me toward Lindsi's room, I'll be off to bed."

Mom and Dad stare at you, eyes wide with horror. Dad lets out a little "humph," his face dangerously red. Jesus, is he going to have a heart attack? You only half-remember CPR.

"We, ahem"—Mom clears her throat delicately—"we thought you'd share with cousin Jimmy. Since you're still... *unmarried*." She can't seem to help wrinkling her nose. Dad is just staring at you, obviously confused and upset. Awesome. "Though if you'd prefer more privacy, there's a couch in the basement. I'll warn you, the dog likes to sleep down there."

If you want to share with cousin Jimmy, turn to page 47.
If you want to slink off to the basement, turn to page 49.

It's the thought that counts.

You swing into the gas station and pick up the classiest things you can find: a package of those melty peppermints, four different varieties of pocket pie, and a sleeve of gingersnaps. You spring for a roll of colored saran wrap and a package of Santa-themed paper plates and make a little arrangement. Unwrapped, the food looks kinda nice, right?

It's the thought that counts.

A half hour later, you arrive. It's just like Lindsi described: the one with Christmas sweaters on all the bushes. How they persuaded bushes to grow into human shapes is beyond you.

You tap on the door softly, assuming only Lindsi will be up, but the woman who opens it is unfamiliar. No, that's not true; you can see Lindsi looking like this in another thirty years. This woman has the same wide brown eyes, and the same rosebud mouth, but on the doughy, unfashionable, late-middle-aged canvas of a first-grade art teacher.

"You can call me Mom," she says.

It makes that one late-night booty call—when you and Lindsi had just started dating and she hadn't told you her mom was visiting for the weekend—even more awkward to recall.

"I made it!" you say, smiling broadly. Maybe if you're cheery enough, her memory of that conversation will just disappear.

"So glad to see that; there are so many *drunks* on the road this time of year." Mom stares at you, eyes narrowed. Fuck, she totally remembers the call. Well, don't pick up your daughter's cell if you don't want to hear about free moustache rides.

"Oh, and you brought…this." Mom takes the plate, pursing her lips in something approximating a smile. "What a…gesture."

That's another $32.98 down the drain.

You head inside, awkwardly carrying your bag. A man with a white beard, smiling eyes, and the exact amount of belly that makes you trust him emerges. This must be Lindsi's father. God, you hope Mom didn't tell him about that phone call.

"I'm Dad. Lindsi will be right down," he says, smiling warmly.

"She's just making herself *decent.*"

"I know it's late, and I don't want to keep you up," you say. "If you just point me toward Lindsi's room, I'll be off to bed."

Mom and Dad stare at you, eyes wide with horror. Dad lets out a little "humph," his face dangerously red. Jesus, is he going to have a heart attack? You only half-remember CPR.

"We, ahem," Mom clears her throat delicately, "we thought you'd share with cousin Jimmy. Since you're still...*unmarried.*" She can't help wrinkling her nose. Dad is just staring, obviously confused and upset. Awesome. "Though if you'd prefer more privacy, there's a couch in the basement. I'll warn you, though, the dog likes to sleep down there."

If you want to share with cousin Jimmy, turn to page 47.
If you want to slink off to the basement, turn to page 49.

No, you won't go gently!

Luckily, you're not so far down the road that you've run out of options.

"Do you hear that?" You cock your head to one side thoughtfully. Man, you should have been an actor.

"Hear what?"

"That flapping. I think a tire might be flat."

"I don't hear anything."

"Better safe than sorry, right?" You pull over at the next intersection. "Would you mind grabbing the flashlight out of the trunk? I'll pop it for you."

"Okay." The hitchhiker's smile falters, but he opens the door and steps outside.

You wait until he's halfway down the car, lean over the console, and throw his bag—Jesus, is it heavy—onto the ground at the side of the road. Can't be found with the evidence. You hear him shout, "Wait, what are you..."

But you don't hear the rest, because you're speeding away, door flapping in the wind.

You wait until you're at least five miles down the road to pull over and close it. That was a close call. Thanks to your quick thinking, though, you've managed to keep yourself from getting murdered by that freak.

You make it the rest of the way to Lindsi's parents' without incident.

You head inside, awkwardly carrying your bag. A man with a fluffy beard, smiling eyes, and the exact color of sweater vest that makes you trust him emerges. This must be Lindsi's father. A few seconds later a woman with a pursed face and permed hair appears behind him. Ahh, and her mom. Didn't you speak to her once, late, when you thought you were booty-calling Lindsi? Maybe she won't remember that.

"Lindsi will be right down," the dad says, smiling warmly. "She's just making herself *decent*. By the way, call me Dad. And this, of course, is Mom."

"I know it's late, and I don't want to keep you up," you say. "If you just point me toward Lindsi's room, I'll be off to bed."

They both stare, eyes wide with horror. Dad lets out a little "humph," his face dangerously red. Jesus, is he going to have a heart attack? Should you start CPR just in case?

"We, ahem"—Mom clears her throat delicately—"we thought you'd be sharing with cousin Jimmy. Since you're still...*unmarried*." She can't seem to help wrinkling her nose. Dad is just staring at you, obviously confused and upset. Awesome. "Though if you'd prefer a little more privacy, there's a couch in the basement. I'll warn you, though, the dog likes to sleep down there."

If you want to share with cousin Jimmy, turn to page 47.
If you want to slink off to the basement, turn to page 49.

You're being ridiculous. This man isn't going to kill you. How many murder-hitchhikers can there really be out there? The chances of you picking one up have to be pretty slim, right?

Something glints at the top of his bag as you pass under a streetlamp.

It's definitely a knife.

For his protection?

You've never packed a "just in case" knife. Especially not when you were planning to drive yourself somewhere.

The further you go, the less light there is on the road. You can't bother to keep up conversation—you have to focus on not having a heart attack—but the silence makes things even more terrifying.

"You're going to want to—"

"AHHH!" You shriek in terror.

"Are you...all right?" He gives you a strange look. A murder look?

"Yes, fine. Just lost in my thoughts. HA! I guess you scared me."

He narrows his eyes. "I was just saying you'll want to turn up here. The road is hard to see."

No, it's almost impossible to see, since it's totally unlit.

Oh god, this is it. He's taking you to his personal murder hole.

"It's just a little further. The road will curve around and you'll see it."

What could possibly be out here? A shack where he tans the skins of his victims? A shallow grave he dug yesterday *hoping to find you?*

You nose the car around the bend, barely able to breathe.

Then you see it.

The lights of...a hospital?

"Wait, you're going here?"

"Yup."

"Are you unwell?"

He laughs, the tinkling bell sound spiking your fear again.

"Didn't I mention? I volunteer here. Every year. I play Santa on the children's cancer ward. It's expensive, of course, but if you start saving a little bit every week around the end of April, you can buy them some spectacular stuff."

He reaches into the bag and pulls out a bright, shiny, silver… superhero cape.

"They let me bunk in the supply closet. It helps make the experience more authentic for the kids."

"Wow. That's so…generous."

"It's the least I can do. After all, there are so many good people in the world, I have to do something. Look at you, driving me all the way here."

A stone of guilt rolls around the bottom of your stomach. He opens the door and turns to smile at you.

"Thank you. I appreciate what you've done for me tonight. I know the children will too."

Then he grabs his bag and walks into the glare of the hospital lobby.

Holy fuck, did you just meet Jesus?

Turn to page 50.

OH, HELL NO.

You grab your duffel off the seat next to you and run off the bus, telling the first cab you see to take you back to the rental car counters.

"Oh, it's you." The clerk from the first counter sighs and rolls his eyes.

"Yes. I'd like a car?"

"Fine." He taps at his computer. "We have one sub-sub-compact left. It'll be $350 per night plus gas."

"Are you kidding? I was here a few hours ago and it was only—"

"Tomorrow is Christmas Eve. Take it or leave it."

At least you got a holiday bonus at work. Which will *almost* cover this.

You take it.

Traffic on the highways out of town is terrible. By the time you make it to the interstate, it's almost 2 A.M. You're desperately tired, not quite sure where you're headed, and judging from Lindsi's descriptions of her parents' neighborhood, you're looking at some dark, winding roads toward the end of the trip.

But the sign for the next exit does show a motel: "Local Motel."

If you want to push through and just drive the rest of the way to Lindsi's, turn to page 52.
If you want to spend the night at Local Motel, turn to page 54.

32

It only takes you fifteen minutes to realize how ill-advised this was.

The infant is clearly suffering from a long-term injury or serious depression. The homeless man didn't buy a coffee can... but should have. And the old woman brought homemade tuna fish with onions. Which, apparently, she wants to air out for a while.

God, you hope that smell is the tuna fish.

Twenty-six hours, three layovers, and one shit in a coffee can later, you've made it to the Greater Bentneck bus depot.

You step off the bus, feeling grim and knowing you smell like some combination of recirculated air, Combos filling from where you accidentally slept on a package, and fermented ass.

Thank god, Lindsi's here. Your phone died several hours ago, somewhere past Farmhamlettonshire.

Wait, who are all those people around her?

Why do they all look so angry?

Hesitant, you walk over.

"Hey...is this...?"

"My family," Lindsi says curtly. "We've been here for the last three hours waiting for your bus."

"Why did you all come? I could've taken a cab, or just... maybe only met up with you?"

"We thought we'd pick you up on time for caroling, then dinner at Aunt Lori's."

"Oh, dinner would be——"

"Of course, it's too late for that now." A woman with a tight perm and a massive cat-in-Christmas-lights sweatshirt is looking at you with a pinched smile and dead eyes.

It has to be Lindsi's mom. Clearly you're already making a great impression.

"At least we haven't missed mass yet," she adds, raising an eyebrow like a challenge.

Ugh. You hate church. Though possibly not as much as Lindsi's mother clearly already hates you...

If you want to go to mass, despite the fact that you're an atheist and feel like seven kinds of shit, turn to page 55.
If you want to beg off and tell them to go without you, turn to page 57.

WHILE HE'S OCCUPIED IN BACK, YOU GRAB YOUR DUFFEL, WHIP OPEN the door, and start sprinting back the way you came.

"Heeeyyy!" you hear, but it already sounds distant. You veer into the woods at the roadside so he won't be able to spot you. "This isn't Little Hampshireton…"

After about fifteen minutes of huffing in the cold, you spot a farmhouse. Thank god, your cell hasn't been getting reception. If you had to go much further, he'd definitely catch you, probably with some sort of chainsaw made out of axe heads.

You knock on the door. An old woman wearing a raggedy housedress answers, hair in curlers.

"Could I use your phone? I'm lost," you say.

She ushers you into the kitchen. Good thing you're you, and not the axe murderer you were just with.

You call your girlfriend.

"Hello?"

"Lindsi, it's me."

"Where are you?"

"I got stranded outside…" You frown at the woman. *New Dindelwood*, she mouths. Seriously? You mouth it back to her and she nods, smiling. "New Dindelwood?"

"That's at least an hour away!"

"I know; it's a long story. I'll explain when you get here. But I need you—or anyone—to pick me up."

"Can't you catch a cab?"

You turn to the woman. She shakes her head solemnly.

"Lindsi…"

"Okay, okay, I'm coming," she snips, and hangs up the phone.

Turn to page 58.

34

THIS IS YOUR CHANCE! HE'LL NEVER BE EXPECTING IT LESS!

Luckily, you have a full metal water bottle in your duffel. You wiggle it out as silently as possible.

"Here it is," he says.

Now! You have to do it now!

You bang the bottle against the base of his neck as hard as you can.

"Ooooh," he says, then slumps over, out cold.

Thinking fast, you grab the two packs of Combos you bought at the station out of the center console, stuff the water bottle back in your bag, and make a run for it.

You pick your way down the road a ways; better to go forward than back, while you know he's not following.

After a few miles you spot a turnoff for County Road Q.

What was it the radio lady said? "Take a cue from this clue?" It could have meant this.

You turn down it. Your cell has no service, but maybe there's a farmhouse down this way. They'd have a landline. Then you can call the cops on this freak.

You walk on.

Huh, that's weird. Wasn't the third clue something about "sticking you between a rock and a hard place"? On the left-hand side of the road, what must once have been a gentle hill has been sheared off, exposing a wall of bare rock. On the right is a barn with a name whitewashed onto the clapboard in huge letters.

HARD PLACE.

Old-timey farmers were so into their fucking suffering.

Turn to page 60.

YOU THANK THE MAN AND HEAD OUT TO A CAB AT THE TAXI STAND.

"I want to go to On the Beach. Do you know it?"

The taxi driver looks puzzled. "On the Beach?"

"Yeah, I think that's right."

"Are you *sure*? Do you perhaps mean the Sandals *located* on the beach?"

"I'm certain it was called On the Beach..." Had you read it wrong? He raises an eyebrow, shakes his head, and drives.

The cab stinks of weed. How authentic!

You shoot an approving smile toward the rearview mirror. The driver squints at you suspiciously.

"So, you a big Bob Marley fan?"

He shakes his head in contempt. So much for talking.

You look out the window. Kingston isn't exactly what you thought it would be. Instead of cabanas with thatched roofs and rows of swaying palm trees, all you see are sickly-looking stray dogs and viscous puddles with plastic bags coated in filth floating on top.

You check again to make sure the door is locked and the windows are fully rolled up. You're starting to wish you'd borrowed your dad's fanny pack.

You've almost made it down an entire block when a scruffy-looking man opens the far door of the cab and sits down beside you.

Adrenaline rushes straight into your heart. Oh god, this is how it all ends...

"Camp Road."

"Yeah," the driver says without batting an eye.

What? What the hell is going on here? This guy already has a passenger—you.

You place your hand over your pocket, cradling your wallet lightly. Steady, now. Did you mistake this for a cab and somehow get into a...what, Jamaican carpool?

After driving at a snail's pace for another five minutes in inner-city, bumper-to-bumper traffic, nothing happens. The stranger doesn't murder you. No street kids even manage to crawl in through a window. You start to relax.

Just then, a rough-looking pedestrian jumps into the front seat of the cab.

"Spanish Town Road."

"Yeah," the driver says. He turns and looks you square in the eye, almost a challenge.

"Detour."

Your heart beats heavily.

This is no Jamaican carpool. It's almost definitely an elaborate ruse to kidnap you! Who can blame them? It's obvious to anyone that your Ray-Bans are real. Wearing these is basically like asking to be ransomed.

If you want to jump out and make a run for it, turn to page 61.
If you want to sit tight, turn to page 62.

IT FEELS AS THOUGH YOU'VE DIED AND GONE TO TROPICAL HEAVEN. You've nearly maxed out your credit card, but you couldn't be more pleased. Everything about this place is perfect.

Armed with a John Grisham thriller and a pair of totally real-looking Ray-Bans, you lie down in a hammock and swing back and forth. Someone immediately brings you a mojito.

From a distance, you see someone who looks like a mid-nineties Cindy Crawford sitting by the pool.

Oh shit, she's made eye contact. And now she's walking over to you. Think fast. Would a lazy eye be a good enough cover for ogling? Can you fake lazy eyes?

"Hey there, stranger," she purrs.

"It's a childhood thing..." you say, pointing toward your eye.

"Um, okay. Do you mind rubbing a little lotion on my back?"

Is this really happening?

"Sure thing," you say, your voice almost steady.

She giggles and hands you her sunscreen.

"Don't miss any spots. Oh, pool boy? Could we get another round of mojitos?"

Magically, she not only stays through that drink, and the next, she seems to think you're funny. Like, really funny. Even when you're talking about your childhood cat's diabetes.

"Want to go back to your room?" she asks as you're sipping your fourth drink.

Is this *still* really happening?

"Yes?"

"Great. I'll grab some drinks for the road."

You head up to your room and she hands you the drink in her left hand.

"Cheers."

You take a big swig.

"Drink up," she coos.

You do. You'll do anything she says. But why is the room getting so dark? Is this what pure ecstasy...feels...like...?

THUD.

• • •

You wake from a dreamless sleep with the worst hangover of your life.

You look around from your spot on the floor. The room is empty, at least of all your things. The woman is gone. Your suitcase is gone, and—you pull yourself to your knees to check the edge of the dresser—yup. Your passport is definitely gone.

You try to muster up some hate for the woman who just drugged and robbed you, but you can't. She's too hot.

But you'll definitely need a passport to get home. And the leisurely pace of Caribbean life probably doesn't lend itself to resolving these types of issues quickly. Especially over the holidays.

Head still throbbing, you call down to the front desk.

"Can I get a cab to the embassy?"

When you arrive the wait time is approximately five…days. Which means you'll be spending what's left of your vacation trying to prove that you are indeed who you say you are.

The End.

IT'S THE THIRD TIME YOU'VE FALLEN ASLEEP TRYING TO FINALLY MAKE it through *Clue*. You really don't know why Kasia, your hipster friend from college, is so into this hunk of crap.

You reach over to the bedside table and toss a few soggy egg rolls into your mouth from the most recent delivery of Chinese food.

You swallow and simultaneously fart. You should be disgusted with yourself, but whatever. That's just what happens on a steady diet of crab rangoon.

Only a few more hours until your girlfriend gets back to the city. At least she doesn't have to know how you *really* spent Christmas. Specifically: lying in bed for three straight days without changing your underwear.

Excited by her return, you call her cell to see if she wants to come straight over.

RING, RING, RING.

No response. Oh well, at least you tried.

You rewind *Clue* to roughly the part where you last fell asleep and hit play. Tim Curry is great in almost anything, right? This time you'll definitely get why Kasia thinks this thing is so funny.

Your eyes slowly start to close.

Turn to page 64.

"Hey, Debby?"

"Merry…" You hear her chewing on something hard and brittle-sounding. Maybe a brittle? "Christmas! *SNRCK!*"

"So, I know this is last minute…" Now that you actually have her and her chewing sounds on the line, you're not sure hanging out is such a good idea. Do you even like Debby? But what are you going to do instead, stay in your apartment alone? You don't even have any brittle to snack on. "Are you doing anything tonight?"

"Am I doing anything," you hear more chewing sounds, "tonight? Well, I don't know. Did FDR pass the New Deal? *SNRCK!*"

You cringe.

At least you're talking to another human being.

"Let's," more chewing, "par-TAY!"

• • •

How much time should you let pass before you actively clarify to people at the party that you and Debby aren't together? Three minutes?

Debby leads you to a walk-up third-floor apartment, chattering the entire way about the Roosevelt White House at the holidays. She knocks, snorting merrily, and a tall, awkward-looking man opens the door and gestures you inside.

"Where's the bathroom?" Debby says, face like a frowning pie crust. "I'm about to burst!" The guy points, and she immediately trundles off, leaving you to fend for yourself.

You take a cursory look around the room.

You don't recognize a single person.

You pull out your phone and start randomly opening and closing apps in an attempt to look busy. You don't even see the sad sack in the formless, baggy gray dress—hair limp with grease, Coke-bottle glasses actually taped in the middle, like some kind of passive-aggressive commentary on her pay grade—sidle up to you.

She sighs heavily. You jump. Jesus, is she like some ninja of misery? How'd she get here so stealthily?

"Looks like you and me are the lonely ones at Christmas, huh?"

If you want to talk to the first person who's acknowledged your existence, turn to page 65.
If you want to escape to the bar, turn to page 67.

"Just curious, why no plastics?"

"There are endocrine-disrupting chemicals—"

"Never mind," you say, already bored. "I'll return these first thing tomorrow."

"Okay," Lauren says. "But let me write you a list of preapproved toys before you leave the house."

. . .

The toy store is even worse the next day.

You pull your sister's shopping list from your pocket, doing your best not to elbow the ten people standing shoulder to shoulder with you.

You start reading:

1. Hogwarts School of Witchcraft and Wizardry LEGO set from Harry Potter and the Philosopher's Stone. *Model D420. Quantity: 1 Made in Denmark*

Jesus, she's like the totalitarian of toys. The…toy-talitarian? Also, LEGOs are *definitely* plastic.

2. Smart Car Robotics kit. Model 662. Quantity: 1 Made in USA

That's it. Those are the only approved toys.

You manage to find the car, but the Harry Potter LEGO sets are sold out—all of them.

You stroll through the aisles, mulling over options that wouldn't violate any of your sister's stupid bans. You see a boxed set of the Harry Potter books at the end of an aisle. Harrison must like them if he wanted the LEGO version, right? That could work…

But then you see them, three rows down.

Moon Boots.

You rush over, picking up the box. They're metal and rubber—perfect, they don't even contain plastic!

Though you have a gut feeling Lauren wouldn't approve of something so obviously awesome.

If you want to buy the complete Harry Potter book set, turn to page 68.
If you're going for the Moon Boots, turn to page 69.

44

"I THINK THERE'S BEEN A MISUNDERSTANDING," YOU SAY.

"No plastics. And no guns," Lauren says curtly. "What aren't you understanding?"

Already your sister is wearing on your last nerve.

"The toys are for charity."

She raises an eyebrow skeptically, trying to gauge whether you're lying. God, she pulled that maneuver right out of Mom's old playbook.

"Then why did you bring them *here*?" she asks.

If you want to tell her you purchased them before leaving the city, but you're going to the toy store now to get the boys their real presents, turn to page 70.

If you want to tell her you want to give the boys the greatest gift of all: the experience of giving to someone less fortunate, turn to page 72.

"WHAT SHOULD I DO WITH THIS *EXPENSIVE* TRUFFLE OIL?" YOU SAY.

"We already have some," Lauren says, waving a hand dismissively. "Gregory mail-orders the *real* kind."

You hang your jacket, teeth gritted.

"Maybe we'll use it for marinade," she adds, moving in to rearrange your coat on the hanger.

"Okay. Well, it's the thought that counts, right?"

She rolls her eyes.

"Are you finished? I had to push everything back to wait around for your…*unexpected* arrival."

Jesus, what have you gotten yourself into? It's only been two minutes, but already you feel yourself reverting to the middle schooler who hated his bitchy older sister.

It would be so great if you could still pull her hair.

If you want to lob a devastatingly accurate insult, turn to page 76.
If you want to turn around and leave, turn to page 77.

46

YOU DRIVE TOWARD THE TOWN'S MAIN INTERSECTION, SEARCHING hotels on your phone.

The only one with any vacancy is in that seedy neighborhood near the Kmart that closed in the early nineties.

Christmas wasn't supposed to be like this.

After getting turned around twice exiting the highway, you finally arrive.

The hotel's shaped like a prison block and is the color of bleached turds. The neon sign over the entrance is missing letters. It just spells HOL. There are pink frosted trees all over the lobby, and a pair of "sexy" Mrs. Claus and Santa tapestries. They look handmade.

Didn't a kid from your high school kill himself here right before senior finals? Maybe just seeing the place made him go through with it.

If you want to go upstairs and fall asleep to fast-forward your stay,
turn to page 78.
If you want to go to the bar and drink until it seems less depressing,
turn to page 79.

"Oh, um, I'm happy to share with cousin Jimmy. Great way to get to know the family better," you say, realizing the second it comes out of your mouth how creepy it sounds.

It seems even creepier when you get upstairs and realize two things: cousin Jimmy is *maybe* fifteen years old, and there's only one bed.

Also, the room smells terrible, sort of like fermented farts.

"Well, we'll leave you to it," Mom says, looking at you with something near disgust. "I trust you'll respect our house rules."

"Yes, of course. I'm just glad to be here. It's so kind of you to welcome me into your home." She sniffs and walks away. That went well.

You turn to Jimmy. He's gangly, with greasy hair flopping over an acne-riddled forehead. He's currently in the process of digging a bony finger into his largish nose, staring at you the entire time.

"Uh, hi, Jimmy," you say, extending a hand, then withdrawing it quickly. Who knows which hand he might choose? "Nice to meet you. Do you know where I can find some extra blankets? I don't mind taking the floor, since I'm already putting you out."

"The floor?" His voice has all the inflection of a GPS system.

"I mean…" His face is utterly blank. "Unless you prefer the floor? I assumed…"

"The bed is more than large enough for two adults, and though I'm tall for my age, I'm not yet at my adult proportions, meaning the sleeping arrangements will be even more spacious."

"Well…that's true." How can you explain to this kid that there's something objectively weird about an adult man sharing a bed with a teenaged boy?

"I take it from your silence that you're concerned about the implications of sharing a bed. This concern, however, is unfounded, as I have no sexual interest in men."

"Me neither."

"That's reassuring," he says, voice flat. "Of course I was not concerned. Most sexual predators prefer to know their victims and to condition, or 'groom,' them to sexual activity. A crime of

48

opportunity, as this would be, carries too much risk."

You frown deeply. You're not sure you've ever been in a more unnerving conversation.

"Also, I do not move in my sleep. For all of these reasons, not to mention ergonomic concerns, the only logical solution is to share the bed."

"Okay…"

If you're taking the floor anyway, turn to page 80.
If you want to be "game" and bond with the family in a totally *not-rapey way by sharing a bed with Jimmy, turn to page 82.*

YOU DON'T EVEN KNOW COUSIN JIMMY. WHAT IF HE SNORES, OR sleep-farts?

"I'll be fine on the couch. I don't want to disturb anyone."

"Bit late for that," Mom says with a bright laugh, like she *didn't* just verbally bitchslap you. "But we don't mind. We like to assess the young men Lindsi dates." The fuck? "Follow me." She heads down the hallway.

She wasn't kidding about the dog liking the couch. Literally every inch of its surface is coated with a fine layer of hair. And you can already tell from the burning, itching, oozing sensation around your eyes that your usually mild dog allergies are going into hyperdrive.

"You'll find linens in the cupboard," Mom says. "Please help yourself to anything you need upstairs, keeping in mind that sound travels through the house and we're all incredibly light sleepers." She smiles widely, eyes narrowed.

"Sure. Thank you, Mrs.—"

"No, no, call me Mom." Her voice is so devoid of warmth you actually shiver.

"Thanks…Mom." You force yourself not to wince. In the last twelve hours this relationship has upgraded itself from "may or may not last until summer" to "you basically have in-laws," without your consent or input.

You lay two sheets and a blanket over the couch, trying to cover some of the surfaces, but it's too late; your allergies are already blindingly painful. You lie down, hoping that closing your eyes will help, but your eyelids feel like they have shards of glass stuck inside.

Maybe because the dog has sauntered up and is panting heavily inches from your tenderized face. You're not certain, but you think you feel welts forming where its spit is hitting your skin.

If you want to lock the dog up somewhere to try to help your symptoms,
turn to page 83.
If you want to take an entire bottle of allergy meds and hope for the best,
turn to page 85.

50

You drive to Lindsi's parents' house half-dazed. Her parents show you to the couch in the basement, where you drift off into the best sleep you've had in months.

The sleep of the beatified.

• • •

When you wake up, the feeling of peace that washed over you the night before has only grown. Instead of living in fear, shouldn't you do more good deeds, like Santa-Jesus?

You almost run up the stairs, you're so eager to find Lindsi.

She's sitting at the kitchen island, drinking coffee.

"Good morning!" You hug her from behind. She laughs slightly.

"Hello to you, too. What's going on?"

"I dunno, I just feel good. And I have an idea!"

"Yeah?"

"Why don't we go down to the hospital to volunteer? They have a children's cancer wing. I think we could do a lot of good!"

"I don't know, I'm pretty busy," Lindsi says vaguely.

"They're so sick, and it's a hard time of the year if you're not in a good place." You come around to face her. She looks down, refusing eye contact.

"The hospital, though? Probably they have lots of people already."

"Or we could do a soup kitchen. I know hospitals wig some people out. There must be some nearby. Do you have your phone, or—"

"Just stop, will you?"

"Why? It would feel so good to do something for others. We'll go together, it will bring us—"

"Shut *up* with this shit." Lindsi scowls.

"Lindsi, what's the problem?"

"The problem is people getting in the way of natural selection."

"What?" You can't have heard that right.

"The gene pool doesn't need the weak and weak-willed scumming it up and choking off everything good, okay?"

"Lindsi, what are you—"

"Some people are *supposed* to die!" she shouts.

Whoa.

You knew Lindsi was a little shallow but you wouldn't have jumped right to eugenicist. Is this something you should know about someone by the four-month mark?

"I think I should go," you murmur.

"Listen, it's not like that," Lindsi starts.

"I'm going home."

"What will Mom say?"

"I really don't care."

You gather your things and practically run to the car.

God, how could you have been with someone so morally disgusting and not even known? Not even had a *hint*? What does that say about you? Do other people feel the way Lindsi does? Is humanity really such a disgusting cesspool?

You make it back to the city with plenty of time to head to the soup kitchen, but you feel too bitter and revolted to do anything. Fuck Lindsi for making you feel this way. Fuck Christmas and its "do a good deed" bullshit. It just teaches you awful truths about people. You hate this stupid fucking holiday.

The End.

52

You've made it too far to stop now. Plus, with the size of the hold the rental place put on your card, you're not certain you can afford another charge.

You drive through the darkness. After an hour, the lines on the road start to get wobbly. You blink hard, but that just makes them disappear entirely.

You feel your head nod against your chest. Should you pull over? The GPS says you're only forty minutes away.

Yawning, you plow ahead. Before you know it, the car has taken off into the air and is driving itself on a black strip of sky! This is amazing—you barely need to steer; the vehicle knows what to do. Maybe if you wish hard enough it will grow wings and—

THUMP.

You jolt awake. Fuck, what was that? You screech to a stop.

Behind you in the dark roadway you see a mound.

Please don't be a person. Please don't be a person.

It's only slightly better. It's a dog. A big, beautiful golden retriever whose tongue is lolling out of its uncrushed head like it's happy to see you, but whose entire torso has been destroyed by the car.

It could have been feral, right?

Though feral animals don't tend to wear dog-sized reindeer antlers…

You look around, but don't see anyone. Terrified, and unsure what to do, you run back to the car. There's blood and some hair smeared on the cracked front headlight, but otherwise things look good. You grab some snow from the roadside, wipe off the blood, and drive—finally fully awake—the ten miles or so to Lindsi's.

When you get there you feel so morally disgusted you can't speak. Her parents frown—can they see what you've done?—then usher you to the room you'll be sharing with "cousin Jimmy."

The room smells like death. Or is that coming off you?

"Do you prefer the right or left side of the bed?" Jimmy, Lindsi's gangly-thin, acne-ridden teenaged cousin asks without inflection. "I am indifferent."

Seriously? They expect you to share a bed with an innocent child? You, a dog murderer?

"I do not believe you to be a sexual predator," Jimmy adds, staring straight at you. "Besides, it seems unlikely you would attack me so soon after we'd met, even if you were."

You're not, but it feels like he's seen something fundamentally true about your disgusting, grimy soul.

If you're taking the floor, turn to page 80.
If you'll share the bed—things can't get worse than
they already are, after all—turn to page 82.

IF YOU DON'T STOP, YOU MIGHT KILL SOMEBODY. OR WORSE, yourself.

You pull into Local Motel and park near the lobby.

Inside, a lone attendant sits behind a desk that's all peeling veneer. His hair is greasy, whether from his acne-blanketed skin or vice versa, it's unclear.

"Could I get a room?"

He sighs exaggeratedly and holds a hand out. Eventually, you realize he wants your credit card. He runs it, grabs a key from the wall, and walks outside. You follow him down a narrow strip of roofed sidewalk.

You reach the room. A long stripe of something brownish is smeared across the door, stopping abruptly at the doorknob, as though whoever cleaned figured wiping down just the doorknob was enough.

"Ice is through there." He points languidly. "Vending machines too."

You thank him, and he leaves, sighing again.

You're struggling to get the door open when you hear footsteps. You turn to see a massive, muscled man with a handlebar moustache towering over you. He's wearing a John Deere hat and flipping a coin with his right hand.

He's looking, however, straight at you.

"Nice to have company," he says.

"Mmm. Uh, yes. Company," you sputter.

He laughs wheezily, but doesn't move. Unsure what else to do, you open the door and rush inside.

You don't hear him leave.

And it seems your fumbling with the key has broken the lock. There's just a flimsy chain between you and this man. And maybe his friends?

Stop being a pussy—he was just trying to make conversation. Turn to page 87.
Fuck that, you're getting a different room. Turn to page 88.

"OF COURSE, LET'S GO TO MASS. I'M SO HAPPY TO SHARE THAT PART of Christmas with you," you say, ignoring the ominous bubbling in your guts and the fact that you haven't showered in...is it three days now?

In the last thirty hours, all you've eaten is Combos. On the plus side, you didn't go hungry, since you bought at least a dozen packages. On the minus, you've eaten a dozen packages, even the Seven-Layer Dip Tortilla flavor.

As you walk into the church, your stomach cramps painfully. You grimace, shaking the hand of the elderly woman Lindsi's introducing you to. Maybe if you sneak to the bathroom now, you'll be able to relieve some of the pressure?

But there's no time; the VanWhittingtons are ushering you to their "traditional pew" near the center of the chapel. Dammit. If you were at the back, you might have been able to duck out during the homily.

Your stomach feels like an overinflated balloon. You heave a shuddering breath out.

You're barely five minutes into the service and you feel like you're going to die. You have to take a shit like never before...or at least fart.

You can't do that, though: you're in church.

Though presumably a churchgoer wouldn't call you on it. And the majority of the congregation has to be over seventy; don't olds lose the ability to fully control their bowels? You remember visiting your grandma's as a kid and tracking her through the house by the *toot-toot* she made with nearly every step.

Another cramp grips your stomach, squeezing so hard you're afraid you might vomit.

You have no choice. While everyone's standing to give the responses, you let the tiniest fart slip out, hoping the noise of a few hundred people will cover it.

It does. Unfortunately, you were wrong about a crucial element.

56

Sometimes a fart is a gamble. And sometimes when you gamble, you lose.

You've lost. It was a shart.

The responses are over. People will sit back down any second. And that clammy feeling on your cheeks tells you sitting would be like doubling down...

If you want to stay standing, turn to page 90.
If you want to sit into the shart, turn to page 91.

"You know what? Go on without me."

Lindsi's mother sniffs and raises an eyebrow.

"Really, I'm not feeling very well—I haven't had any real food in the last day or so—and I don't want to make myself sick by pushing too hard."

"Okaaay," Lindsi says, rolling her eyes. "I guess you can just hang out at the house, then."

"Great. I'll see you in a few hours. If I'm not already conked out by then!"

You're the only one who laughs.

Still, it was the right decision. Not only is the Combos shit you have at the house utterly terrible—that strange mix of chemicals and organic rot really does penetrate a space—there's only one bathroom on the first floor. Think if you'd had to do that with someone around? Or hold it in through a church service?

You're drowsing on the couch, flipping through channels in the hopes of finding something *other* than a televised church service, when you hear it.

THUD.

It sounds like it came from directly overhead. Like, the room where Lindsi explained you should leave your things.

Is someone burgling the house? Through your window?

You creep up the stairs, but you don't hear anything. Summoning all your courage, you push open the door, screaming to throw the intruder off guard.

"YAAA!!!"

No one's there.

No one except the family dog, lying on the ground, motionless.

It's clearly gotten into your leftover Combos. And—you go over to check for a pulse—oh yeah, it's definitely dead. Why did *you* eat so many of these things?

You hear the sound of boots tramping inside. There's no way you'll be able to hide the dead dog from the family.

But you could hide the evidence…

If you want to confess about the Combos, turn to page 92.
If you want to hide the Combos and play stupid, turn to page 94.

58

The drive to Lindsi's house is utterly uneventful. After all, Lindsi cursing you out under her breath has never really qualified as an "event."

You head downstairs the next morning, but the only person up is a permed, heavyset woman in a teddy bear Christmas sweater who you assume is Lindsi's mom. Her mouth pinches into a tight, judgy little smile at the sight of you.

"I'm surprised to see you up so early, since you got Lindsi out of bed in the middle of the night." She narrows her eyes. "I'm Lindsi's mother, by the way. Call me Mom." You've never seen a less motherly expression accompany that phrase.

"Sorry about that. I told Lindsi last night, I got a ride from the bus station, but the gentleman driving the car made me really nervous. I had to get out for my own safety."

"Hmm. Poor judgment *and* an overactive fear response," you hear her mutter. That's awkward. Not wrong, just...who says that?

Mom flips on the television and turns her back on you.

The morning news is on. They're running a story about... wait a second, "Local Man Finds $50K Radio Prize, Planning to Donate Half to Charity."

That's the guy you hitchhiked with!

Which means he wasn't lying about the clues...

He appears onscreen.

"I'm planning to give my half to charity, of course, since I was guided by spirits to the location of the golden ticket. But I was traveling with a nice man who must have been confused about where we were turning off, and I promised him half the prize, since we were going to search it out together. That offer still stands!"

"What a Good Samaritan," Mom says. "Just one look at him tells you he's trustworthy."

Now, in daylight, with TV makeup, he does seem like a pretty nice guy. The fact that he's offering you $25,000 doesn't hurt either.

"You know what's weird——" you start, but Mom cuts you off.

"It's too bad you couldn't have caught a ride with him. Not only would you have been $25,000 richer, you wouldn't have had to be afraid. I mean, who could be nervous around that face?"

"Yeah…"

"What were you saying?"

You think back to your hasty departure, your terror, Lindsi's mom basically calling you a pussy just now…

"Nothing. He just looks like someone I knew in high school."

At least if you don't claim it the money will probably go to charity, right? You wonder whether you can write that off on your taxes…

The End.

60

You pass between the outcropping and the barn, eventually reaching a little covered bridge—it has to be the point of that bridge clue. On the other side, almost totally hidden by snow, is a sign next to a tiny footpath.

"Holly Berries for Sale."

The third clue was just a choral rendition of "The Holly and the Ivy!" You sprint down the path...there, at the end, is an old, falling-apart shed covered in ivy leaves. You open the door. The ground inside is soft, like it's been dug up recently. You spot a trowel hanging from the wall, much too shiny for this abandoned shack.

You dig.

About six inches down you hit something hard. It's a cheap plastic treasure chest, covered in stick-on gems. Inside are three dozen KWAL Radio! stickers and a shiny gold piece of paper with *Redeem at KWAL headquarters!* printed on it.

Fuck, the driver was telling the truth. About everything.

You pick your way back to the main road, walking in the direction of the car.

It's still there. And he's still slumped over, exactly where you left him.

Double fuck. You're pretty sure he's breathing, but you're no expert on what permanent brain damage looks like...

If you want to leave the ticket as a "sorry"
to the injured man, turn to page 96.
If you want to keep the ticket—it's not like anyone
knows you were ever in that car—turn to page 98.

You bolt out of the cab, slamming the door behind you.

Luckily, you kept your suitcase on your lap. Unluckily, it feels like it's packed with cinder blocks, and you're literally running for your life.

Running for your life is hard. Like, really hard. You're barely a block away from the scene of the inevitable—or at least potential—crime, and you're already considering taking a knee.

You cut through a few back alleys at what you think is still a pretty good clip.

You're safe now. Probably.

That was a close call. Probably.

Where exactly are you?

You wander the streets of Kingston aimlessly for hours, hoping you'll come across a Starbucks, or even a McDonald's. Unfortunately, you see neither. You'd ask for directions, but you can't bring yourself to trust anyone. Not after what just happened. Probably.

God, is it hot.

You've got a horrific case of swamp-ass and you can feel your skin attempting to peel away from your body. At some point, you're going to have to trust someone to give you water. Wait, can you trust the water here? Why did you not research this place *at all?*

Another hour passes. You might have to part with your suitcase soon. It only makes you a bigger target.

BEE-BEEEEEEP!!!

A car pulls up beside you.

"This is not your hotel!" shouts the driver.

It's the same cab as before. Seriously?

Sunburned and dehydrated, you resign yourself to the fates and slouch back in.

Turn to page 100.

You're sweating so hard you can feel your ass sticking to the seat through your underwear, but...nothing happens.

You drop off the first interloper, pick up another, and stop by a jerk chicken stand—which you try; it's so *authentic*—but eventually, after several hours of detouring, the driver deposits you at the hotel.

Unfortunately, On the Beach isn't as advertised...on that piece of handwritten copier paper.

It's in the back of an inner-city alleyway. There's a strip of filthy sand running around a tiny pool out front, but it's got too many needles floating around it for your liking.

"Keep the change."

The cabbie nods, like it's his fucking due. Dammit, you should've asked for the change.

"By the way, On the Beach..." the taxi driver pauses dramatically, "isn't safe." Then he speeds away, cackling.

That was disconcerting. But where else can you possibly go now?

You check in with an especially shifty-looking receptionist, though to be fair, that's probably because of the glass eye. He said he had one, but you're not sure which is which. They're both twirling separately, seemingly at random.

The minute you close the door to your room you look around for the safe. You need to stuff as many of your belongings as possible into it.

There isn't one. Fuck. At a loss, you start sticking things in random places: the pillow cases, between the mattress and the concrete slab the mattress is on, inside a plastic bag in the toilet tank.

You hear a murderous scream in the distance. That must just be the cries of all the hungry street cats, bellowing out in unison, right? Sure. That's logical.

Night starts to fall. You feel your stomach lurch...then liquefy. You really should have stopped at one helping of street chicken.

You run to the toilet and explode. The minute you feel capable of shuffling back to bed, you need the toilet again. Eventually, you just commit to staying in the bathroom.

Around 2 A.M. your stomach quivers again.

Sighing, you hoist yourself onto the toilet.

Sitting there, not quite sure if you're done spurting yet, you hear the door to your room creak open.

"Hello? Who's there?" you call out, mid-dribble. "Hello?"

The bathroom door cracks open. Jesus! If you weren't already shitting yourself, you'd shit yourself!

The cabbie's face peeks around. He holds his nose delicately. Like you didn't know you're being fumigated by your own filth right now.

"I told you, On the Beach isn't safe," he says with a laugh.

He closes the door. From the banging sounds on the other side, you guess he's robbing you blind. You could chase after him, but your pants are down by your feet, like ankle handcuffs. Also you're a coward.

The rest of the night you huddle inside the bathroom. The door is paper-thin, but at least it's *something* between you and other potential robbers. Not that you have anything left to rob.

The next morning you peer out to assess the damage.

Yup, everything is gone. Everything except for your passport. Good thing you stuck it in the toilet tank instead of your goggles, as originally planned. You grab it and run to reception.

"Get me to the airport!"

The End.

RIIIIIIIIIINNNNNNGGGG

You roll over and grab your phone. What time is it? What day is it?

"Hello?" you mumble groggily.

"Um, hello?"

"Lindsi?"

"You sound terrible," your girlfriend says.

"Thanks," you mutter.

"I've been doing a lot of thinking…"

"What time is it?" you ask, still half asleep.

"We need to have a serious talk."

"Okay." That can't be good.

"There's no easy way to say this, so I'll just say it. It's time to end things."

"Huh?" You'd been planning to give her a drawer when she got back. A *drawer*.

"Being home and talking with my family really opened my eyes. They helped me realize that if you were serious about me, about *us*, you would have come to Christmas at my parents'."

"I told you." You fumble to mute the TV, which seems to have gotten stuck showing *Clue* on never-ending loop. "I had to get caught up on work stuff. But I have, so we can spend all kinds of quality time together when you get back." You hear a hint of desperation creeping into your voice, but you don't know how to repress it.

"I just can't waste time at this point in my life on relationships that aren't going anywhere," Lindsi says, sighing. "I'm sorry."

She hangs up.

You stare at the ceiling, pressing your knuckles against your temples. Loneliness hasn't set in yet, but it will soon.

And you already bought those nonrefundable tickets to the New Year's Eve gala. Those were really fucking expensive.

At least all your drawers are still your own. That's the best Christmas present you've gotten in years.

The End.

"I GUESS SO." YOU FROWN. WHAT KIND OF CONVERSATION OPENER is that?

"I think Christmas is one of the *worst* times of the year," Sad Sack says with an exaggerated sigh.

"Tell me about it," you mutter distractedly.

"Well, there's lots of reasons for me. Last year, of course, I had to put my beloved cat Bimbleton down on Christmas Eve. She had really bad cancer. And cat AIDS."

Jesus. You hadn't expected an answer. Especially not one so miserable. You just met this person.

"Um, sorry to hear that."

"It's okay. Christmas tragedies are nothing new to me. Two Decembers ago, my dad lost both his arms in a milk truck accident."

How the hell do you even respond to that?

"He died several days later from a related infection."

Fucking hell.

"That's...just terrible." You frown deeply. Suddenly the idea of having no one to talk to at the party seems distinctly appealing.

"Nice to meet you, by the way," Sad Sack says.

"Likewise." You dutifully stick out a hand to shake hers. It's cold, clammy, and totally limp. "Listen, I haven't had a chance to eat anything all day. I'm gonna scope out the spread at the snack table." You take a step away from her. "I'll find you in a bit."

"That's fine, I'll come with," Sad Sack says. "Even though my doctor says I'm prediabetic and shouldn't eat after six."

"Okay then..." You push your voice right up against the edge of impolite.

On the way over you recognize Brad from your old office. Man, he was always so cool. And so funny. If only Brad had been your work friend.

"Actually, I'm just going to say hello to a friend first, okay?"

"Okay," Sad Sack responds. "I'll come with."

You force a smile. "Of course you'll *come with*," you mutter under your breath.

On the way, you get stuck in a bottleneck of people-saying-hello-to-Brad traffic, which pushes you and Sad Sack even closer together, up against the edge of the doorframe.

You catch sight of something waving just overhead. You look up. Shit. Hopefully nobody notices you're both under the—

"Mistletoe!" someone yells, pointing at the two of you.

If you want to be a sport and kiss Sad Sack, turn to page 101.

If you want to laugh it off and step away, turn to page 102.

"HA. I GUESS YOU'RE RIGHT," YOU SAY TO SAD SACK. "IF YOU'LL excuse me, I'm gonna get a drink."

Sad Sack looks even more lonely and disappointed than before. Which is actually kind of impressive. Whatever, you want some eggnog before the brief eggnog-drinking window snaps closed again.

You approach the bar. You still fail to see any faces you recognize. You really expected to see more people from your old office. Even Debby seems to know everyone here. It's like you're the only awkward person in the room. Besides Sad Sack, obviously, but that's not happening.

You grab a rum and eggnog and pull out your phone again. Of course you have no texts or emails, so once again, you're just poking around the home screen at random.

You're so fucking lame and transparent right now. You have to start a conversation with someone. Anyone.

"Merry Christmas," you say to the next person who walks by.

The guy stops dead in his tracks, looking confused. Oh fuck, you must have gotten it wrong. You weren't thinking, or looking.

"Or, you know, Happy...Kwanzaa."

"What? Kwanzaa?"

"Um, I dunno, I just thought..."

"Because I'm black." He glares down at you from behind thick-rimmed glasses. He's at least three inches taller than you. You swallow hard.

"No, no. I dunno, I just thought...it didn't seem like you were responsive to 'Merry Christmas,' so I..."

Oh god, you sincerely hope no one is listening to you verbally drown in this sea of stupidity.

"Dude, I was just trying to figure out if we'd *met* before." He shakes his head, nose wrinkling up in disgust.

RUN AWAY! ABORT! Turn to page 134.
He's got you all wrong. Explain yourself on page 104.

IT HAS TO BE THE BOOKS. LAUREN WOULD CRUCIFY YOU IF YOU brought home something as sweet as Moon Boots.

"You know, those are half-price at the used bookshop," an elderly woman says, shuffling by.

"Oh?"

"Yup. The shop used to deal only in murder mysteries. It was called Booked for Murder. If you make a left on Main, and…"

She rambles on. It's probably been days since she's actually spoken to anyone.

You're definitely not going to the used bookshop. These are cheap enough as is. In fact, they're so inexpensive you're not even going to return the Super Soaker.

You'll donate it to charity. At least some kid out there can have a truly awesome Christmas present.

"…then it's a right on Front Street. Now then, would you like a Werther's?"

You nod eagerly. You knew it was worth humoring this old.

You leave the store, sucking on your candy, feeling pretty damn good about yourself. Too bad now you have to go back to your sister's house.

If you want to wrap the gifts yourself, turn to page 105.
If you want to ask Lauren to wrap the gifts, two for her sons,
and one for charity, turn to page 106.

You're sticking with the Moon Boots. What kid wouldn't love them?

Besides, they only get you six inches off the ground. Honestly, how much damage can even the stupidest child do at six inches above the ground?

You approach the checkout.

"Parkdale High? Go Lions?" you hear behind you.

"Excuse me?"

"It's Jim! Jim French. Remember?"

Jesus, that can't be the same Jim French from high school, can it? It looks like someone's injected a factory's worth of Silly Putty into his cheeks and neck.

"Whoa, Jim! Long time, man. You look great."

"What are you doing back in town?"

"Uh, well, Christmas…"

"Oh yeah?" He looks interested. Seriously? "Well, you'll have to swing by my place tonight for our annual Christmas party. Jones will be there."

"Our?"

"Me and Mary. Mary Weickmann—you remember her, right?"

You nod. You haven't the faintest clue who she is.

"Rogers will be there. Tom Robinson, of course. He's in municipal politics now." Jim waggles an eyebrow, like you're supposed to be impressed by this. "Alex Carter…"

You're not in touch with any of these people. Their names aren't even familiar.

"Well…." you say, hesitant.

You're supposed to be in town to see Lauren's family…but you're fun! Why do you have to be on house arrest?

"Sure, I'll swing by."

Turn to page 107.

"I BOUGHT THESE BEFORE I LEFT THE CITY," YOU SAY. "I WAS GOING to buy the boys *their* presents tomorrow morning."

Lauren folds her arms.

"Honestly. I wouldn't buy anything without consulting you first," you say. She absolutely loves when you suck up to her like this. "What do they need?"

"I'll draft a list of approved toys later tonight," she says.

• • •

The toy store is even worse the next day.

You pull out your sister's shopping list, doing your best not to elbow the ten people standing shoulder to shoulder right beside you.

You start reading:

1. *Hogwarts School of Witchcraft and Wizardry LEGO set from* Harry Potter and the Philosopher's Stone. *Model D420. Quantity: 1 Made in Denmark*

Not to split hairs, Lauren, but aren't LEGOs plastic?

2. *Smart Car Robotics kit. Model 662. Quantity: 1 Made in USA*

That's it. Those are the only approved toys.

Hopefully you can get store credit on that Super Soaker. Donating it to Toys for Tots is a nice thought, but you're not made of money.

You manage to find the car, but the Harry Potter LEGO sets are sold out—all of them.

You stroll through the aisles, mulling over other options that wouldn't violate any of Lauren's bans. You see a boxed set of the Harry Potter books at the end of an aisle. Harrison must like them if he wanted the LEGO version, right? That could work…

But then you see them, three rows down.

Moon Boots.

You rush over and pore over the box. They're metal and rubber—perfect, they don't even violate Lauren's rules!

Though you have a gut feeling she wouldn't approve of something so obviously awesome...

If you want to buy the book set, turn to page 68.
If you want to go for the Moon Boots, turn to page 69.

"...BECAUSE I WANTED THE BOYS TO EXPERIENCE THE TRUE MEANING of Christmas," you say.

Lauren crosses her arms and narrows her eyes. You can tell the gauge on her bullshit meter is spiking into the red zone.

"Really."

"Yeah, I wanted to teach the boys about—"

"We're not religious."

"Thanks for letting me finish my sentence." She rolls her eyes. "I wanted them to bring these to Toys for Tots. So they can understand how fortunate they are."

"Well..." She unfolds her arms reluctantly. "I'll wrap them tonight, then. But don't go to Toys for Tots, okay?"

"Oh?"

"Put them under the Christmas tree in the atrium of the boys' school."

"Why there?"

"So the other mothers will know we donated."

• • •

The next morning you take the boys to their school.

"Like I said, these are for kids less fortunate than you."

Otto squints, obviously confused.

You fling the Super Soaker and the costume on top of the mountain of gifts beneath the elaborately decorated Christmas tree.

"There you have it, the true meaning of Christmas..."

The boys look at you in disbelief.

"But there's already millions of presents under the tree!" Harrison protests. "Who are they all for?"

"I don't know," you sigh.

"You don't know?"

"No."

You usher the boys out of the building.

You've got to make it up to them. Unless, of course, you want to be known as the *uncool* uncle.

If you want to take the boys to Santaland, turn to page 108.
If you want to take the boys to see the Mickey
Christmas Carol, *turn to page 109.*

"…BECAUSE I WANTED THE BOYS TO EXPERIENCE THE TRUE MEANING of Christmas," you say.

Lauren crosses her arms and narrows her eyes. You can tell the gauge on her bullshit meter is spiking into the red zone.

"Really."

"Yeah, I wanted to teach the boys about—"

"We're not religious."

"Thanks for letting me finish my sentence." She rolls her eyes. "I wanted them to bring these to Toys for Tots. So they can understand how fortunate they are."

"Well…" She unfolds her arms reluctantly. "I'll wrap them. But don't go to Toys for Tots, okay?"

"Oh?"

"Put them under the Christmas tree in the atrium of the boys' school."

"Why there?"

"So the other mothers will know we donated."

• • •

You pull up in front of the boys' school.

"Like I said, these are for kids less fortunate than you."

Otto squints, obviously confused.

You fling the Super Soaker and the costume on top of the mountain of gifts beneath the elaborately decorated Christmas tree.

"There you have it, the true meaning of Christmas…"

The boys look at you in disbelief.

"But there's already millions of presents under the tree!" Harrison protests. "Who are they all for?"

"I don't know," you sigh.

"You don't know?"

"No."

You usher the boys out of the building.

You've got to make it up to them. Unless, of course, you want to be known as the *uncool* uncle.

If you want to take the boys to Santaland, turn to page 108.
If you want to take the boys to see the Mickey Christmas Carol, *turn to page 109.*

"WOW. IT'S AMAZING. YOU'RE EXACTLY. LIKE. MOM." YOU GRIN triumphantly.

"Take that back," Lauren hisses.

You have her on the ropes. Time for the knockout blow.

"Actually, that's not fair to Mom. She got drunk sometimes, and was actually *fun*."

"GET OUT!" she screams.

"And her food didn't taste like dirt," you add, slamming the door behind you.

You stomp to the car feeling equally triumphant and disappointed in yourself.

Christmas wasn't supposed to be like this.

You could go to a hotel and try to repair things tomorrow morning, but fuck it. It's not like Lauren will be any less bitchy tomorrow.

• • •

After a long, slow drive home through a snowstorm, you arrive at your apartment at 3 A.M.

You have no food and no plans for the holiday, but it's too late to worry about that now.

You open your Netflix, turn on the movie *Clue*, and almost instantly pass out on the couch.

Turn to page 39.

WHY EVEN ENGAGE IF SHE'S GOING TO BE LIKE THIS? YOU'RE TOO old to deal with this shit.

"I'm sorry for arriving late," you say, trying your best to sound mature and reasonable. "Christmas traffic is heavy. I think it's best if I stay at a hotel. I'll be out of your way, then."

She looks guilty. That's satisfying.

"Wait, you don't—"

"Goodnight. Tell the boys I can't wait to see them."

You grab your coat and walk out.

Turn to page 46.

YOU HEAD UP TO YOUR ROOM AND LIE DOWN ON THE DINGY BEDSPREAD with your clothes on. You pull out a sacrificial T-shirt to use as a pillowcase cover. You spend a few minutes wondering if that suicide happened in this exact room before nodding off to sleep.

The next morning, you wake up feeling much more relaxed about things between you and your sister.

You decide to call and extend an olive branch.

"'Morning," you say. "I was hoping to take the boys off your hands this afternoon."

There's a long pause.

"I don't know."

Jesus, why does she always have to be so difficult?

"I promise we'll do something fun *and* educational," you say.

"Like?"

"We…could see how they make traditional maple syrup?"

"I've already told you, this family doesn't eat sugar."

"Right." She sounds extremely testy. "I'll just swing by the house and we'll make a plan when I get there," you say.

"Fine." She hangs up.

What can you do that even Lauren can't have a problem with?

Wait, you have an idea. A *perfect* idea. You just have to swing by the toy store on your way to Lauren's…

Turn to page 74.

You choose the only vinyl-covered stool at the bar that's neither cracked nor streaked with mysterious, sticky substances.

"Can I get a rum and eggnog?"

The combed-over bartender flashes a gummy smile and grabs a dingy-looking glass.

"Alone on Christmas?" he asks.

"Not really."

He splashes something from a plastic bottle into yellowy cream. He slides the drink across the bar, spilling a quarter of it.

"I was about your age when I started spending Christmas alone."

"Oh?" You look around the dim, threadbare-carpeting-and-wood-panels bar, then back to the bartender's pouchy, pockmarked face, and shudder.

"Yup. Just couldn't seem to get along with my family. Especially my bitchy sister. Eventually, I just stopped bothering with family at the holidays."

You nod awkwardly and move to the back of the room, where you proceed to down several more rummy eggnogs. No one enters the bar the entire night. Eventually you stumble upstairs and pass out.

You wake up with a horrific, noggy hangover.

Everything about your room seems infinitely worse by daylight. The windows are grimy. The wallpaper is water-stained and peeling. Dear god, that better be *your* vomit splashed all over the nightstand…

If the idea of staying here is too much and you want to go back to your apartment, turn to page 110.
If you want to try to repair things with your sister, turn to page 112.

"THAT'S ALL GREAT," YOU SAY, "BUT I'D FEEL MORE COMFORTABLE on the floor."

"Perhaps you have latent psychological issues that you have yet to fully deal with," Jimmy says in his nasal monotone.

"Yeah, probably."

"Even if your body were to react sexually in the night, that wouldn't necessarily mean that you were—"

"You know what, Jimmy?" You throw a pillow on the floor and grab a quilt folded at the bottom of the bed. "Let's not talk about it anymore."

"I see that you prefer silence."

"Yes."

"And that—"

"JIMMY."

"I will be quiet now."

You hear him lie down on the bed, and then you don't hear another thing. Not a move, not a breath, nothing. At least there's one thing about your roommate that doesn't suck.

• • •

You wake up confused, your back radiating pain into every limb.

You've barely slept, you're in massive amounts of pain, and you can tell that one wrong move is going to fully throw your back out.

You should never have come here.

You trudge downstairs and pour yourself a cup of coffee.

"Finally up?" Mom says, pinch-smiling at you.

"Mmmm." You don't even bother telling her it's only seven thirty, or that you were driving half the night. Actually forming words would lift the seal off your bubbling pissiness.

"Well, luckily you haven't missed out yet," she says.

"Mmmm?"

"In our family the men all go out on Christmas Eve day to cut down the tree. Even though they don't know you yet, they wanted to include you. They're generous that way."

"Mmmmmm."

*If you want to go along, if only to avoid Mom
for a few hours, turn to page 113.
If there's no way you're chopping down trees when your
back is an inferno of pain, turn to page 114.*

82

"OKAY, JIMMY. YOU'VE CONVINCED ME," YOU SAY. HE HASN'T, BUT the alternative is the floor, and the scent seems to be stronger down there. "We can share the bed."

"Excellent. I was concerned momentarily. Anyone who would be unwilling to platonically sleep next to another male might have serious issues. Sexual pathologies perhaps, or an unhealthy bodily—"

"Jimmy, can we just be quiet now?"

"Yes." He lies down on his back, closes his eyes, and says nothing else. You can't even hear him breathing. Okay…

If you want to mummy yourself in a sweater to make sure things don't get weird, turn to page 116.
If you want to try your best to fall asleep on the farthest edge of the bed, turn to page 117.

THERE'S NO WAY YOU'LL SLEEP—OR BREATHE—WITH THIS DOG IN the same room.

You head to the hallway near the stairs, the dog trotting behind, wagging its fluffy yellow tail, spreading infinitely more dander in its wake. The thing would actually be cute if you could see it without screaming pain.

The first door you open is the bathroom. You might need that later; the dog can't go in there.

The next is a closet filled with crossbows, camouflage bodysuits, and more Bowie knives than you've ever seen in one place. Jesus Christ, what kind of family does Lindsi have? You close the door.

The third opens onto a cement-floored room with a drain in the center. A washer and dryer are along the side wall.

Perfect! If the dog needs to pee it will even clean up after itself. You leave the dog inside, close the door, and return to your couch, hoping to sleep.

• • •

"YYYYAAAAAAAAAAAAAAHHHHHHHHHHH!!!!!"

You awaken to the loudest, shrillest scream you've ever heard.

It's coming from the laundry room.

You get up and creep cautiously down the hallway.

"Who put him in here? Who would do such a THIIIIIIINNGG?" Lindsi is clearly upset. And in the room where you left the dog. Gulp.

"What's going on?" you ask as casually as possible as you walk into the laundry room.

Oh dear god. There's blood everywhere, all over the sides of the washer and dryer, on the detergent bottles, and of course trickling in a narrow stream from the mangled head of the dog, crumpled in a yellow heap in the corner, into the floor drain.

Jesus fucking Christ.

"What happened?"

"Obviously Toodles ha-ha-had an epileptic f-f-f-FIIIIIIT," Lindsi wails.

"Epileptic…" you trail off, mesmerized by the dead animal. You've never actually seen anything dead before. At least, nothing larger than a parrot. Grandma's funeral was closed-casket; your mom "didn't want to see her miserable fucking face ever again."

"This is the only room in the house he's not allowed to stay in unmonitored. Every surface is hard. It was a recipe for, for, for DISASTERRRRRRRR!" Her weeping rises to gale force again. And it's drawing a crowd. You see Mom down the hallway, smiling cryptically. Between her and you are half a dozen traumatized-looking relatives you've never met.

"Who put him here? Who would do that to a poor, defenseless animal?"

Everyone is looking at you. They know you, dog murderer. And they're all about ten feet from an arsenal of crossbows.

You wonder: if you return the rental car early, will they give some of your money back?

The End.

AT THIS POINT, IT'S NOT GOING TO MAKE ANY DIFFERENCE WHAT YOU do: this dog has blanketed every available surface in allergens.

You dig through your bag until you find the magic combo: a quadruple dose of allergy medicine and a couple Ambien to make sure you don't wake up once it wears off.

After an extremely uncomfortable half hour, you feel the drugs kicking in. Thank god. You need a good night's rest if you're gonna face this family.

• • •

Where did this dragon get a monocle? He raises it to his eye with scaly fingers and peers at you, lips curling in scorn.

"You've gained weight," he hisses.

"That's just this suit of armor. It adds ten pounds." You step back, embarrassed. As soon as you do, the ground lets out a high-pitched beep.

"No, you definitely have. I've rigged the floor to be weight sensitive. It only beeps for fatties." He grins sardonically, narrowing his yellow eyes. "And you know what I do to fatties."

Before you can back away, he's breathing fire straight at your arm. How does he target it so well? And how does he make it look like a...like a...

You look down. There is no armor, no dragon, only a full-grown coyote, teeth sunk into your bloody, naked arm. You look around, confused and terrified. You're outside, barefoot in the snow, wearing just your flannel pajama pants. And you're stepping on something soft and squishy. What is that? Ahh. A baby coyote. That makes sense.

Fucking Ambien. Why can't you ever get the fun side effects, like sleep-driving twenty miles to sleep-fuck an ex?

The coyote growls and bites down harder. You shriek in pain. Unsure what else to do, you punch the animal in the side of the head as hard as you can. Stunned momentarily, it releases your arm and drops into the snow. But it's clearly ready for round two.

You step backward, hands up to defend your face, and trip over a rock buried under the snow. Cursing, you reach for it, swinging it through the air toward the coyote leaping for your head.

CRUNCH.

You actually feel the skull crack. Jesus, you're like Conan the fucking Barbarian. But with more Ambien. And less pecs.

The coyote shakes violently, blood spattering from its head wound onto the white snow, then collapses, tongue lolling out. You step toward it cautiously, wanting to make sure it's really dead.

What's that grayish stuff leaking out the side of its…oh, definitely brains.

You vomit profusely onto the still-twitching corpse.

You're wiping your mouth when you hear a door creak open behind you.

Fuck.

"What are you doing out here?" It's Mom's voice.

You have no answer.

"Is that…a dead coyote? What happened?"

If you want to tell her you were defending yourself, turn to page 119.
If you want to tell her you found it this way, turn to page 121.

OH, FOR CHRIST'S SAKE, YOU'RE NOT IN SOME B MOVIE; YOU'RE IN A shitty roadside motel. The worst that's going to happen to you tonight is contracting some unknown form of scabies.

You head to the vending machine. Pickings are slim— just sugar-free gum and a few flavors of Combos, mostly the shitty flavors.

Still, it's better than nothing. You buy all the Combos and head back to the room for a feast.

You put a T-shirt around the pillow, leave all your clothes on, and fall asleep on top of the crusty paisley bedspread.

Several hours later you jolt awake. Light is pouring in your open door, silhouetting a broken chain swinging from its moorings... and a huge figure wearing a trucker hat and a bathrobe.

He takes a step into the room.

Just don't piss yourself. This could be any number of things, right?

Unless you *should* piss yourself. It could be the thing that saves you.

But you only have this one pair of pants for the entire week.

He takes another step toward you. You imagine you can smell his musky, feral scent, though that could just be the bedspread.

"Hey, sorry to intrude this way, but I had to know..." the monster-giant-trucker begins.

At least your weeping won't stain your pants.

If you want to hit him as hard as you can over the head with the bedside lamp, turn to page 122.
If you want to just curl up and pray he won't hurt you...
too badly...turn to page 124.

88

YOU KNOW WHAT? BETTER SAFE THAN SORRY. BESIDES, THE WHOLE reason you pulled over was to get some sleep; if you spend the entire night nervous about the weird trucker you saw outside, that won't happen.

You head back to the front desk.

"I'm sorry, but the lock on my room is broken. Is another room available?"

The attendant rolls his eyes dramatically and snorts. When you don't leave, he stands, grabs another key, and walks toward the door.

"This way."

A few minutes later you're inside a room at the opposite end of the motel, one with a working lock and no lurking terrors. Perfect.

You put a T-shirt over the pillow and are just lying down to sleep when you hear a piercing shriek.

Then another piercing shriek. Then a couple of expletives. Clearly the people next door are fighting—dramatically—and the walls aren't thick enough to drown out the noise.

Soon, the shriek-fighting turns to shriek-fucking, which somehow involves much more noise, including wall thumps.

After thirty minutes of staring at the ceiling, wondering whether that stain is black mold, you get up. You're hungry and bored. At least if you grab a snack from the vending machine it will be something to do until this couple wears themselves out.

The only options are four types of Combos and gum. You buy as many Combos as you have money for and head back. On your way, you notice the door to your previous room swinging open. That's unnerving.

The entire night, whenever you're about to nod off, some snore, or grunt, or renewed fucking from next door wakes you. Finally, around 6 A.M., you drift into a fitful sleep.

Hours later, a truck horn blares outside and you jerk awake. It's after eleven—fuck, you meant to be on the road hours ago. You grab the rest of the Combos and rush out.

You don't have time to stop for food; Lindsi will be wondering where you are. You power through, fueled by rest stop coffee, Combos, and frayed nerves.

Turn to page 126.

YOU CAN'T CHANGE WHAT'S ALREADY HAPPENED, BUT YOU CAN control how you respond to it.

Your response is clamping your butt cheeks together as hard as you can and staying standing; sitting would spread this everywhere, and you only brought one pair of pants.

The congregation sits after the responses.

You don't.

Lindsi tugs your sleeve. You turn a brief smile on her before facing forward again. Pretend this is what you do in church. You're just a guy who loves standing.

"You may be *seated*," the priest says pointedly from the pulpit. You nod, so he knows you got the memo. He frowns.

"Sit. Down," Lindsi hisses.

You can feel beads of sweat forming on your brow from the effort of holding your cheeks together. The shart is preventing the skin from forming its own vacuum seal.

Worse, you can smell the barest hint of processed-cheese-filling fart starting to permeate the area around you.

"What's wrong with you?" Lindsi starts pulling insistently on your hand.

Why did you eat so many fucking Combos?

One thing's obvious. Standing is no longer a viable option for containing this shart.

If you want to run to the bathroom to deal with things, turn to page 128.
If it's time to go hard, harder even than a wet fart—that's right,
we're talking full-on pants-shitting—turn to page 127.

WHY BOTHER GAMBLING AT ALL IF YOU'RE JUST GONNA FOLD THE minute the stakes are raised?

The responses end and the priest gestures the congregation to sit.

You do.

That was another losing bet.

The smell explodes into the air around you, a viscous blend of spoiled potatoes, morning breath, and jungle rot. It's so bad it's almost palpable.

And clearly you're not the only one smelling it.

You side-eye Lindsi's family. Her mom is crinkling her nose in pure disgust. Dad is frowning, as though in physical pain. On the other side, Lars, Lindsi's Herculean blond brother, is discreetly attempting to pull his shirt over his nose. Lindsi's full-on gagging.

You feel like that guy in the Kenny Rogers song…except with farts instead of poker.

If you want to excuse yourself to deal with this in the bathroom, turn to page 128.
If you want to pretend it wasn't you and hope it goes away soon, turn to page 129.

YOU HAVE TO CONFESS. THE GUILT IS TOO MUCH; IF YOU DON'T, you'll wind up blurting it out over dinner, or during sex with Lindsi, or at some other, even worse moment.

You run downstairs.

"I'm so glad you're here, I just found him," you pant.

"Found him?" Lindsi frowns.

"The dog. He's...I think he's dead," you say. Everyone pushes past you up the stairs. Lindsi's mom makes it to the dog first, checking his pulse. She shakes her head. Some trick of the light almost makes it look like she's smiling.

You have to confess now, or you'll never have the guts.

"I have to tell you something else," you start. "I feel... responsible for this."

"No, no," Lindsi's dad says, patting you on the shoulder.

"Yes. You see...the dog got into my leftover Combos."

Everyone stares at you blankly.

"They're a snack food? They come in lots of great flavors, like Buffalo Blue Cheese, and Sweet and Salty Caramel Creme Pretzel?"

"Of course we know what Combos are." Lindsi's brother Lars shakes his head, clearly lost. "But that's not what killed Toodles."

"No, they have to be! When I got here, I was very ill myself, and it's clear the Combos were at fault."

"Honey, Combos can't kill a dog," Lindsi says.

"You didn't smell the shit I had while you were gone!" You know you're going too far, but you need them to understand, so they can absolve you. "It smelled like the inside of an old person's mouth mixed with swamp gas. It was horrible. I almost passed out it was so bad. And I didn't even touch the Cheddar Cheese Pretzel flavor the dog got into. It says right there on the packaging, it's their wildest yet..." You keep babbling about the brutality of Combos, and the shits they bring on, but no one seems to understand.

"Stop," Lindsi's mom says, holding up a hand. "Just stop."

"But you don't understand. The cramping alone was—"

"No, we all understand. Graphically. What *you* don't

understand is that Toodles was epileptic."

"Epi...what?"

"Our dog had epilepsy. It's clear from the bite marks on his tongue that he had a fit. You couldn't have known, but this is absolutely not from your snack foods. So please, *please* stop explaining."

Lindsi's family nods agreement, obviously horrified.

"Oh. Okay."

You all stand in silence for a few moments. You have to break the ice somehow.

"So...who wants nog?"

The End.

QUICKLY, YOU STUFF THE COMBOS UNDER THE CLOTHES IN YOUR bag, arranging a dirty T-shirt under the dog's head so no one will see the crumbs. Satisfied the evidence is hidden, you call down.

"Hurry, I just found him. Maybe you can help!"

"Found who?" Lindsi's voice echoes up the stairs.

"The dog! I don't think he's breathing!"

The entire family troops up to your room, Lindsi in the lead.

"Oh no, Toodles!" She lets out a plaintive moan as she rushes to cradle the dog's head in her arms.

"Thinning the herd," you think you hear her mom mutter under her breath. You stare at her and she smiles blandly. Did that really happen?

"We'll have to give him a real sendoff," Lindsi chokes out between sobs. "Tonight."

"Linds, the ground is frozen solid," her brother Lars says.

"I know. We'll pyre him."

Lars nods. Have you lost some fundamental element of your hearing? Nothing being said in this room makes any sense.

"I'll get it built." He troops past you, face grim but determined.

• • •

You stand outside, shivering next to the mountain of wood Lars has somehow stacked in the last hour.

Apparently your hearing is fine.

Lindsi's dad climbs the side with the dog under one arm and lays it gently on top. Once he's back with the family, they all begin to step backward. Unsure what else to do, you join them, walking backward through the snow until you're pressed against the deck.

"You can do the honors," Lars says, turning to you. "You found him, after all. That's no way to start a Christmas. It's only right that you should do this."

"Do…what?"

"The lighting."

Lars hands you a crossbow and a lighter. Jesus Christ, you're going to Viking funeral the dog?

Everyone looks at you expectantly. Unsure what else to do, you flick the lighter at the end of the arrow. It flames up immediately. You take aim…it lands about twenty feet short.

You try again.

And again.

You never knew how hard it would be to hit a mountain of wood from fifty feet away. Crossbows are definitely *not* easier than regular bows.

Finally, coughing embarrassedly, Lars grabs the bow and shoots it, one-handed, at the pyre. It crackles to life.

Then pops. Loudly. Like, little gunshots.

"What is that?" you murmur, horrified.

"Just the organs exploding in the heat." Lars almost sounds bored. "Nothing to worry about."

You swallow the bile rising in your throat and stand there with the family as the mountain of wood and dog burns.

You look down.

A flaming scrap has landed at your feet. It's charred, but you can still make out the word written there.

Combos.

The End.

FIFTY THOUSAND DOLLARS IS A SHIT-TON OF MONEY.

Still, would you ever be able to enjoy it knowing you'd attacked—maybe murdered—someone to get it? Someone who was willing to split that money with you, a total stranger? What if he wakes up to astronomical medical bills? Or just persistent headaches? He was the one who knew where this treasure was, not you.

But $50,000...

No, you can't take it. You'll never live down the guilt.

You find a scrap of paper in the car, write *You were right! Consider this my thank you for the ride,* and tuck it, along with the ticket, between the man's seatbelt and his body. He'll find it there for sure.

Unable to get reception, you walk back toward the last town you spotted. You can call Lindsi once you find a signal.

Though that makes you feel guilty, too. What if she drives by the man in the car? Will she check on him? Would she recognize your writing on the note?

You opt for a cab instead. The hour-long drive costs just over $300, but your conscience, at least, is in the clear.

• • •

When you head downstairs the next morning, the whole family is huddled around the TV.

"Local Man Wins $50K Radio Prize" streams across the bottom.

"Morning! Can you believe this? Hell of a Christmas present, eh?" a bearded man with a warm smile says. He must be Lindsi's dad. You smile, cherishing the secret of your amazing kindness. You'll have to find a way to let slip what you did. Maybe over dinner?

A man comes onscreen and starts talking about how he found the prize.

"I'm a pig farmer in the area and I just knew all the

landmarks," he says.

That's not the guy who drove you.

This guy is terrifying—bald, teeth black around the edges, smile weaselly, like he's deciding where to strike.

Something in the pit of your stomach lurches.

"Best of all, the money is very much needed. Mr. Warren was unable to purchase pig feed this winter because funds were so low, but says this injection of cash will put his farm back on track."

The story ends. Another comes on.

"A Dodge Stratus was found abandoned near County Road Q this morning. Traces of blood were found inside the vehicle, though there was no sign of the driver. Police suspect foul play."

You were in a Dodge Stratus. Near County Road Q.

And your water bottle definitely didn't draw blood.

The pig farmer's leer flashes through your mind and you shudder.

It's not your fault, though, right? Leaving the driver incapacitated, with the golden ticket on his lap…in pig country…

The End.

JUST BECAUSE HE WAS RIGHT ABOUT THE TICKET DOESN'T MEAN THIS guy *wasn't* going to murder you. Plus, you can see his fingers twitching. He'll be awake soon. Why feel guilty? It was self-defense.

Also, that's a lot of money.

You walk away from the car rapidly, until you reach a point where your cell gets service, then look up a cab company. The ride to Lindsi's parents' will be exorbitant, but who cares? Tomorrow you'll be a fifty-thousandaire.

• • •

You wake up eager to tell everyone the good news (they were in bed long before you arrived). You rush downstairs, smile lighting up your face, to find Lindsi's family clustered around the kitchen island, glued to the local news.

"Morning, VanWhittingtons. I have some fantastic news! But first, let me introduce myself; I'm——"

"Shh." Lindsi snaps a hand closed in the air behind her. "Let us finish watching this story."

The TV cuts to an image of a guy in a wheelchair, head wrapped in layers of gauze. He looks kind of famil——

Oh Jesus, it's the guy who gave you the ride. The story lede, "Local Do-Gooder Attacked for Good Samaritan Ways," doesn't bode well.

"Even with the bills, and my lack of insurance, I'm not worried about myself. I know God will provide." He smiles creepily at the sky. "I just hope the man who was with me is safe," he says to the blonde reporter interviewing him. "We were going to split that money, and considering the kind of shape I'm in, I'm worried he might be seriously injured, even dead."

"Do you know the man's name?"

"No." You exhale deeply. "Just a description. He was tall, but kind of malnourished-looking, with slightly thinning hair." That's a lie——your hairline is *awesome*. "And he really liked Combos. He must have eaten six packets while we were in the car together." Oh c'mon. "Oh, and his teeth were pointier than a normal person's. Which I sympathize with; dental care is expensive." Dammit, you've always worried your teeth were too pointy.

The segment ends and Lindsi flips off the TV.

"How horrible. How could anyone attack such a kind, charitable man?" Lindsi's mom shakes her gray perm no. "And on Christmas, no less. I don't know how people like that live with themselves."

"Agreed," Lindsi says, then turns to you with a smile. "But let's talk about something pleasant. Like your good news. What was it, sweetie?"

You think back to the golden ticket, specifically the fine print on the bottom: *Must present in person to redeem prize. Claiming prize indicates willingness to appear in publicity materials for KWAL.*

You have fifty thousand reasons to tell the truth…and one possible assault charge's worth of shutting the fuck up.

"Nothing," you say, forcing a smile. "Just happy to be here."

You knew nothing good would come of this fucking holiday.

The End.

100

AFTER ANOTHER HOUR WINDING AROUND WHAT FEELS LIKE THE entire fucking island, you finally arrive at the hotel.

Unfortunately, On the Beach isn't as advertised…on that handwritten piece of copier paper.

It's in the back of an inner-city alleyway. There's a strip of filthy sand running around a tiny pool out front, but it's got too many needles floating around in it for your liking.

You think you can hear gunshots in the distance, though it might just be a car backfiring. Either way, the single, haggard woman working the desk doesn't seem fazed.

You clench and unclench your fists, unable to force yourself to walk through the door. A passerby on a bicycle gives you a leering wink. Maybe he meant it to be friendly, and maybe he's only twelve, but it adds to your uneasiness.

You jog back to the cab and knock on the window.

"On second thought, could you take me back to the airport?"

"Really?"

"Yes. And please hurry." You hope he didn't hear your voice crack. You feel both vaguely guilty and giddy with relief.

At the airport, the cab driver claims he spent the entire afternoon looking for you, ergo the fee he's trying to charge isn't, in fact, "exorbitant."

But the truth is, you don't care. You don't even mind paying a change fee that costs more than your rent in order to get a same-day flight home.

All that matters is that you're inside a safe, air-conditioned airport where they serve Starbucks.

The End.

"I'm game if you are," you say, trying to play it cool.

"Well I have no particular objection, though the tradition is a bit…"

You cut off whatever depressing thing she was going to say with a quick peck on her cheek.

Brad starts cheering. "Woot WOOT!!"

People around him join in.

"Of course, if it were me, I would have *really* kissed her!" Brad waggles an eyebrow suggestively.

The crowd erupts with a middle-school-worthy "Ooooo-OOooohh!"

Brad's looking at you expectantly. This is it. Your chance to impress Brad, and all the people who like Brad…i.e., everyone, obviously.

"Mind if I take a mulligan?" you ask Sad Sack, already leaning in.

"Again? Fine, but only if you haven't eaten peanut products in the last twenty-four hours, because I'm deathly—"

You cut her off midsentence with a passionate, open-mouthed kiss.

The crowd is absolutely *loving* it.

"YEAHHHHHH!" Their roars are deafening. This is what it must feel like to be a professional athlete. Or a movie star who was formerly a professional athlete.

From the corner of your eye you see Brad pull out his phone and snap a photo.

"This will be the perfect Holidaygram!" he says, laughing.

"You're so right, Brad! This *will* be the perfect Holidaygram," someone repeats. You see phones whipping out, flashes going off.

Fuck. How did you not think about the fact that you have a girlfriend until exactly this moment? A jealous, occasionally juvenile girlfriend. One who asked you to visit her for Christmas.

If that picture starts get shared online, Lindsi will lose her shit.

If you want to ask Brad to delete the photo, turn to page 131.
If you want to stay quiet to look cool in Brad's eyes, turn to page 130.

"Settle down, guys," you shout over the chanting crowd. "I have a girlfriend!"

You turn back to Sad Sack. Dear god, she's puckered her lips and is already leaning in.

"I'm taken, sorry."

"Oh…"

Sad Sack pulls away in obvious embarrassment.

"BOOOOOO!" roars the crowd. "BOOOOOOO!"

Oh come on, are you all twelve?

"Grinch!" you hear someone yell from the back of the room.

"Well, I'm not taken!" hollers Brad.

The crowd parts in two, like some ugly-sweatered Red Sea, as Brad walks over to Sad Sack.

He saunters up, smiles, then dips her to the ground and kisses her dramatically. Everyone pulls out phones to take photos.

"Classic Brad!" someone says nearby.

"He's just so cooooool," someone else responds.

Brad twirls Sad Sack around as everyone enthusiastically claps.

You sneak to the snack table and start stuffing your face with spinach dip. Sad Sack has been folded into Brad's entourage. They must find her miserable attitude hilarious or something.

You glance around the room. Everyone but you seems to be having a great time. Even those guys at the other end of the snack table, looking like the reject table in a John Hughes movie, are deep in conversation.

Wait a second. Did one of them just reference the seven charisma spells of the half-goblin sorcerer Ozshan? You may have just stumbled upon a bunch of fellow Dungeons and Elves nerds.

Up until now you've made a pretty concerted effort to hide your longtime love of D&E, but god, you could add so much to that conversation.

And it beats spinach dip and loneliness.

You head toward the D&E crew. Wait until they hear you once played a multiclass rogue-druid drow…*and* have a girlfriend.

They're gonna be so envious.

As you near them, you spot Sad Sack out of the corner of your eye...

...and she's standing under the mistletoe again.

If you want to redeem yourself and kiss her, turn to page 133.
If you want to hang with the D&E crowd, turn to page 134.

"I JUST WANTED TO COVER ALL THE BASES," YOU SAY. "EVERYONE'S SO
PC about hitting every holiday nowadays, you know?"

"Oh, totally," he nods and sticks out a hand. "John, by
the way."

You grip it gratefully and introduce yourself. Phew. You take
a sip of your drink.

"I'm just confused that you didn't start with Hanukkah."

Shit, you thought you'd gotten away with it. Of course he
had to bring up Hanukkah.

"That was gonna be my next guess. Well, not *guess*, it's not like
it's a game…"

"It *is* a much more common holiday."

"Is it? Yeah, you're probably right," you say, trying to sound
fair-minded and reasonable. And like you have any idea what
you're talking about. "I suppose the number of Jews…Jewish
people, I mean, is more…numerous than the number of…
Kwanzaa…people…"

"Do you even know what Kwanzaa *is*?"

No, no you don't. Turn to page 135.
Yeah. Sure. You probably know enough. Turn to page 137.

YOU START WRAPPING THE PRESENTS.

By the time you're done, it looks like you pulled them out of a landfill. The paper is crumpled and uneven, part of every box is showing, and there's tape everywhere.

Whatever. No kid has ever cared about a wrapping job, right?

You can hear your sister stomping around the kitchen angrily.

"No, that's all wrong!" she screams at her husband, Gregory. "It's like you've never even seen a balsamic reduction!"

You can't help but feel a little guilty.

If you picked up some of the workload, Lauren might settle down…slightly. After all, she is hosting you for Christmas.

On the other hand, if you toss the presents under the tree and sneak out the door right this second, you might be able to grab a drink without being judged.

If you want to stick around and offer to help your sister, turn to page 139.
If you want to sneak out to the bar, turn to page 140.

106

"SHOULD I USE MASKING TAPE?" YOU ASK LAUREN, POINTING TO HER "wrapping nook." "I want to wrap these as well as you would. Like Martha Stewart would. Same difference, right?"

Lauren gives you a big dumb smile. Oh god, you can't believe that actually worked.

"Maybe if I staple on some yarn it will have that cool, old-fashioned look?" You try not to wince at how stupid that sounded.

"Just put them on my bed," she says. "I'll wrap them later."

Success!

The rest of the evening seems much easier. Somehow admitting your inferiority has thawed her icy heart.

You even share drinks over dinner. And with a couple of glasses of wine in him, Gregory is actually funny...ish.

"Whoo! It's *way* past our bedtime," Lauren says as she loads the dishwasher.

You look at the clock on the wall.

8:07 P.M.

"See you in the morning," says Gregory. "*Gute nacht.*"

You're still a bit tipsy from the drinks at dinner. You don't want to call it a night already.

There's gotta be something fun to do around here, right?

If you want to peek at the presents, turn to page 141.
If you want to take your nephews sledding, turn to page 143.

YOU WALK IN THE DOOR TWENTY MINUTES LATER. ALL THAT SHOPPING has made you hungry. Weirdly, Lauren is already making dinner.

"Don't eat those," she says, batting your hand away from a bowl of nuts. "You'll spoil your appetite."

Seriously? It's not even four thirty.

"Um, okay."

You pull out a bottle of wine you picked up while you were out.

"Do you have a corkscrew?"

She gives you the hairy eyeball.

"Relax. It's Christmas. Gregory, you in?" You nod to Lauren's husband, sitting at the kitchen island. Who knows, maybe he'll be less insufferable after a couple of drinks.

He grins. "You know what? Why not!"

You pour him a glass, much to the annoyance of your sister.

"Just the one, okay? Dinner's almost ready."

You sit down—at four forty-five—to one of the most forgettable meals of your life. No sugar, no sauces, barely any salt…it's really just sustenance.

You pour Gregory a second glass of wine.

"What about you, a little splash?" you ask Lauren.

"I don't need alcohol to enjoy my Christmas," she responds, drenching the word alcohol with judgment.

"Suit yourself." You act like you don't notice. It's the perfect counterattack. "I was thinking that after dinner, I'd swing by this party."

"Party?" asks Lauren.

"Yeah. I ran into Jim French at the store." You double down on the casual tone. Bring it, Lauren.

"Jim French? That's a name I haven't heard in ages." Lauren snorts. "I didn't know you even liked him."

Fuck her, you're GOING to this party. Turn to page 147.
The party isn't the point; it's annoying your sister that matters. Stay at Lauren's and attempt to grab the upper hand on page 145.

108

You head to Santaland.

And what a charming land it is: miniature log cabins with costumed elves offering free jam cookies, stores with ridiculously adorable crafts, and a cute baby reindeer that grazes right out of your hand.

If this is what parenting is like, maybe you're not against having kids after all.

"Who wants cocoa?" It's Lauren who has the rule about sugar, not their *cool* uncle.

"ME, ME!" the boys scream.

You buy them cups, tossing in a candy cane each so they can stir the marshmallows around. You're nailing this.

"A bouncy castle!" Harrison yells.

"Go for it, boys!"

After jumping around for fifteen minutes, they race back out.

"Let's go on the candy cane jungle gym!" screams Harrison.

Hmmm, you thought they'd be more worn out after all that jumping.

Oh well.

As you make your way across the village, you pass an extremely attractive elf attendant standing in front of an ornament stand.

She winks at you suggestively.

"LOOK! IT'S SANTA!" screams Harrison, pointing past her.

If you want to approach the hot elf, turn to page 150.
If you want to get in line with the kids to see Santa, turn to page 151.

THE BOYS WALK UP TO THE HOUSE, TREMBLING.

"Why was Goofy…*SNFF!*…covered in chains?" Harrison asks between sobs.

"Because that's how the story goes. It's a classic."

Who knew that a Disney cartoon could be so traumatizing? Or that any child, ever, could be this sheltered?

Lauren is waiting at the door. Both boys run straight to her.

"Where did you take them?" she asks, holding one against each leg.

"Just a movie. It was rated G." The boys continue to sob uncontrollably. "I thought you read them Harry Potter?"

"Boys, go upstairs and get ready for a bath," your sister says.

"Ooo—*SNFFFF!*—o-kayyyy."

Lauren glares.

"I read Harry Potter *to* them."

"Right. It's much scarier than *Mickey's Christmas Carol*."

"Not after my edits."

The End.

You'd take a shower, but the thought of what's lurking in the bottom of the bathtub makes you feel nauseous. More nauseous.

Instead, you take a cologne-and-deodorant shower, check out, and hop into your car, setting the GPS for your apartment in the city.

Better to spend Christmas alone than in this shithole.

But you don't want to be *alone*-alone. Who's spending Christmas in the city?

The only person you can think of is your former colleague, Debby. You can't imagine her having anything good to do. But then, wouldn't that mean she'd be more likely to agree to see you?

You dial her number.

"Hey, Debby?"

"Merry—" she slurps thickly. The idea that it's eggnog turns your stomach. "—Christmas! *SNRCK!*"

"So, I know this is last minute…" Now that you have her and her slurping on the line, you're not sure hanging out is such a good idea. Do you even like Debby? But you're out of other friend-ish options. "Are you doing anything tonight?"

"Tonight? Did the WPA get Depression-era America back on its feet? *SNRCK!*"

You cringe.

"Let's," more slurping, "par-TAY!"

• • •

How much time should you let pass before you actively clarify to people at the party that Debby's *not* your girlfriend? Two minutes? Less?

Debby leads you to a walk-up third-floor apartment and knocks on the door, snorting merrily. Someone opens it and gestures you two inside.

"Where's the bar?" Debby says, her face like rising bread dough at its coyest. "It's time for SHOTS!" The person points, and she immediately trundles away, leaving you to fend for yourself.

You take a cursory look around the room.

You don't recognize a single person.

You pull out your phone and start randomly opening and closing apps in an attempt to look busy. You don't even see the sad sack in the shapeless gray dress—hair limp with grease, Coke-bottle glasses actually taped in the middle—sidle up to you.

She sighs heavily. You jump. Jesus, is she some kind of misery ninja?

"Looks like you and me are the lonely ones at the party, huh?"

If you want to talk to the first person who's acknowledged your existence, turn to page 65.

If you want to escape to the bar, turn to page 67.

YOU HAVE TO MAKE UP WITH YOUR SISTER. AFTER ALL, EVEN SHE'S better than another night in this miserable hole.

RING!

"Hello?"

"Hey, sis."

"Oh…hello," Lauren says frostily.

"I just wanted to call to patch things over from last night."

"I'm surprised you managed to find a hotel room." She sniffs.

"It wasn't too much trouble." You stare at the vibrating mattress coin box beside the bed. "Anyway, how's the gang this morning?"

"We're fine. Though I think you really hurt Otto and Harrison by not saying hello to them last night." You grit your teeth. "Anyway, if you still plan on eating Christmas Eve dinner here, there are a few things you can do to help out."

This is as close to an apology as you'll ever get from Lauren. You might as well take it. "Okay."

You spend the rest of the day running around trying to find the right "GMO-free, long-life healthy, ethical" groceries she needs.

By the time you're finished, it's late afternoon and you're starving. You probably should've eaten more than that solitary dry bagel at the "continental breakfast buffet."

You walk into your sister's house, carrying a sack of windfall beets in one hand and three biodegradable bags of unpasteurized pasture-raised milk in the other.

"I can't wait to eat," you say.

"You're late," says your sister, obviously annoyed.

"What?" You're truly puzzled. "It's four o'clock?"

"Look. If you have a problem with me, that's fine. But don't take it out on my family this way."

Is she for real?

You drop the bags of milk and the sack of beets to the floor and walk out. Fuck this—if this is family, you'll spend Christmas alone.

Luckily, you know a bar nearby with plenty of nog…

Turn to page 152.

"THANKS FOR INCLUDING ME," YOU SAY. YOU, LINDSI'S DAD, 'DAD,' her brother Lars, and her brother-in-law Michael have been trudging through the woods for about twenty minutes, after a solid half-hour drive to the tree farm, but no one has spoken a single word yet.

"Mmm," Lars grunts, nodding at you. He seems friendly enough. Apparently the kind of men who cut their own trees with smallish-looking hand-axes don't need excess words.

It should be awkward, but the silence of the woods, the beauty of the snow-covered trees, and the freshness of the air is making you feel better. Even your back is starting to feel less brutalized. Maybe this is exactly what you needed to get back on track.

"Mmmm." Lars elbows you, tilting his head to the right. You look in that direction and see a magnificent buck staring back, totally unfazed by your presence.

"Wow," you murmur. Lars nods, smiling.

"Not too often you see a twelve-pointer as healthy as that," he whispers back, looking at you appraisingly.

"Oh, for sure," you agree. That makes you sound like you know what you're talking about, right? Like you've seen deer outside of petting zoos before? Apparently so. Lars smiles again and thumps you on the shoulder in a chummy, manly fashion.

Could this day go any better? You're even getting along with Lindsi's brother. Shit, he spoke a full sentence to you; you might as well be blood brothers.

This is the kind of Christmas you'd always been missing. Maybe you actually *love* this holiday. Maybe you love Lindsi. You've never felt more at one with the world around you.

Turn to page 155.

"Wow, that sounds amazing," you say, heaping as much sugar onto the words as you can, "and I'm honored that you'd include me, but honestly, I don't think I'm up to it."

"Really." Mom stares at you. Technically you suppose she's smiling, but she somehow manages to convey utter disgust.

"Yeah, unfortunately I have a really terrible back. I slipped a disk playing high school hockey." That's not true—you never made the team, and your doctor said your back pain was most likely "excessive-sitting-based"—but it sounds better.

"Mmm. All right then, if you'd rather stay home with the *women*."

Apparently the VanWhittingtons don't do progressive gender roles.

You spend the morning on the couch while Mom and a couple of Lindsi's nieces make gingerbread in the kitchen.

"Why's he so lazy, Grandma?" the smaller one whines loudly enough for you to hear. Screw you, kid, that snub nose isn't gonna look cute in another year.

"Some people don't have a work ethic, sweetie," Mom says, her voice brutally cheery. "They don't like helping when they visit someone's home."

Goddammit.

"Hey, guys," you say, grimace-smiling as you push off the couch. You still feel like the interior of your back has been replaced with a colony of pissed-off fire ants, but that gauntlet-throwing was too much to ignore. "I'd love to help out with the cookies since I'm *far too injured* to chop down a tree."

"I'm making a you-gingerbread," Snub Nose says, holding up a cookie. It's wearing a pink frosting skirt and...c'mon now, you don't have man-tits, do you?

"Oh! It's just like him!" Mom laughs, balancing a plate of cookies on one elbow while she lifts the entire upright mixer with the other hand. Jesus, is everyone in this family made of tree trunks?

"Let me help," you say.

"No, no, I wouldn't want to *strain* you." She rolls her eyes dramatically. You think you hear her mutter, "Never survive a proving," but that doesn't make any sense. Maybe the pain is causing aural hallucinations?

You grit your teeth. A timer dings.

"I can at least grab those cookies," you offer. "So they don't burn."

"Fine, if you insist." She tilts her chin toward the counter, where two potholders are stacked. They're frilly and embroidered with the words *The Ladies Are Cooking*. Awesome.

You lean down to grab the cookies, but the minute you reach your arm into the oven, it feels like your spine has been torn in two, like a wet toilet paper tube.

Fuck. You've fully thrown out your back.

*If you want to jerk upright and hope you don't pass
out from the pain, turn to page 157.
If you want to claim you've burned your hand
to buy time, turn to page 159.*

ANTS! THERE ARE ANTS CRAWLING ALL OVER YOUR BODY, FIRE ANTS, biting you, your entire chest is a carpet of...

You blink several times, confused. Where are you? And why is your entire body in pain?

Oh, right, you put your sweater on last night without the arms. It seemed like a good idea at the time—it would guarantee you couldn't accidentally grab Jimmy's balls or something.

But now your entire body feels like one massive wool rash. Worse, pinning your arms in place means you must have slept in some really weird positions; you're still lying flat and already you feel your back radiating pain into every limb.

Awesome.

You pull the sweater over your head and trudge down to the kitchen.

"Finally up?" Mom says, pinch-smiling at you.

"Mmmm." You don't bother telling her it's only seven thirty, or that your chest looks like it has pinkeye. Actually forming words would lift the seal off your bubbling pissiness.

"Well, luckily you haven't missed out yet," she says.

"Mmmm?"

"In our family the men go out on Christmas Eve day to cut down the tree. Even though they don't know you yet, they wanted to include you. They're just generous that way."

"Mmmmmm."

If you want to go along, if only to get away from Mom's passive aggression for a few hours, turn to page 113.
If you'd rather stay home and try not to completely throw out your back, turn to page 114.

You lie down on the edge of the bed farthest from Jimmy's motionless body and close your eyes, certain you're facing a sleepless night.

• • •

You wake up with your arm around your girlfr—

Fuck, you knew you shouldn't have trusted sleep-you.

You roll away as quickly as possible and dress over the edge of the bed. By the time Jimmy wakes up—eyes flapping open all at once, like some terrifying humanoid doll—you've managed to shrug into a sweater and jeans.

"Last night I dreamed I was fighting a gelatinous sea monster." Jimmy hasn't moved; he's staring at the ceiling, reciting this to… well, presumably you.

"Okay."

"It seemed about to overwhelm me, but I punched it in the side of the head with my gauntleted fist. Then it understood I was its master and lay down coyly for me."

Oh god, is this going to be a sex dream?

"But I was still filled with blood lust and sliced it into a million tiny blobs with my scimitar."

Phew.

"Then I had sex with the blobs. Which explains the large quantity of ejaculate now present on my boxers, pajamas, and one corner of the quilt."

Wow. That was…specific.

"It seems as though my semen production must have increased, judging from the spread of the—"

"JIMMY."

He stares at you, eyes dead, then nods once.

"You must help me dispose of this evidence."

"Dispose of…what?"

"My mother sees me as a child. She is uncomfortable with the idea of my burgeoning, uncontrollable sexuality," Jimmy says flatly. "If she knows this happened, she'll be inconsolable."

"No offense, Jimmy, but that's not really my pro—"

"She'll probably assume you were sexually inappropriate with me."

Well, fuck.

"I mean…don't you know how to do laundry? It's not hard."

"No. I have never been required to launder my clothing or bedding."

"But it's simple, really. It—"

"Doing laundry now, the very day after we shared a bed, would surely draw suspicion."

He has a point.

If you want to help him deal with the jizz shorts…
and sheets, and comforter, turn to page 160.
If Jimmy's mom's gonna have to learn that he blows
loads sometimes, turn to page 161.

"No. Well, I mean, yes, it is, but…" What can you say that will make this seem less horrifying? "I was out here for some…air, and it attacked. Out of nowhere! I had to defend myself."

"You're saying *you* killed the coyote?" It's hard to make out her expression, since she's backlit by the house, but it doesn't *look* like the depths of horrified disgust.

"Well, in a manner of speaking…yes?"

"How?" You're still loopy from the Ambien, but it almost sounds like there's wonder in Mom's voice.

"It had latched onto my arm, and the only thing I could think to do was punch it in the side of the head."

"Yes." Mom takes a step toward you. "It's perfect technique."

Was that weird? You can't tell what's weird anymore because of the drugs. And the murdered woodland animal at your feet.

"It released briefly, and, I dunno, I managed to grab hold of a rock. Then I just…smashed its skull in."

You can feel the skull crushing beneath your hand again. You swallow hard against another wave of vomit.

"I'm so sorry," you say when you're fairly certain you've mastered it. "I never meant for this to happen."

"Sorry? It's a natural proving." She's close enough now for you to make out her features. She's looking at you with something approaching awe.

"Natural…what?"

"Please, come inside; let me make you breakfast. You've earned it."

You're not sure how getting drugged up and slaughtering a coyote has done it, exactly, but it's clear: Mom has stopped hating you. She might even love you.

● ● ●

All day the entire family treats you like some sort of hero. Mom insists that you pick the Christmas meal. Dad gives you a crossbow he claims has been in his family for generations "as an early Christmas gift," and Lindsi has never looked at you more adoringly.

You could get used to this.

After an evening around the fire where every one of your jokes seems to land, you stretch, yawn, and head for the basement door.

"I should get some rest; I was up early this morning," you say, giving Mom a meaningful look. "Thank you so much for a lovely day."

"Our pleasure," Mom says, smiling warmly. "But where are you going?"

"Uh." You're not sure what she's getting at. "The basement? I assumed I'd be sleeping there the entire—"

"No, no, no," Mom shakes her head, smiling indulgently. "That's ridiculous. A man like you can't sleep in the basement, like the hired help."

"A man like…?"

"A man with your instincts and natural dominance should be sleeping in a place of honor. With my daughter."

Lindsi looks at you eagerly. You can almost smell the horniness coming off her.

"Well done, Killer," Mom says as the two of you climb the stairs. "Welcome to the family."

You're going to have to make it seem like you're interested in that offer, at least until you're out of range of all those crossbows…

The End.

"I was, uh, stepping outside for…some air? And I found this coyote."

"You…found it?"

"Yeah, I saw something dark against the snow," you're warming to your story now, "and I wanted to see what it was, and then you came out."

"Mmm." Mom's walked up beside you. "Apparently after you vomited on it."

"Oh, yeah. I…ate a lot of Combos on the drive. They must have upset my stomach."

"Mmmm." Mom's obviously disgusted, though it doesn't seem like the vomit's the issue. She stares at *you*, lip curling upward, until you feel almost obligated to speak.

"Is something wrong?"

"Not necessarily." She sighs heavily. "It's just that in this house we have a hunting tradition."

You nod, trying to look not-that-terrified. You're suddenly very, very happy you never told Lindsi about that time you fainted in biology after watching that video about dissection.

"Of course, I don't use that term lightly. Tradition means following the ways of our forebears. It means traditional tracking techniques. And traditional weaponry."

"That seems more fair," you say, trying to add anything to this baffling monologue.

"YES. Yes." She nods vigorously. "Exactly. Guns are for the weak."

"I've always said that," you lie. You don't even have an opinion on gun control.

"Would you be open to something like that?" Her eyes look momentarily less judgy. "To bond with the men in our family?"

"Something like…"

"A traditional hunt with the men? Or maybe on your own?"

Visions of impaling your foot with a crossbow flutter across your mind. You're pretty sure it's not the Ambien anymore.

Yup. It's the only way. Turn to page 163.
No, that's barbaric. Turn to page 165.

HE TAKES ANOTHER STEP TOWARD YOU. YOU SHRIEK AND GRAB THE table lamp near the bed. Adrenaline pounding through your veins, you run toward him and swing as hard as you can.

The lamp connects with his head. In the dim light, you see a look of pure shock cross his face before he collapses to the floor, out cold.

Huh. You always figured yourself for a "flight" guy.

Once you can breathe normally again, you grab your phone and call 911. They can deal with this monster. The operator says an ambulance will be by shortly. Just as it pulls up, the trucker starts to come to.

"What…what happened?"

"This man attacked me," you say to the officers walking through the door. "I had to defend myself."

You hear a sob from the lump on the ground.

"I didn't attack you!" He grips his head, weeping louder.

"You broke into my room in the middle of the night."

"Because I needed your help."

You raise an eyebrow.

"I have *diabetes*." He coughs. "You'd bought out the vending machine and my blood sugar was low. When I knocked, the door just came open on its own."

"Well…why are you wearing that?" You gesture at the bathrobe that's fallen open, revealing a giant-sized diaper. "That's some kind of weird fetish thing; what was I supposed to think?"

"This? It's for *incontinence*." He weeps louder. "It's a side effect of—of—of…my diseeeeeeease."

One of the cops shakes his head in disgust.

"My sister has diabetes. How could you be so intolerant?"

"Oh, come on, what would you think if this guy broke into your room?"

The cop steps over. "Please extend your hands, sir."

"What?"

"We have to keep you in county until this man decides whether to press charges."

"You can't be serious."

"Are you resisting?"

You stick out your hands.

• • •

The first hour isn't so bad.

Then the eggnog drunk shows up and promptly destroys the toilet in the corner of the holding cell.

Good thing you went at the motel.

An hour later they bring in a man who's totally naked except for penny loafers and reindeer antlers.

"Merry...Crizz....mahhh—" he says to you, then promptly vomits all over his own feet. For reasons you can't even begin to fathom, the puddle is red and green.

You wonder if Lindsi will believe you hit a tree...

The End.

YOU SHRINK AS FAR BACK INTO THE BED AS YOU CAN MANAGE. MAYBE if you appear infinitesimally tiny he won't hurt you as badly.

You feel his weight at the other end of the bed. Here it comes. He starts to wail.

"WAAAA! Baby wants a ba-ba!"

You open your eyes. He's lying at the foot of the bed, all four limbs waving in the air. He's removed the robe and hat. Beneath the first is the largest diaper you've ever seen; beneath the second is a giant, lacy bonnet.

"Baby's BORED!"

He gets louder.

"You want me to…"

"Give baby toys! Give baby ba-ba!"

"Okay, I don't have a, uh, 'ba-ba,' but I have a big kid cup." You tiptoe around the bottom of the bed, giving him as wide a berth as the room will allow. He calms slightly. You cross to the sink and fill a filmy plastic glass with murky water. "Can you drink like a big boy?"

"Okaaaayyyyyyy."

You hand him the cup. He promptly spills it everywhere. He turns to you, lip trembling.

"Oh, uh…whoopsie-daisy," you say. He giggles maniacally, biting on his fist.

"AGAIN! AGAIN!"

"Whoopsie-daisy."

"HEEEEEEE!!!!!!!!"

You grit your teeth. It's better than getting raped. Remember that.

• • •

After an hour, he stands, puts his robe and hat on, nods, and leaves.

You wedge a chair beneath the doorknob but you barely sleep.

There's no way you can face Lindsi after tonight. It'll show on you somehow. It will be a funny story in a few weeks, maybe.

Or a few years. But right now? You need to get home, shower for a year, and make sure every lock is secure.

As soon as it's light you pack up. On your way out the door you notice something on the dresser.

It's a wad of crumpled twenties.

It makes the idea of telling people about last night even harder to imagine.

And it begs the question…where was he keeping these?

You grab them gingerly and stuff them in your pocket. Just call it babysitting money.

The End.

As soon as you hit the highway traffic is at a standstill. You should have expected it—it's Christmas Eve day, and you're in prime "Grandma lives a few hours from here" territory.

Still, it's maddening. At least you have the Combos. You know it's gross to be eating so many—are you on your tenth bag now, or your thirteenth?—but they taste so *good*.

Several hours later you pull into Lindsi's parents' driveway. You walk into the kitchen to see her entire family sitting tensely around the table, staring at you.

Why do they all look so angry?

"Merry Christmas," you say hesitantly.

"This is my family," Lindsi says curtly, introducing you to everyone in turn. "Now, are you ready to go?"

"Go?"

"We've been waiting for the last few hours so you wouldn't be alone when you arrived. We thought we'd bring you caroling, then for dinner at Aunt Lori's."

"Oh, dinner would be—"

"It's too late for that now." Lindsi's mother's smile is tighter than her terrible perm. Clearly you're already making a great impression. "At least we haven't missed mass yet," she adds, raising an eyebrow like a challenge.

Ugh. You hate church. Though possibly not as much as Lindsi's mother clearly already hates you…

If you want to go to mass, despite the fact that you're an atheist and feel like seven kinds of shit, turn to page 55.
If you want to beg off and tell them to go on without you, turn to page 57.

THE ONLY WAY OUT OF THIS IS TO GO WAY, WAY DEEPER.

You have to full-on shit your pants. After all, what adult human would deliberately do that? The VanWhittingtons may hate you afterward, but they'll be sympathetic. Or at least fear you.

You figure it might be difficult to shit your pants in public—everything in you wants that to never happen—but as soon as you push out a little of the Combos foulness you've been holding back, it becomes a torrent. Half farts, half bubbling wet shit, you can tell this will be a doozy.

"Oh god," you say to Lindsi, wincing in pain for effect. "I'm so sorry—I think I have food poisoning." You hang your head. "Please, let me out, I'm so sorry."

She turns to you, briefly confused, then edges backward, face tight with horror.

You shamble down the aisle, shit dripping from your ankle, too horrified to look at anyone. You hear the sound of someone retching a few pews up, near the site of the devastation. Someone else joins in. You turn once, as you're pushing through the doors of the chapel. The scene is horrific—dozens of people are leaning into the aisles, vomiting profusely. A child is shrieking somewhere. In the middle of the church you see a man frozen in horror, vomit dripping down the front of his sweater and khakis, everyone around him bent double.

You hurry to the bathroom.

The only option is to abandon your pants…and underwear, and socks. You scrub the shoes a few times, then put them back on, feet squelching ominously.

Now what?

You head into a stall and grab a roll of toilet paper, wrapping it around and around yourself to cover your nakedness.

Not gonna keep anyone from knowing who Pants-Shitter Zero was, though.

Turn to page 153.

128

YOU SQUEEZE OVER LINDSI AND LARS AND HURRY DOWN THE AISLE, ignoring the frowns and wrinkled noses in your wake.

You try to keep your butt cheeks as together as possible, but it takes about ten minutes of wandering the halls before you find a bathroom.

By the time you get there, you know things have gotten much, much worse.

You step into a stall, fully remove your pants, and hang them over the door.

Now for the moment of truth.

You peel away your underwear.

Dear god, the smell was already bad, but now it's absolutely cataclysmic. The entire bathroom is filled with the curiously processed smell of digested Combos. You glance down at the underwear.

The entire back is coated with a layer of slick, oily, bright orange shit.

You step out of them, wrapping your hand in a few squares of toilet paper to pick them up. Fortunately, church toilets are superpowered—the olds must have even more serious issues than you do—and the offending underwear easily flushes away.

You clean up as best you can, carefully pressing your ear to the stall door before dashing to the sink to make toilet paper wet wipes. Your balls flap into the shart residue, forcing you to repeat the process. Finally, however, you manage to clean yourself fully.

But now you have no underwear.

And you're not sure the Combos sharts are done with you.

If you want to take your chances and go freeball, turn to page 167.
If you want to fashion some toilet paper underwear for
pants protection, turn to page 168.

It will have to dissipate soon, right? That's just the law of farts.

But with each passing second, the foul, rancid odor seems to get stronger, as though more and more poo-lecules are working their way out of your pants.

And of course Combos sharts smell particularly horrific. The chemical element adds a specific, painful tang to the befouled air.

Lindsi leans in to whisper in your ear.

"What's that smell—oh—" She chokes slightly. "It's even worse by you." She gags a little.

"I don't smell anything."

She frowns, her eyes watering.

"How can you—*ohmahgahd GROSS.*"

She vomits at your feet.

A lot.

A tiny, shrunken woman with a bird's nest of white curls turns at the sound, gasps, covers her mouth, then vomits all over the pew she's standing in.

The person next to her vomits seconds later.

Soon it's passing through the entire church, like a holy wave of puke.

Somehow you manage not to join in.

Turn to page 169.

BRAD WALKS UP AND GIVES YOU A HIGH FIVE.

It lands perfectly.

SMACK!

It's clear you're now the envy of the party.

"You're right, Brad! That picture *will* be the perfect Holidaygram."

He grins and taps at his phone. Too late to turn back now.

But it doesn't matter, not if Brad thinks it'll be funny. There's no reason to worry. It was just a laugh. Besides, what are the chances Lindsi will see it? Slim, right? She barely knows Brad.

You set out to enjoy the rest of the party, which is pretty easy, since Brad's absorbed you into his entourage. He even introduces you to the cool-looking black dude at the bar!

By the time you're ready to head home, you're pretty drunk. Who knew Brad's beer pong skills were so razor sharp? Who knew people your age still played beer pong?

As you stumble into the street, your phone rings.

You drunkenly fumble it out of your coat pocket.

"Hello?"

"Oh, good. You're answering."

It's Lindsi. And for whatever reason, she sounds absolutely livid.

"Hey Linzzzzzz," you slur.

"I thought you were staying home to 'get some work done.'"

"Huh?"

"I saw that photo. You and that...*slut* making out."

You sincerely doubt Sad Sack is a slut, but now's probably not the best time to come to her rescue.

"Obviously the kiss was a joke, Linzzz. Did you see that loser? She'za complete charity case!"

You hear a sharp wail just feet behind you. You turn around. Shit, it's Sad Sack. She clearly heard every word you said.

"WE'RE OVER!!!" Lindsi screams into the phone.

The End.

ONCE THE CROWD SETTLES DOWN, YOU WALK UP TO BRAD.

"Hey, man, I'm sure it's a hilarious photo, but if it's all the same to you, could you maybe delete it? Or at least not post it online? My girlfriend would be pissed if she saw that."

Your heart is racing. You've never been this assertive with someone like Brad before. You're not even sure you and he have had a real conversation before.

"I totally understand," he says. "It's gone." He actually pulls out the phone and trashes the photo on the spot. By the time the rest of the party got their phones out the kiss was over. You're safe!

Wow, you never expected Brad to be so understanding. And easygoing. No wonder he has the reputation for being the king of cool.

"This party is getting pretty lame, right?"

"SO lame," you instantly blurt out, still giddy from relief. Brad not only deleted the photo, but he likes you enough to shit on this party with you. Maybe you're cooler than you thought!

"We should go do something fun. You know, somewhere else. Me, you, and Blitzer."

Blitzer? Does he mean *Wolf* Blitzer? Was he invited to this party?

You know what? It doesn't matter. Whoever Blitzer is, you're in. You've never felt so chosen before.

"Totally. Cool," you say.

"Hey, everyone!" Brad yells.

Someone turns down the music. Everyone turns to Brad, waiting to hear what he has to say.

"Thanks for the good times, but I gotta jet."

Wow, that was pretty aggressively douchey.

But no one else seems to think so. In fact, look of disappointment is sweeping the crowd, like some sort of sorrow wave. Maybe it was cool? Brad *did* do it, after all.

You follow Brad and Blitzer—a tall black guy dressed like some kind of hipster catalog model—down to the street. A Porsche is parked there.

"Someone's having a midli—"

"Squeeze in," Brad shouts, grinning widely. Oh, okay. You're glad you didn't finish that sentence.

You have to basically sit on Blitzer's lap because there are only two seats. This is seeming less cool by the second.

Brad speeds away, sailing through a few stop signs before making a quick left-hand turn. He stops in front of a church. It has a nativity scene on the lawn.

"I've got an idea," Brad says, looking at the two of you with a wicked grin. "Let's get the baby Jesus."

What are you, twelve?

"Oh, dude, that would be *EPIC*," Blitzer says from beneath you.

Seriously?

You clamber out of the Porsche. Whatever, Brad can vandalize all the churches he wants; you'll just watch. If you play along for the night, you'll be in. And Brad does seem to get invited to some really killer parties…

"So?" Brad's walked around the side of the car and is looking at you expectantly.

"What, you want me to…?"

"I mean, unless you're chicken."

"Oooooooh," Blitzer says, eyebrows raised.

Do they really expect you to do this?

If you want to fake an injury to get out of it, turn to page 172.
If you want to steal church property, turn to page 170.

"MISTLETOE!" YOU YELL CHEERILY, RUNNING OVER TO WHERE SAD Sack's standing.

Everyone turns to look as you pucker your lips and close your eyes, swooping in—in what you hope is a very Brad-like motion— for a kiss.

Sad Sack jerks her head back at the last second. Oh god, you've overshot the landing. You lose your balance and tumble to the floor.

"You already had your chance," she says, stepping over your body.

"Ohhhhh...BURN!" yells Brad.

Everyone erupts into laughter.

"Swing and a miss," you say with a self-deprecating smile. You pop up from the floor quickly, even though you think the fall might have ruptured your spleen.

You grab some ice from the punch bowl and try to inconspicuously press it against the small of your back. Once you feel confident you can make it down the stairs without exacerbating your maybe-injury you leave, annoyed, embarrassed, and sore.

You check your phone back at your apartment.

Thirty new Facebook mentions?

You click the first notification.

Someone's posted a video of you going in for the kiss and falling. The second and third notifications show the same scene shot from different angles.

No need to read all twenty-seven...no wait, fifty-six...eighty-three? Jesus, why are so many people commenting on this thing?

The newest one is from...oh, man, Brad. You should have known Brad wasn't really on your team.

There's a new one from...your third-grade teacher? When did you even become friends on Facebook? And why would she say you were "always socially awkward"? That's not true, is it?

Oh come on, your mom is piling on? You should have never let her and Dad go on a Christmas cruise; they're clearly mean drunks.

The End.

BE HONEST WITH YOURSELF: THAT GROUP OF ANEMIC-LOOKING DUDES by the snack table is more your speed.

You almost run over; even if you have no conversational in, you can grab a few mini-quiches. Everyone loves a mini-quiche.

"Sorry you feel that way, but my alignment's chaotic evil. I couldn't help you even if I wanted to…because I'd never want to," a slightly overweight, schlubby guy with long, curly hair says. Someone nearby snorts.

"That's bullshit; you were just pissed I got more XP from the orc battle," the weedy guy with the vampire coloring and glasses pouts.

"Whatever."

Dungeons and Elves nerds! You have more than an in here— you have your entire adolescence to discuss. That will get you through to…at least 10 P.M., right?

"Did your character die?" you say to Vampire. He looks over, startled at being addressed by someone outside his circle.

"Yeah. This asshole killed me." He points at Schlubby, who's grinning smugly.

"That sucks. I once leveled a paladin up past fifty then got decapitated 'cause my DM was pissed I made out with his sister."

Vampire nods understandingly. "Whatever, I need to roll a new character tonight anyway. We were gonna play the special Christmas edition module over there," he nods to a corner, "but we need a fourth player. Victor won't DM for a party of two." The guy who hasn't spoken yet, a short guy with hair so pale he looks eyelashless, nods in agreement. Presumably that's Victor. "You in?"

You want to be so badly; nights in Jim Ikola's basement, battling trolls and demon armies while you got drunk off cordials from his parents' liquor cabinet, are some of your happiest memories.

But you left that part of you behind in college. No one there knew you as a D&E nerd, and you were more than happy to step away from "social reject" into the role of cool, hiply nerdy guy.

Fuck it, you're nerding out with these guys. Turn to page 174.
No, the risk is too high; people here could know Lindsi, after all.
Tell them no on page 175.

"ACTUALLY, I DON'T REALLY KNOW MUCH ABOUT KWANZAA. I WAS just trying to be culturally sensitive to all...religions?"

"You mean you were profiling, right?" John shakes his head. "Since we're being honest."

Out of the corner of your eye, you see someone approaching. Oh no, it's Brad, the coolest guy at your old office! You should have known he'd be at this party. Everyone loved Brad.

"Hey bros, what's the word?" he asks.

"This guy," John says, sticking his finger directly in your chest, "just wished me a happy Kwanzaa."

"Oof. You Kwanzaaed John?" Brad laughs, hitting John on the back chummily. Of course they're friends. Classic Brad.

"I might have. A little." You swallow hard. "But it was an accidental Kwanzaa-ing," you add. If Brad's using the word as a verb, you can too, right?

"Dude, you just admitted you didn't even know what it was. Maybe try understanding the tradition before you start throwing it around."

"You really don't know anything about Kwanzaa?" Brad looks legitimately surprised. Oh, come *on*.

"Well, no. Seriously though, who really knows about Kwanzaa?"

"Kwanzaa, the holiday, first celebrated in 1966, that grew out of the black power movement?" Brad smirks slightly.

John nods solemnly. Seriously? There's no way everyone would know about Kwanzaa if it were that recent.

"Kwanzaa, which in Swahili—a language chosen for the holiday as a cultural unifier"—Brad leans in like you're pals— "translates as 'first fruits of the harvest'?"

"Mmmhmm," John agrees.

As if Brad even knows where Swahili is. You'd point that out, but you're not actually sure where it is, either.

Brad keeps going, listing "fact" after "fact" about Kwanzaa. You're starting to think he and John are playing an elaborate joke on you, but there's no single point you're certain enough of to bet on. You already Kwanzaaed the guy once. If you're wrong now, that's it.

"Anyway, you should read up on it." Brad smiles broadly. "It's really an interesting celebration." He turns to John, leading him away. "You can't blame people for not checking their privilege," you hear him say as they walk off.

Fucking Kwanzaa...

Turn to page 177.

"OF COURSE I KNOW WHAT KWANZAA IS," YOU SPUTTER.

That's not entirely untrue, though explaining it to someone who *really* knows might be a bit beyond your capacity. But John's looking at you expectantly, so you go on.

"Some people think of it as a sort of African American Christmas," you start.

"*Christmas* is black Christmas," John says, annoyed.

Fuck.

"Of course, I don't dispute that. That's just how ignorant people think of it." Nice backtracking. "Which is what I was *going* to say before you cut me off."

"Sorry."

Focus now. Try to remember those five minutes of that one day in elementary school.

"Kwanzaa, as I'm sure you know, stems from…the rich… *bake* sale tradition…in Creole culture." Oof, that can't possibly be right.

John frowns slightly, but doesn't correct you. Might as well keep going, the damage is already done now.

"It's a common misconception that the holiday arose as a reaction to the brutal campaigns Andrew Jackson led throughout the South in the War of 1812."

The War of 1812? You possibly know even less about that than about Kwanzaa.

"Right, right," John says, rolling his hand in a "go on" gesture. You try to conceal your shock. Somehow you've been right up to this point. Can you possibly come up with more?

"But in fact, some of the earliest traditions aren't Creole at all, as they're so often portrayed. They're not even Native American. The, um, milking of the goats ceremony…" Is that even remotely close to a thing?

"My grandma was always so into the milking of the goats." John shakes his head ruefully.

Phew.

"Anyway, the genesis of the milking ritual goes back to ancient

Rhodesia," you say.

"Known today as Kenya, of course."

"Of course," you agree, feeling more confident now. "It could only happen at the end of harvest, as I'm sure you recall, largely due to time constraints…"

• • •

Perspective Switch: You Are John

The milking of the goats ceremony? That sounds vaguely familiar, but you are 99 percent certain this guy just pulled it out of his ass. But what can you say? It's not like you can counter with some *real* part of Kwanzaa.

You seriously need to Wikipedia Kwanzaa the second you get home.

Then at least the next time this happens, you'll be able to call out ignorant assholes when they're so clearly bullshitting. For now, though, you basically have no choice but to play along with this idiot. After all, it would be just your luck to call out the one thing he's actually getting right.

You should mention yams, follow it up with something vague about Pan-Africanism, then get the hell away from this conversation.

Fucking Kwanzaa…

The End.

"ANYTHING I CAN HELP WITH?" YOU ASK LAUREN.

Hopefully she'll know you're just trying to be polite.

She hands you a multipage list.

"Sulfite-free? Does eggnog even contain——"

"You'll find that in the next town over. I've listed the address of the creamery," she says. "It's the only eggnog the boys can drink."

You look at the list, repressing a sigh. You can't even pronounce half the words on it.

"Just curious—what's this?"

"Oh, Gregory loves his spicy Austrian cheese spread."

"Is there another option I can pick up somewhere nearby, or——"

"I'll just do it myself," she says, snapping her fingers for the list.

"No, no, no. I'd be more than happy to go to the Austrian specialty shop in"—you look down—"Bakersfield." That's fully four suburbs away.

If you stick around any longer, there's no limit to what Lauren might ask you to do.

You grab the gift you're donating to Toys for Tots and rush out the door.

Turn to page 178.

You sneak out the back door before Lauren can force you into indentured servitude.

You walk around your hometown.

It takes all of fifteen minutes before you're bored. Plus, it's starting to get cold.

There's only one option that will eat up time *and* keep you warm: the bar.

Before you go, you stop at the Toys for Tots bin. Donating to charity means you've earned a few Christmas drinks, right?

You walk in and order a beer.

You feel calm for the first time since you've arrived.

But you also feel like a shit for not helping out around the house…

If you want to head home out of guilt, turn to page 179.
If you want to stick around for a few more drinks, turn to page 180.

YOU LOOK AT THE CHRISTMAS TREE. IT'S SO SOULLESS, EVERY ornament like a page out of a Crate & Barrel catalog. Whatever happened to homemade ornaments and pounds of tinsel?

You squat down and start reading a few of the tags.

Weird. Apparently this one is from you to Harrison. The box is way too small to hold all seven Harry Potter books in their decorative cardboard case.

You pull a strip of tape back and peek under the wrapping paper. What the fuck? A junior geologist's kit?

You quietly hunt around the house in search of the book set, checking all the cupboards and crawl spaces.

Finally, tucked behind a stack of books about the Austro-Hungarian Empire in the laundry room, you find the Harry Potter set.

You wrap it and replace the geologist's kit under the tree.

• • •

"Harrison, it's your turn," Lauren says. You're all gathered around the tree, waiting patiently while each present is opened. Otto looks like he's about to self-asphyxiate, but he says nothing. Clearly Lauren has the boys trained.

Harrison homes in on your gift, ripping the paper off hungrily.

"HARRY POTTER! YES, YES, YES, YES!"

He jumps around the living room, holding the books over his head.

"THANK YOU, THANK YOU, THANK YOU!"

Lauren gives you the stink-eye and pulls you out into the hallway.

"What were you thinking?" she hisses. "Those books haven't had any of the inappropriate material redacted."

Seriously?

Harrison sets the books down in front of the fireplace and runs over to give you a big hug. Lauren takes the opportunity to slip across the room.

"Oh no. Look what you've done, silly," Lauren says, kicking the books into the fire. "You've accidentally burned them."

Harrison turns around, obviously confused.

"I didn't…what?" He stares, horrified, then bursts into tears and starts rolling around the carpet.

"NOOOOOOO!"

Your sister is staring daggers at you. She mouths, *Don't. Say. Anything.*

You keep your mouth shut as the books go up in flames.

The End.

YOU TIPTOE INTO YOUR NEPHEWS' SHARED ROOM, HALF EXPECTING them to still be up playing.

They're dead asleep.

"Psst." You give Harrison a gentle pat on the back. "Harrison. Wake up."

"Is it Christmas already?" he mumbles

"Even better. We're going on a Christmas Eve adventure."

"But it's bedtime."

"Bedtime can wait. Right now I need you and your brother to get into your winter clothes, okay? Then meet me downstairs." You put a finger to your lips. "But shhhh. Your mom and dad are sleeping."

Harrison looks confused.

"But we have to tell them if we wake up in the night."

"That's okay. I'm giving you a free pass. I can do that as your uncle." Maybe that will plant a tiny seed of rebellion. God knows he needs one.

The boys sneak downstairs, massive grins on their faces. You double-check to make sure they're properly equipped to go outside.

Hats. Check. Gloves. Check. And…a triple layer of snowpants? Okay, better than none.

"Where're the sleds?"

Harrison points to the shed outside.

You throw on a coat and head out to the shed. The drinks are keeping you pretty warm. Inside, you grab a bright orange sled with four helmets attached to it.

"What's the best hill around here?"

Harrison points to a mound in front of the house that's maybe ten feet long.

"Mom says this hill is safest."

"That's not a hill."

You point to the real hill behind their house.

The boys are obviously impressed. "Can we really?"

"Of course. You're with your cool uncle."

144

You take a couple of runs down the hill, everyone laughing, then Harrison tumbles off his sled at the bottom and somehow manages to cut his lip.

"I'm bleeding!" he screams.

You examine the cut. It's pretty minor. But he's near tears; clearly any sort of injury is rare in this household.

If you want to tell Harrison that it's no big thing, turn to page 182.

If you want to fix his cut yourself, turn to page 183.

If you want to tell your sister, turn to page 184.

You stab your fork into the chia seed soufflé.

No matter how much you eat, you don't seem to make a dent.

"Oh, I *knew* Jim French," you say. Hmm, that came off a bit sexual. "Gregory, let me refill your wine."

Lauren shoots you a death stare. Clearly the party isn't the best way to annoy her; getting Gregory to have fun is.

By the time you finish eating, you've polished off a couple of bottles together.

"Gregory, any interest in playing a little pickup hockey after dessert? There's a rink down the block, right?"

"We have to get ready for bed, Gregory," Lauren says sharply.

"Gregory is a grown man. Let him speak for himself."

"Well…" He seems to consider.

"Gregory, you'll be out well past nine." Lauren taps her watch meaningfully.

"I think a little exercise will do me good," Gregory says, grinning. "It's just a shame that rink isn't to international standards."

You're not sure what he's talking about, but it sounds like you're winning.

"Great!"

Your sister storms out of the dining room.

• • •

"I used to play in college," you say, lacing up Gregory's extra pair of skates. "But I haven't since."

"Not to worry. I only ever got as far as the intramural team."

"Which school were you at again?"

"University of Salzburg, in Austria."

"Right."

You assume Gregory's being modest, but as soon as he steps on the ice, it becomes clear that he can barely skate.

"European ice is so much smoother," he says, tripping on

nothing and nearly face-planting. "It's the process of freezing there. It's much more refined."

Well, you're here, you might as well play, turn to page 185.
If you want to leave while you still can, turn to page 187.

YOU STAB YOUR FORK INTO THE MOUNTAIN OF SPELT SALAD LAUREN'S
served you.

No matter how much you eat, you don't seem to make a dent.

"Oh, I *knew* Jim French," you say. Hmm, that came off a bit
sexual. "Gregory, let me refill your wine."

Lauren shoots you a death stare. Clearly the thing that's
bothering her even more than the idea of you enjoying yourself
at a party is the idea of Gregory having fun at all.

It gives you an idea.

"Gregory, any interest in coming along to Jim French's?"

"We have to get ready for bed, Gregory," Lauren says sharply.

"Gregory is a grown man. Let him speak for himself."

"Well…" He seems to consider. "I suppose it would be nice
to get out of the house for a bit."

"Great!"

Lauren storms out of the dining room.

• • •

You walk through the door to Jim French's. It's immediately clear
you know—or at least remember—no one in the room.

You fiddle with your phone, trying to look busy. Gregory,
however, is surprisingly popular.

"…as it turns out, he was wearing the hat the entire time!"

Everyone laughs hysterically at Gregory's joke.

Considering how much he's had to drink, you're impressed
he's able to hold the room so well.

A little while later, Jim French walks up to you.

"Enjoying yourself?"

"Of course. Thanks again for the invite."

"No worries. Hey, so, this might be weird, but do you have
any rolling papers on you?"

"I dunno," you say. "Let me check my coat."

You know you don't, but at least it gives you something to do.

You go to the coatroom and push open the door.

148

Gregory is spread-eagling the bed, naked, with your high school prom date, Sarah.

Man, she used to be so hot before never bouncing back from her first kid.

You lock eyes with Gregory.

You're mortified.

RUN! Turn to page 188.

YOU WALK THROUGH THE DOOR TO JIM FRENCH'S. IT'S IMMEDIATELY clear you know—or at least remember—no one in the room.

You fiddle with your phone, trying to look busy. Gregory, however, is surprisingly popular.

"...as it turns out, he was wearing the hat the entire time!"

Everyone laughs hysterically at Gregory's joke.

Considering the possible head injury, you're impressed he's able to hold the room so well.

A little while later, Jim French walks up to you.

"Enjoying yourself?"

"Of course. Thanks again for the invite."

"No worries. Hey, so, this might be weird, but do you have any rolling papers on you?"

"I dunno," you say. "Let me check my coat."

You know you don't, but at least it gives you something to do.

You go to the coatroom and push open the door.

Gregory is spread-eagling the bed, naked, with your high school prom date, Sarah.

Man, she used to be so hot before never bouncing back from her first kid.

You lock eyes with Gregory.

You're mortified.

RUN! Turn to page 188.

150

You find yourself pulled toward this sexy elf, like she's magnetic north.

"Merry Christmas," she says, smiling.

"You have to tell me. Am I on Santa's naughty list?"

She blushes, then giggles.

Yup, still got it.

"Well, I'm not sure about you, but your son is definitely on the nice list."

Son? Not that they're yours, but you did come here with two...fuck.

"Harrison, where's Otto?"

Harrison glares at you, eyes glassy. "I want more cocoa!" he screams. "NOW!"

"Where's security?" you ask the elf, completely flustered.

She points toward the concession stands.

You grab Harrison's hand and start running like a madman toward the security booth.

"He was with me literally two minutes ago," you tell the guard.

"We'll make an announcement right away."

Each second passes like an hour. How the hell do you lose a human being?

You start preparing your speech to Lauren. "He just vanished...Poof." God, she's gonna cut your face off and shit in the wreckage.

You take a deep breath. Tears start rolling down your cheeks. It would be almost impossible to fuck up harder than this.

The best option is to drop Harrison off at home, then come back and resume the search with no one else to lose.

You push through the turnstiles and jog to the car, thumb-dialing 911. Just before you hit send, you see a child climbing a Christmas tree near the entrance.

You race to the tree, nearly pulling Harrison's arm off.

Oh thank fuck. It's Otto.

Never mind that he's not wearing pants or socks; you found him. In one piece. And without a second to spare.

Turn to page 189.

YOU WAIT IN LINE FOR A PAINFULLY LONG HOUR, THE KIDS ACTING like feral, sugar-fueled beasts.

You've just reached the front when a douchey banker type cuts in front of you.

"Excuse me, the line's back there," you say politely. He sneers and stays put.

"That's no fair!" Harrison cries. Both boys look at you as though you can somehow fix this. Sorry, kids, there's no cure for douche.

"It's okay, guys, some people act rude because they don't have the Christmas spirit, but we're better than that, right?"

The douche turns around. "You think you're better than me?"

Before you even have a chance to respond, he slugs you square in the nose.

Blood from your nose gushes into your mouth.

You hit the ground…hard.

• • •

When you regain consciousness, that sexy elf from earlier is standing over you.

You touch your nose. It feels like a hot dog has been stapled to your face.

"Are you okay?" she asks.

"Where are my nephews?"

"They're at the candy store with a security guard. We couldn't reach their mother, so we gave them some free gumdrops and gingerbread cookies to stop them from crying."

Oh god. Not more sugar….

"Your nose looks broken," says the elf. "And I think you might have wet your pants when you were out."

You don't even have to touch your crotch to know she's right.

But maybe it's a blessing in disguise. Just a week ago, you might have said you wanted kids of your own.

The End.

152

You wake up Christmas morning with a new, creamy-colored pile of vomit waterfalling over the particleboard nightstand. At least you're pretty sure that one's your fault.

You think back to Christmas growing up. You and your sister and brother would jump on your parents' bed at five in the morning, screaming about how Santa actually ate the cookies you left for him.

It would be nice to reminisce with Lauren about those years.

But she'd probably hang up the phone if you called. Fuck the bitch she's turned into. Fuck memories. Fuck this terrible holiday.

You get out of bed and spray yourself with cologne before heading downstairs for breakfast.

It's 10 A.M., but the restaurant is still packed with people squeezing in a free meal before the cutoff.

You grab two dry bagels and an orange.

You sit down and squirt a packet of cream cheese onto your first bagel.

Alone.

Just like everyone else in the restaurant.

Just like the guy who's making zero effort to conceal the fact that he's dumping vodka into his orange drink.

Just like the fat woman spilling out of a Dalmatian-themed Christmas sweater. Look at her smearing all those butter packets over her Wonder Bread. And eating all those jams with a spoon, one after another, like a GIF of herself sent to depress you on Christmas.

You're not this pathetic, are you?

No. Fuck no!

You have a girlfriend. A reasonably *hot* girlfriend!

Sure, you were only 60/40 on Lindsi before you came to visit Lauren, but the idea of being lonely forever spurs you into action.

You have to lock her down.

The future's simply too grim without her.

Turn to page 190.

AFTER A HALF HOUR OF PEEKING FURTIVELY OUT OF THE BATHROOM, then ducking back into a stall, you finally spot Lars in the hallway.

"Lars," you hiss-whisper.

He turns. "Oh, thank goodness, we were so worried." He jogs over. "Do you need me to call an ambulance?"

"No, I'll be fine, but my pants...won't." Lars nods knowingly. How is it possible that Lindsi has such an understanding brother? Who's also, apparently, had some pants-shitting experience? "Is it safe to sneak out to the car quick?"

"Yup, the congregation's cleared out. I'll tell Dad you're on the way. Hold tight for a second."

He comes back shortly to hurry you to the car. You take the window seat and everyone coos over your toilet paper bottoms.

"Poor baby," Lindsi says. "But you seem fine now."

"Well." You can't have them thinking you faked it. "I don't want to be difficult, but I may need to pull over."

They do, so rapidly your stomach lurches. How fortunate. You now have no trouble forcing out another slick Combos shit, wiping with the remnants of your toilet paper diaper.

Fuck, now you're out of dick coverings.

You pull your sweater off, then your T-shirt, which you step into as a new diaper.

The rest of the ride home, you grip the neck together so your dick won't fall out.

Not your finest moment, but at least no one doubts your story.

• • •

The next morning, you feel fine—Combos really only have one good bout of diarrhea in them—but every time you try to join the family, Mom pushes you back to bed more insistently...and weirdly, with a wider smile.

"You lie down," she says when she sees you at the head of the stairs again. "I'll bring you more crackers and ginger ale. What a constitution! Ready for phase two already," she adds approvingly.

"Okay," you say as weakly as you can, shuffling back to the bedroom they've put you in.

It's not the most exciting Christmas, but you have to admit being waited on hand and foot *is* relaxing.

And apparently it's bought you a permanent in with Lindsi's family.

Not a bad haul for a deliberate pants-shitting.

The End.

YOU APPROACH A CLEARING. NEARBY, DOZENS OF FAT, PERFECT Christmas trees stand in well-spaced rows.

"Dad," Lars says. Dad turns and looks at him. Lars raises a bushy blond eyebrow, tilting his head back over his shoulder. Dad squints, obviously deep in thought, and turns to Michael, the brother-in-law. Michael lowers his eyelids meaningfully. A smile spreads across Dad's face and he nods.

Seriously, you've never seen a more eloquently nonverbal collection of people than the VanWhittington men.

"We think you should chop down the tree. As a sort of 'welcome to the family' treat." Lars grins.

"Oh, you don't have to do that." You smile ingratiatingly. Your back tenses up in fear. You've never swung an axe before. Shit, you didn't even play baseball as a kid. "I'm a city boy, after all. Leave it to the pros, right?"

"No, it's easy. Any idiot can chop down a tree." Lars laughs, a rich, deep baritone sound. Dad and Michael join in. "I mean, if you can't chop down a fir tree, how will we feel comfortable leaving Lindsi with you, am I right?"

"HA!" You force out one brief spasm. Your back twinges ominously. "Totally. Yes, couldn't leave your sister—your daughter—with a man who doesn't know how to use an *axe*." Do they know how creepy that sounds?

Apparently not, because Lars is handing one your way— Jesus, did he really have that thing strapped to his thigh this entire time? Whose thighs are big enough to hide an axe head?

There's nothing to do but give it a go.

You throw the axe to the side, trying to twist from the hips so you won't rupture your spine. You swing back forcefully, hoping to impress Lindsi's family, but you've misjudged. The axe head is heavier than you thought, and your hands have started to sweat, probably from axe-fear.

Your grip is weakening. You feel the weight of the axe pulling it through your fingers. *Please don't amputate my foot*, you think, hoping to somehow make it true.

You don't amputate your foot.

Instead, you slam the axe head into your kidney, hard.

You crumple to the ground, screaming like a small child. It's hard to see—your vision is literally red, you're in so much pain—but it looks like Lindsi's family is utterly unimpressed.

If you want to try to play it off like you're not in crippling pain, turn to page 194.
If you absolutely have to go to the ER, now, turn to page 195.

Maybe if you jerk up fast enough, your back will fix itself. That's what they always recommend, right? Sudden, jerky motions?

No way to know but to try: you stand as fast as you can, cookies in hand.

You hear a pop, feel something like a stab directly into your spinal column...

THUD.

You collapse to the floor, back spasming. You hear glass splintering near your head, and if you open your eyes—you can just manage to squint through the pain—you can see the tray of gingerbread upside down a few feet away.

You might actually be dying. No, scratch that: dying would be better than this.

Mom leans over you, pure hatred in her eyes. You'd say something, but you can't form words; the pain is too intense.

"D-d-d-d...I wa—wa—wa..." You grit your teeth and scrunch up your entire face, forcing yourself to concentrate on verbalizing your need.

"D-d-doctor. Please."

"Doctor? Doctors aren't open *today.*" Mom picks up the tray, shaking her head in disgust at the broken gingerbread on the floor. "It's Christmas Eve."

"Emergency...room?"

"I don't think anyone's going to want to spend Christmas there." She hasn't made any move to help you. Apparently the gingerbread is her bigger concern.

You lie there for a few minutes, incapable of shifting from your fetal curl.

"I have a neighbor who might be able to help," Mom says, obviously annoyed that you haven't moved. "A chiropractor. Lives next door."

"Yes. Thank you, yes." You push up to your hands and knees, trying not to cry out at the new spasms in your back. You just have to make it next door.

• • •

After forty-five excruciating minutes of bent-double shuffling, you arrive.

"Come in, come in," says a kindly voice above your head. "Marlene said you'd be coming."

The man-voice leads you into a room with a worn leather couch, which you immediately flop onto. You appear to be in some sort of den. You see a few framed diplomas on the wall.

What's the "Hollywood Correspondence School for Psychic Chiropracty"? Is that certified? Is the Office of Lou Diamond Phillips really qualified to give out "chyroprakter's" licenses? Jesus, that "Masters in Dog Yoga" doesn't even have a school name printed on it.

"Sorry, but would you mind telling me a bit about your qualifications?" Luckily, your face is too full of couch for him to embarrass you with eye contact.

"Well, I took a lot of courses from the local Y in undergrad," he begins. "Practiced for a few years up past Fresno. Had dozens of happy clients. At least until '92, that is."

"What happened in '92?"

"Oh, regulatory snafu. Paralysis is a normal, if unfortunate, side effect, but those pencil-pushers wouldn't listen."

You can feel your face starting to sweat, sticking clammily to the leather.

"So you haven't practiced since the early nineties?"

"No, no, I've been practicing this whole time."

"Without a license?"

"You don't need a license for dogs."

If there's no way this guy is touching you, turn to page 196.
If you have no choice, now, but to go through with it, turn to page 198.

"Oh, uh, ow! Oooooh, owww." You shake your hand in the air, still bent over the oven.

"What's going on?"

"I've burned my hand. It's pretty bad." You grip one hand in the other, wincing in very real pain.

"Let me take a look."

Fuck, she'll know you're lying. You can hear her clomping toward the oven.

Thinking fast, you grip the baking rack with your entire hand. You pull it away, the crisscross marks of the wire rack already swelling and blistering your palm. You see a little piece of skin stuck to the rack, sizzling in the heat from the oven.

"Did you just…" Mom bends down, squinting in confusion.

"No, no, like I said—"

"I *saw* you."

Fuck, this is the end. It's one thing to be a weak, pathetic, genetically poor specimen, but deliberately burning your own hand? That's outright psychotic.

"That was just incredibly…" She sounds dazed. Horror does that sometimes. She shakes her head slowly. Here it comes. "Impressive."

The fuck?

"I must have underestimated your back pain. Anyone who would undertake such a heroic action just to prove his mettle, well…" She leans down slowly and very deliberately wraps her hand around the oven rack. She doesn't cry out. She doesn't even grimace. Jesus, who *is* this woman?

Slowly, she releases. Her hand is oozing and inflamed. She presses it to your mangled, burnt palm, looking straight into your eyes.

"That's someone I want in my family. It's an unconventional format, of course, but I think my husband will be happy to count this as a proving."

A proving?

What the fuck is *wrong* with this woman?

If you want to leave this place NOW, turn to page 199.
If you're just happy that Mom has finally warmed up to you, turn to page 201.

"FINE," YOU SIGH DRAMATICALLY. JIMMY NEEDS TO KNOW YOU ARE being *extremely* cool right now. "Bundle everything together and I'll take care of it."

"Thank you," he says, stripping naked and throwing his clothing in the middle of the pile of sheets. Jesus, is Jimmy more hung than you? Check out that...NO, STOP LOOKING AT THE NUDE TEEN.

When you turn back around, he's dressed, and the laundry is contained. You grab a few shirts from your luggage to make it more plausible and head down to the basement. Everyone's washing machine is in the basement.

You've just managed to figure out the machine settings when Lindsi's older sister, Luanne, walks in. You haven't met yet, but she looks like Lindsi with ten more years of stress wrinkles and a body that never fully bounced back from pregnancy. It's like looking into the future. God, you hope a future with Lindsi wouldn't mean your very own Jimmy.

"Need some help with that?" she offers cheerfully.

"No, I'm fine, I think I've got it figured out."

"Let me just check. This machine's tricky, the colors cycle isn't good for certain fabrics, and—oh."

She's peering into the machine, right at a big pile of sheets and one pair of Pokémon boxers. She plucks them out.

"But these are—oh." She drops them hurriedly, scrunching up her nose in disgust before squinting at you suspiciously.

Oh yeah, she's definitely noticed the semen.

Turn to page 203.

"I FEEL FOR YOU, BUT YOU'RE GONNA HAVE TO DEAL WITH THIS one yourself."

"But surely if you were a hardened sexual predator you wouldn't leave such obvious evidence behind." His inflectionlessness has taken on a note of desperation. "Anyone would realize that. They wouldn't assume—"

"Dude. Not my problem."

You pick up your clothes and head to the bathroom. You don't want to have any more "sexual predator" discussions before coffee.

The rest of the day passes uneventfully. Apparently you slept through the men leaving to cut down the tree—thank god, that sounds fucking terrible—and Lindsi seems so grateful that you're there, she's going out of her way to run interference on Mom. By the time you sit down to dinner, you're actually starting to think this was a good idea.

Until Luanne—Lindsi's sister and Jimmy's mother—opens her mouth.

"Jimmy, is there something you've been keeping from us?"

"To what do you refer, mother?" He stares at his brussels sprouts intently.

"I found your boxers in the laundry this morning, and I was worried."

Jesus, he just threw them in with the laundry? He might as well have tied a bow on them and left them on his mom's fucking pillow.

"Obviously you're having some discharge; can you describe it for me?" Luanne says.

"Oh no, Jimmy, is something wrong?" Mom chimes in, looking worried.

"Nothing is wrong." Jimmy is making markedly little eye contact, even for him.

"I saw traces of blood," Luanne says, looking around meaningfully. "I was looking on WebMD and they say blood in pus could be a sign of gangrene, even something worse."

162

Oh come on, she's really floating dick gangrene as the answer?

"Have you noticed anything, Jimmy? Any sores or necrotic flesh?"

"Nothing has changed."

"Then we have to go to the ER. Should I call an ambulance, or—"

"For Christ's sake," you say with a snorting laugh. "Stop embarrassing the kid. We all know it was a run-of-the-mill wet dream, right?"

Everyone stares at you, mouths dropping open in horror.

"Right?"

Apparently not.

If you want to apologize to try to smooth things over, turn to page 204.

If you're just gonna let this one hang, 'cause Jesus fucking CHRIST you can't listen to this idiocy anymore, turn to page 206.

"Umm…" You can't imagine anything you'd be less good at than hunting—it's always killing Bambi's mom, you don't care what anyone says—but this is the first time Mom has looked at you with anything less than pure and utter loathing. "Sure, yeah. That sounds…fun."

"Perfect. Come on, I'll wake Lars. He'll explain things."

Mom grabs your arm—she doesn't even shudder at the gore—and hustles you inside, sitting you down at the kitchen table. The microwave clock reads 4:32. Poor Lars.

But when he appears in the doorway, he looks eager. So does Lindsi—she's right behind him. They sit while Mom makes coffee.

"So I'm not sure if Mom explained," Lars begins, folding his huge hands together on the table. Jesus, each finger is at least as big as a carrot.

"Explained that you're a hunting family?"

"Well, yes, but I meant something more specific. We call it the proving."

"The proving," Lindsi echoes. That's weird. Maybe she's just too sleepy to get her timing right. Though you could swear you heard Mom say it, too. In unison with Lindsi.

"It's a sort of…how do I put it?" Lars smiles ruefully, rubbing his blond hair. "Like a test of manhood in our family? It used to be a big deal, but now it's just a fun tradition. We all do it."

"They do," Lindsi leans forward, eyes fever-bright. "It's how they show they care about the family."

"Anyway, the idea is you have to bring home a kill by the end of the night, prove you can provide and the like."

"My family respects people who can fend for themselves," Lindsi says, nodding rapidly.

"You should try it. You'll have a blast, I promise," Lars says, leaning down slightly to gaze into your eyes. He looks so friendly, like some kindly Norse myth, that you find yourself nodding along with Lindsi.

"So," Mom says, setting three mugs of steaming coffee on the table. You can't help but notice yours is the largest. "What do you say, are you up for it?"

You're not, absolutely not. But how can you say no?

"Of course! I can't wait to…prove?"

"The proving," they all say in unison.

Turn to page 192.

"What? No. God no. That's barbaric."

Mom actually shrinks back from you, her disgust is so deep. It appears the Ambien is really fucking with that "having any filter between your brain and your mouth" thing.

"Sorry, that was a poor choice of words. What I meant was that it's not really for me. But I eat meat, so, you know, no judgment."

"No need to explain," she says, waving her hand dismissively. She's already halfway back to the house, clearly uninterested in anything else you have to say.

• • •

You wake up the next morning to the sounds and smells of breakfast being made. Lindsi should have woken you—she has to know you'd want to help. You head down to the kitchen.

"Good morning! How can I pitch in?"

No one responds. Weird. Maybe the frying noises drowned you out?

You clear your throat loudly.

"'Morning, everyone. What can I do to help?"

Once again you're met with silence.

"Lindsi?" You walk up and tap her on the shoulder.

She turns, her expression like a dozen sucked lemons.

"Is everything okay?"

"Come with me," she hisses.

She pulls you, by the arm, to the front door.

"Why is everyone being so…distant?" you ask.

"Mom told us, obviously."

"Told you?"

"That you refuse to hunt!" She wrinkles her nose like you're a bad smell.

What do you say to that? Seriously, who cares if you hunt?

"If you won't hunt, how can my family trust you to provide for me?" she asks sternly.

"*Provide?* What? I just got promoted…and you *work*."

"You should go. It was nice of Mom to even let you stay the night."

"Are you serious?"

"Uh, *yeah*. And don't call again."

"Lindsi, whether or not I hunt can*not* be that big a—"

"You're weak stock, okay? It's that simple." She turns to walk back to the kitchen. "I should have known better when he ate that quinoa salad," she mutters.

The End.

YOU ONLY HAVE TO MAKE IT THE FEW MILES TO THE VANWHITTINGTON house. And the time in the bathroom has really cleared things out. You'll be fine going freeball for half an hour.

You exit the bathroom to find the entire VanWhittington clan waiting.

"I was just about to come in after you!" Lindsi's dad says, grinning.

"Yes, you were in there *quite* some time." Lindsi's mom glares. "I suppose you had a fairly good reason for interrupting the entire service?"

"Sorry, stomach problems. From travel, I think. I'm feeling better now, though."

"That's convenient." She turns on her heel and marches toward the exit. You all follow, packing into the car.

It's a tight squeeze with five adults, especially since one of them is Lindsi's brother Lars, a man whose body seems to have been fashioned out of multiple tree trunks. You squeeze up against the door, half hovering so as not to get too friendly with Lars.

Lindsi's mom turns around to say something, then stops with a horrified sniff. Her hand flies to her mouth and her eyes are wide. She's staring straight at your fly. That's weird…

Oh *fuck*, somehow it's come down since you left the bathroom. And scooting around the car has caused the tip to flop out onto your pants.

You zip up so fast you catch your dick in the teeth.

"AHHHH!"

You swat at your junk, trying to get the zipper to unclench.

Of course, now *everyone* has noticed your little…peep show.

Turn to page 207.

REALLY, IT'S PRETTY MIRACULOUS YOUR PANTS ARE EVEN INTACT. You've managed to work some things through your system in here, but it would be playing with fire to put them on with *nothing* between you and the fabric.

You'll just have to fashion some temporary underwears out of toilet paper.

You start wrapping one leg, then the other, then around the entire middle to get some junk coverage, then repeat the process. You've barely built a single layer before you've totally emptied the roll in your stall.

You peek beneath the divider, but you don't see any feet. Quickly, you open the door, jerking your pants off the back and shambling over to the next stall, careful not to move your legs too quickly lest you tear through the layer you *have* created. Fuck, no toilet paper in there either. But there's one more stall. You start toward it...

The door opens.

"I was just coming in to check on you; you've been gone a long—oh."

It's Lindsi's father.

He's definitely noticed the toilet paper underwears.

If you want to just tell him the truth, turn to page 209.
If you want to tell him the first lie you can think of, turn to page 211.

FINALLY, THE VOMITING STOPS.

Lindsi's mom turns to you, eyes steely and cold.

It. Was. You, she mouths.

You gulp. You could deny it, but somehow you know it won't make any difference.

She picks her way between piles of sick to the front of the church, where she consults with the shell-shocked priest. After a few moments she waves you over.

"I was just telling Reverend Mather that we'd be happy to help him clean up this horrible mess. Since you and I obviously have stronger stomachs than the rest of the congregation."

"Oh, but this young man isn't even a member of the church. And it's Christmas Eve. We'll find…a way…" The priest's eyes glaze over as he stares at the congregation limping away from the devastation they've—you've—wrought.

"No, he's glad to help." She smiles a reptilian smile, her narrowed eyes never leaving yours. "Aren't you?"

"Yes. Sure. Least I could do."

"Good. Let's get started." She walks away, presumably to find mopping supplies.

Hours later, the clock hits midnight.

It's officially Christmas morning, but you're still swabbing puke off the vast church floor. You don't even have the comfort of having Lindsi with you—her gag reflex was too strong for her to stay.

"You missed a spot between those pews," her mother says sharply.

You sigh, heading back to where she's pointing. You still have at least thirty rows of vomit to mop up.

The only thing stronger than the smell is the potency of the hatred you can feel pouring out of Lindsi's mother.

The End.

You trudge through the snow with Brad and duck inside the faux stable.

You grab baby Jesus. He's stuck. Maybe even nailed in place? Huh. That's kinda ironic.

"Hurry up, bro!" Brad yells.

You position your right foot on a Wise Man's crotch for leverage, then start pulling the Jesus's head, the only part you can get a good grip on.

Something's giving way...

POP!

Oh Jesus, you've decapitated...Jesus!

Two meaty hands grab you and toss you to the ground. From your prone position you can see Brad and Blitzer sprinting toward the Porsche.

"You're under arrest for a committing a religious hate crime!" screams a police officer.

You feel the officer's knee digging into the small of your back.

"AHHHHH!"

"SHUT UP!"

"MY BACK!!!"

The officer slaps on a tight pair of handcuffs. You shift slightly; one of them cuts into your wrist.

The policeman starts reciting your Miranda rights.

"Brad. BRAAAAAAADD!!!!"

• • •

After a sleepless night in the drunk tank, you're released. Apparently "minor vandalism" isn't actually a hate crime after all. Though the fine's pretty fucking steep.

Your first phone call when you get home is to your girlfriend, Lindsi.

You tell her the story, sprinkling in a few white lies to make yourself come off better.

Somehow, it fails to elicit sympathy.

"How could you do something so stupid?" she spits.

"I dunno," you mumble, opening up Facebook.

Huh, look at that. Brad's posted a new video to his timeline.

"You don't *know?*"

And it features you…getting tackled by a police officer.

"What do you mean you don't know?"

A new comment appears on the video. It's from Brad: *#ChristmasChampion.*

"Hello?" Lindsi screams into the phone.

The video is racking up tens of likes. It even has two shares. A smile spreads across your face, warming you from the inside. You've never had a post perform so well.

"Are you still there?" Lindsi yells. "HELLO?!"

Wow! Brad just clicked "like" on his own post!

"You know what? GOODBYE!" screams Lindsi.

You can't believe it. Brad's called *you* out as cool. Publicly, even! It's a Christmas miracle!

The End.

YOU TRUDGE THROUGH THE SNOW AND DUCK INSIDE THE FAUX STABLE with Brad.

You've never vandalized anything before. You've never even shoplifted. And now you're supposed to steal baby Jesus, from a church, on Christmas Eve? That's like going from straight-edge to heroin without stopping off at booze.

Could you fake a seizure?

No, they might send you to the hospital, and your insurance is pretty shit. Plus, your acting skills are also pretty shit.

You take an exaggerated step forward and pretend to stumble over an exposed part of the crèche display.

You scream in pretend agony. "AHHHH! I think I've sprained my ankle!"

Maybe that was a bit too specific. Whatever, too late now. You writhe around in pretend pain.

Blitzer and Brad just stare at you. It doesn't look like they're buying it.

You get up, brush the snow off your pants, and pretend-limp over to Brad.

"You okay?" he asks.

"I'll be fine. But I think it's a pretty nasty sprain."

Brad rolls his eyes.

"Blitzer, grab the baby Jesus."

Blitzer yanks the statue out of the crib and tucks it under an arm.

"Huh. I think it was nailed on," Blitzer says, turning it over and displaying two long nails.

"Good work, man," Brad says.

After that Brad drops you at home, where you ice your non-injured ankle in an attempt to justify your cowardice to yourself.

• • •

The next morning, you open Facebook. Maybe someone will have a good "Christmas puppies" video.

Oh, Brad's posted…a video of you rolling around in the snow like a fucking Pentecostal that's just been touched by the spirit.

Brad and Blitzer chuckle in the video.

"What the fuck is he doing?" whispers Brad.

"Besides looking like a fucking idiot?" Blitzer snorts.

Jesus, you've never seen so many "likes" on a video before. And look at all those comments.

Blitzer: *Didn't know we were going to a show last night*

Some guy named Jeff: *Who's the spaz?*

Julian: *Did you guys get drunk with a homeless dude?*

Oh god, Brad: *LOLZ*

You tear up a bit. *Et tu*, Brad? It's going to be a long morning.

Just as you're about to click the window closed, you hear a beep. There's a new comment on the video…from your girlfriend.

Lindsi: *Jesus, what a pussy*.

The End.

"So?" Vampire raises an eyebrow. "We want to get started; this module outline estimates at least ten hours' playtime."

"Sure," you say, feeling lighter than you have in years. "Let's do it."

"Great. Let's roll up some characters."

"By the way," Eyelashless says in a soothing voice, "class and race options are limited because the module's pretty simplified."

"Total Christmas edition move," Schlub says with a snort-laugh. You join in. Why did you ever leave this behind?

"All right, well, I'm playing a female bard," Vampire says. "And let me guess—you'll be a half-orc rogue?" Schlub shrugs his agreement. "We could use a ranger. Or maybe a cleric." He turns to you expectantly.

You hate rangers—their play style is so simplistic—but you always wind up as some sort of cleric. You sigh. You'd kinda been hoping this would be your chance to go full-on Berserker.

"I can be a cleric. High elf, I suppose."

Vampire smiles, nodding eagerly.

"And what's everyone's alignment?" Eyelashless whispers.

If you play it lawful good, like everyone expects, this will be the least exciting reentry into D&E ever…which is saying a lot.

But playing chaotic evil, when it's clear that Schlub's choice of that alignment is already causing tension in the group, is a serious risk to take.

Be the good guy. The lawful good guy. Turn to page 212.
MWAHAHAHAHA! IT'S FINALLY YOUR CHANCE TO LET
OUT YOUR INNER DARKNESS! Turn to page 214.

You have to let that go. You've moved beyond D&E. And since you have, your girlfriends have been rolling natural…well, twelves or thirteens, at least, in hotness. And they have modifiers, too. That's not something you can turn your back on.

You meander to the other end of the snack table. Awesome, there's shrimp hiding down here! You hadn't seen that when you first came over. You're always too cheap to buy shrimp for your own parties; whenever you see it elsewhere you try to get your fill.

No one approaches. After about ten minutes of concerted shrimp eating, you wander over toward Debby. She's talking to Brad—perfect, this will be your in with him!

"So, Debby, it's been a while since—"

"One second, Brad and I have to finish these parody Rudolph lyrics. *SNRCK!* They're hi-*lar*-ious." Debby's nose is gumdrop red and she's swaying into Brad, like one of those blowup car lot balloons, but wearing more red and green velour.

"Oh. Where are you stuck? I could—"

"It's kinda our thing?" She smiles, then turns her back on you.

Unable to find anyone else, and so full of shrimp even *you've* had enough, you see no option but to leave.

• • •

You wake up with the gorge already three-quarters of the way up your throat.

You run through your apartment to the bathroom, but your hands are so sweaty you can't get a grip on the toilet seat cover. Jesus, it's coming. NOW.

You vomit violently into the sink. A lone undigested shrimp floats atop the scrum.

It's like a murderer leaving a signed picture behind.

All night you lie on the bathroom floor, writhing in agony, trying to find a cool spot on the tiles. After vomiting, you have about three minutes of feeling normalish…then five of feeling weird…then another five of feeling hideously nauseated, during which you pray to actually die…then you vomit again.

The next day, you're too weak to cook anything with the few staples you left in the fridge during what should have been your island vacation. The only options delivering to your area, according to Foodler, are Chinese places.

The thought of eating Chinese right now—there's definitely shrimp in fried rice, right?—is enough to make you vomit. Again. Into the bucket you're keeping at the end of your couch.

The End.

YOU LEAVE THE PARTY, EMBARRASSED AND ANNOYED.

The first thing you do when you get home is Google Kwanzaa. You are *not* going to get humiliated by another Brad at another party.

You open the Wikipedia entry.

Really, 1966? That sounded so implausible. And apparently Swahili is a language, not a country, which makes that sentence structure more logical. Good thing you kept your mouth shut there. Wow, Kwanzaa actually *does* mean "first fruits of the harvest." Brad was right...about all of it, in fact. Even the seven core principles—or as he called them, *Nguzo Saba.*

Dammit! You'd thought he was being a douche, but he was actually just that much more culturally aware than you. Yet again, Brad proves he's cooler than everyone else in the room.

And now he probably thinks you're going out for the Klan.

You've wrecked any chance you had of becoming real friends with Brad, possibly forever.

Fucking Kwanzaa...

The End.

THE ERRANDS TAKE EVEN LONGER THAN YOU EXPECTED.

After several hours you're nearly done. The last stop before you can head home is that ridiculous specialty eggnog farm stand.

As you're waiting in line, someone behind you punches your arm.

"Look what the cat dragged in!"

"Excuse me?" Who is this strange, balding man with the ridiculous smile?

"It's me, Wayne. Wayne Parrish?"

Who the fuck is Wayne Parrish?

"You know, Parkdale High?"

Oh, *that* Wayne Parrish. You've fallen so out of touch that you don't even think you're Facebook friends. Maybe because you were never friend-friends.

"Wayne! Great to see you. How are you?"

"Doing great. Married Anna a few years ago."

Who?

"She's the best," you say.

"Why don't we grab a drink and catch up?"

How can you catch up with someone you never knew?

But there *will* be booze…

If you want to beg off and head home, turn to page 216.
If you want to head out with this former "friend," turn to page 217.

You're too guilty to even enjoy this third beer. Reluctantly, you head home.

It's only 8:00 P.M., but the house is pitch black. Presumably everyone's asleep.

You fumble around in the darkness, looking for something to eat.

There's a note on the refrigerator from Lauren, addressed to you:

Where did you go? You could have at least told us! Please be more considerate or else you'll completely ruin Christmas for Otto and Harrison.

You roll your eyes. How is it that you're related to this person again?

If you may as well go back to the bar, turn to page 219.
If you want to make this up to Lauren and the kids, turn to page 243.

180

After three more beers, you start to feel full of Christmas cheer.

An attractive blonde with impossibly long legs opens the door. She flicks a cigarette out before entering. You haven't smoked since college, but who cares? Smokers always get along with smokers.

"Can I bum a cigarette?"

She looks at you like you're a piece of animated shit.

"Here," she says, passing you one without looking at you again.

Burn. Still, you might as well smoke it. Cigarettes feel awesome when you're drunk.

You step outside. Fuck, it's freezing.

You could probably crack a window in the bathroom and smoke it there. The bar seems seedy enough that no one will mind.

You grab a pack of matches from the bar, walk into the bathroom, and light the cigarette.

KNOCK KNOCK.

"What's taking so long?" someone yells from the other side.

You chuck your cigarette in the trash can and start frantically waving your arms through the air to push the smoke out the window crack.

"Just a minute," you shout.

You're looking for a secret can of air freshener when you realize smoke is pouring out of the trash can.

You turn on the tap, cup your hands under it, and try to splash the bin with water. It's ridiculously ineffective. Maybe you should close the window so the fire doesn't get even more oxygen? How does a person put out a trash fire?

It's getting bigger. If you just leave, will they know it was your fault? Flames lick up the wall, which immediately bursts into flame. At least you're not trapped in a room full of asbestos. You run to the door, but it's stuck. You can't get it open, no matter how hard you pull.

Wait, didn't Lindsi say her self-defense teacher told everyone to scream "rape" instead of "fire"? No one ever responds to "fire," right?

It's too smoky to think of another plan.

"Rape! There's a rape in here. Seriously, RAPE!"

You keep screaming "Rape!" at the top of your lungs. No one comes.

Eventually, the whole wall catches. You cough, choke, then pass out on the grimy, wet bathroom floor.

Turn to page 220.

182

You need to talk Harrison off the ledge before he full-on loses it.

"It's a battle wound! It'll make you look like a tough customer."

"But mom always says…"

"Oh, forget your mom. She has a massive stick up her ass."

Harrison's eyes go super-wide.

"Sorry. I shouldn't have said that."

"What do you mean?" On the plus side, Harrison's completely forgotten his cut lip.

"She can just be a little…uptight at times. Which is why we maybe don't have to tell her what happened? It can be our fun little uncle-secret, 'kay?"

Fun little uncle-secret? Sounds a bit rapey….

"After all, she doesn't need to know *everything*."

You can actually see the lightbulb go on over his head. It's almost nerve-wracking…

Turn to page 221.

"LOOK, CUTS TO THE FACE ALWAYS BLEED A LOT. THEY SEEM WORSE than they are."

Harrison doesn't look reassured.

You try to examine the gash, but you need more light. You shush the boys and lead them into the house to take a better look at Harrison's lip.

Hmmmm…it might actually need stitches. But you don't know how to do stitches.

You remember reading about soldiers in Vietnam using superglue on flesh wounds. That could work, right?

"Harrison, where's the superglue?"

"In the pantry, bottom right. We make balsa wood models of wine vessels with it. We're on the Sauternes glass."

Jesus, there's absolutely zero hope for these kids.

You grab the tube and get to work.

"Hold your lip from both sides and squeeze it together," you say, readying the superglue. Your hands are still pretty cold, but there's no time—you have to act fast. Easy does it, now…

The glue squirts everywhere, coating Harrison's fingers. He tries to pull them away, but they're stuck.

"Aaalp," he splutters.

You immediately panic.

"Just pull your fingers off your face fast. Like a Band-Aid. It will only hurt like a Band-Aid. I promise."

Harrison rips his fingers away.

"AHHHHHHHHH!" He shrieks in pain.

Chunks of lip are attached to each finger.

Blood gushes everywhere.

Fuck.

Turn to page 222.

You HEAD INSIDE, PATTING YOUR NEPHEW ON THE HEAD RHYTHMI-cally so he doesn't start bawling.

"There, there…"

You open the door to the house and start taking off the kids' snow gear. You do your best to keep quiet, but the noise of zippers and tromping boots rings through the empty house.

A light in the upstairs hallway comes on.

Lauren walks down the stairs in her robe and slippers.

Your heart starts racing.

"So…Harrison had a very, very minor accident," you start, voice quivering. "It's my fault; I thought sledding would be fun. I should have known better. But I don't have kids. What do I know?"

Maybe preemptively blaming yourself will steal some of Lauren's inevitable thunder?

"But really, it's fine. He's fine."

She shrugs. "It's just a cut lip. He'll live. Kids aren't made of glass, you know."

Oh thank god. Also, extremely unexpected.

"Anyway, I think it's nice that you took them out and did something fun. You can be their *fun* uncle."

Has she been drugged?

Better not to question it.

"Now, why don't we all have a cup of warm milk and you guys can tell me about tobogganing with your silly old uncle."

Wow. That sounds lovely.

Turn to page 223.

GREGORY'S FLOPPING AROUND THE ICE LIKE A JAPANESE KID THAT'S watched too much Pokémon.

"I used to be a fierce defenseman back in Salzburg. It must be these crummy skates."

You feel embarrassed for him. But you try to ignore it, jumping onto the ice and tossing a puck out.

"Top corner!" you yell. You lower your head and focus on the puck. At that moment, Gregory pushes off the boards and glides slowly, inevitably, into the line of fire.

SLAP!

The puck hits square in his mouth. He drops to his knees, gushing blood. A few teeth clink against the ice.

"*SCHEISSE!*"

"Fuck. Oh, fuck. I'm so sorry…"

"AAAAAAHHH!"

• • •

"There's no one at that office, either," you say, ending the call.

"Keep trying until you find someone," Lauren snaps back.

It's Christmas Day and you're on the phone with dental office number seven.

"Ummmmm," Gregory mumbles, pointing to a bowl.

Your sister places her spoon in the mashed apricots and spoon-feeds him. It disgusts you on multiple levels, but now is definitely not the time to mention that.

"Can we open presents yet?" Harrison wails.

"Not until your uncle finds a dentist that's open today."

"Come OOOOOOOONNNNN!"

"Maawwww, preeeeevv," Gregory mumbles.

"Why did *he* even have to come?" Harrison asks, pointing at you and stomping away.

"You guys can open one present each until your uncle figures this out," Lauren yells. "Just be quiet while he's on the phone."

"Dr. Reid's is closed until the twenty-seventh," you say,

hanging up yet again.

"Dr. Reid? I heard he isn't very good," Lauren says. "We want the absolute best dental surgeon money can buy...*your* money."

You were planning to pay for this, but hearing Lauren demand it infuriates you.

She sticks the spoon back in the mashed apricots and continues to feed Gregory.

You hear a loud shriek from the living room. Lauren jumps into action, sprinting toward her wailing son.

"AHHHHHHHHH! MY ANKLE!"

"YOU BOUGHT MY SON MOON BOOTS?" she screams from the other room.

Awesome.

The End.

GREGORY'S FLOPPING ALL OVER THE ICE LIKE A ONE-MAN HORIZONTAL *cucaracha* dance.

"I used to be a fierce defenseman back in Salzburg. It must be these skates. They're antiques!"

Gregory struggles to stand, skates backward a few feet, then does half a reverse somersault, smacking his head against the ice. *WHACK!*

He doesn't move. Jesus, you haven't even gotten your left skate on and he's nearly killed himself.

"You okay, buddy?" you yell from the bench.

No response. You jump onto the ice, one foot in a skate, one in a shoe.

"Looks like you bonked your head pretty good. You might need to put some *ice* on it," you say.

The joke's lost on the half-conscious Gregory. He lets out a loud moan.

"I bit my tongue pretty…" Blood splatters randomly, like he's some Pollock of the mouth. "Badly."

"It's not your fault." You force cheer into your voice. "You were right; the ice isn't smooth at all."

"It's a death trap!"

"Anyway, why don't we get outta here and head to that party instead…"

Go to the party already! Turn to page 149.

188

YOU RUN OUT OF THE ROOM.

You rapidly down beer after beer, trying to process what you saw. As much as your sister pisses you off, it brings you no pleasure knowing her marriage is a farce.

"Whoa there, save some for the rest of us," Jim French says with a phony chuckle.

You stare at him, dead-eyed, until he's so uncomfortable he walks away.

Twenty minutes later, Gregory reappears, acting as though nothing happened.

"Ready to head home?"

You nod, silent. You have nothing to say to him.

On the way, Gregory starts talking. "So, I guess you know Sarah?"

You say nothing. Finally, getting the picture, Gregory shuts up, too.

Christmas morning you wake up hungover and depressed.

The world feels flipped on its head.

Your almost pedantically perfectionist sister is in a sham marriage and probably doesn't even know it...

If you want to tell, turn to page 224.
If you want to bury this secret deep in the pit of your stomach, turn to page 225.

CHRISTMAS MORNING.

You still feel a little shaken from losing Otto yesterday. If Lauren ever finds out…well, she can't.

"And then we petted some reindeers," Harrison tells your sister. "Their noses were wet and funny."

"All right, boys, your mom doesn't want to hear about… reindeers." You laugh awkwardly.

"Of course I do," she says, frowning at you.

The boys run around like madmen after every present. They're screaming and jumping all over the house.

"I'm not sure if it's the excitement, or if it's the sugar cookies we gave them," Lauren whispers.

"I thought you said you don't allow sugar?"

"Well, it's a special day, isn't it?"

Harrison runs by and pulls on your hair.

"Owwwww, what gives, little man?"

"HAHAHAHHAH!"

Otto follows his older brother's lead, nearly ripping out a hunk.

Their maniacal laughs are becoming deafening. Every second with them is torture. But you have to stay in earshot at all times. They can't talk about yesterday.

They just can't.

The End.

THE DESPERATION IN THE HOTEL RESTAURANT IS PALPABLE. YOU DIAL Lindsi right there.

"Hello?" She sounds like she doesn't know who's calling.

"Lindsi, it's me. I've been doing a lot of thinking."

"So have I."

You scan the diners again, stopping on an old man working to fish his dentures out of his oatmeal with a fork.

You shudder and turn away.

"...And I think we should get married!" you say.

"Oh..." She sounds extremely caught off-guard. "I was thinking maybe things between us weren't really...and I've been hanging out with my ex a lot here...still, that's not important. Yes! Totally! We should totally get married."

You hear her family erupt joyfully in the background.

"Ohmygah, just like in my horoscope!" Lindsi screams.

Horoscope? She really thinks marriage proposals can be determined by horoscope?

"Of course, you'll have to do a proving before it's official," she continues.

You hear voices in the background echo "proving" in unison. Maybe it's just a bad connection?

"I'm hashtag so *EXCITED*!" You cringe. "I have a venue booked for June!"

"Wait. What?"

"Yeah. I got it after our third date. Just in case."

"Oh..."

"Also, I've planned a way you can for-real propose. With a flash mob. I've choreographed most of the moves already."

"Okay..."

"I'll keep practicing looking surprised."

She continues to ramble on. Forget 60/40, you're now at 30/70 on Lindsi, and dropping fast.

You look around again. The old man looks like he managed to get his dentures back into place. Now he's trying his best to stuff jelly packets in his pockets without anyone noticing.

He shoots you a dirty look. "Mind your own fucking business."

"Sorry."

It's probably better to marry someone you're so-so about than end up like that lonely fuck, right?

The End.

192

You look out the window. Snow is falling lightly, dusting the fir trees with picture-perfect clumps of white. You haven't seen another car for at least fifteen miles. You can't remember the last time you saw a house.

"Where are we, exactly?"

Lars laughs. He's been driving for almost an hour, and he's barely spoken a word. This "proving" idea is starting to seem extremely ill-advised.

"We're in the real wild. I shouldn't give you the advantage, but I like you." He thumps you heavily on the shoulder. You force yourself not to wince.

"Cool, thanks," you murmur. "And...what am I supposed to do?"

"Simple: just track a full-grown animal—deer are easiest, they're a good-sized target—kill it, and skin it. Usually we'd have you find your way home with the carcass, but since you're new, you can call and I'll pick you up."

Oh dear god, you're in winter *Deliverance*.

"Okay. How do I do that, exactly?"

"I mean...you just do." Lars frowns, obviously confused. "That's what you're proving. I don't know what to tell you." He shrugs. "I promise, though, it's not hard. I did mine at nine."

You focus on not pissing yourself. That definitely won't make Lars think very highly of you. Plus, animals can smell pee, right?

"All right, here we are!" Lars says cheerily, pulling off to the side of the road. "Tools are in the back." He points to a crossbow and a Bowie knife. You're already dressed in a white jumpsuit they had at the house—Mom called it a "first-timer's bonus."

You grab the weapons and step out of the car. You're about to ask Lars where deer hang out when you hear him slamming the door from the inside. He speeds away before you have a chance to react.

You turn, but there's nothing in sight but trees and snow. Uncertain what to do, you walk toward the nearest clump of forest. That seems right.

You've only made it about twenty yards when you see it. A full-grown deer stepping out of the woods carefully, stopping every few feet to nibble at branches. It's a lady deer. You can tell because it has no horns, and because there's a tiny Bambi behind it.

You grip the crossbow tight. Now what?

Kill it, obviously. Turn to page 282.
There's no way you can kill a deer. Turn to page 283.

"OH, MAN," YOU SAY THROUGH GRITTED TEETH. "I MUST HAVE OVER-rotated on that one. HA. HA." You bark a few laughs out and roll over, your face contorting in pain as soon as it's facing the ground. "I told you, I'm not used to this woodsy stuff."

You scramble up with the help of a nearby tree, barely repressing a cry of anguish.

"That's okay," Lars says, sounding supremely embarrassed. "I'll take over from here."

You step to the side, smile-grimace firmly in place, as Lars fells the tree in one massive swing. You've never felt more emasculated in your life.

"You'll help to carry it, though, yes?" Dad just looks confused, as though he's not certain what kind of creature you are.

"Of course, sure. My aim isn't that bad!" You force out another laugh, stopping abruptly as you feel it ripple through your kidney.

Dutifully, you help hoist the tree overhead, biting your tongue almost in half in your effort not to shriek.

Every step back through the woods is agony. You've never walked a longer half-mile. Why in god's name did you agree to this ridiculous expedition? Lindsi's family sucks. She should have warned you.

By the time you make it to the car, you're shivering all over. You feel weak, achy, and mildly feverish. Did you somehow explode a virus that had been safely stored in your kidney lining until now? That would be just your fucking luck.

If you need to lie down and rest immediately, turn to page 228.
If you want to soldier on in order to maintain some modicum of dignity, turn to page 230.

YOU'VE NEVER BEEN IN SO MUCH PAIN. THROUGH GRITTED TEETH you manage to whimper, "Please, take me to the ER."

"Really? On Christmas Eve?" Dad sounds skeptical. Isn't it obvious you're probably dying?

"I need a doctor. And help getting to the car."

Lars bends over and hoists you up like a baby, one hand beneath your knees, the other under your arms.

"I'll take him," he says. "Michael can drop a car by later."

"All right," Dad mutters. "If you *insist*."

You take back any thoughts about loving this family.

Thirty minutes later, you check into the ER. Lars helps you to a seat. Nearby, an old woman is weeping openly, snot and tears running down her chin, but you can't see anything wrong with her. Do ER doctors treat the misery of old age?

Minutes tick by. A man hugging a bucket vomits twice, loudly, before they've even finished checking him in. Luckily, he decides to camp out in the bathroom after that. Unluckily, you're afraid you might need to pee some blood soon.

After what feels like hours, a nurse calls your name. You hobble over—actually, most of your pain seems to have disappeared now. Will you get out of the bill if you just turn around and go—

"I'll come too," Lars says, stepping up to support your arm.

You'd love it if Lars came. Right now he's your only ally in this family, and he's so freakishly strong and handsome everyone seems to just...*do* things for him. While you were waiting, a nurse gave him a pair of scrubs "for a souvenir." He'll definitely score you the good pain meds. Maybe he'll somehow bring down the bill?

Still, it seems like too much to ask. He already thinks you're such a pussy.

"No, that's fine," you force yourself to say. "I don't want to inconvenience you."

"I don't mind. You probably want the moral support."

If you'd like to graciously agree, turn to page 231.
If you want to insist on going it alone so he doesn't think you're an even bigger wimp, turn to page 233.

You don't care how much pain you're in, there's no way you're letting this "chiropractor" touch you.

"You know what?" You make a Herculean effort not to grimace as you push yourself into a sitting position. "I'm already starting to feel better. I think the walk over must have really helped."

"Sure you don't want just *one* realignment? It did wonders for Sparky," he says, pointing at a picture you couldn't see before. To be fair, you're not certain Sparky wasn't always one of those wheelchair-hind-leg dogs, but the curve of his spine doesn't look natural.

"No, no." You stand. You feel a blood vessel in your eye popping from the strain of holding in all the pain. "I don't want to waste your time, especially at the holidays. I'll just head home. Thanks for your help!"

You somehow manage to make it past his hedge before you collapse onto your hands and knees, crawling through the gray, mucked-up snow the rest of the way back to Lindsi's parents' house.

• • •

You should call out to cousin Jimmy to close the door to the bedroom you're sharing—he left it open behind him—but the effort of yelling that loudly might permanently cripple you. Even speaking shoots lightning bolts of pain around your ribcage, like some sort of corset of fried nerve endings.

"Some stock is just weaker." Mom's voice drifts up the stairs. Is she talking about tasty Christmas stew? Or livestock—this *is* rural country. "It's not his fault, of course; it's his parents'. They should have forced him to develop better musculature in his youth."

Wait, is she talking about...

"You can see it in his eyes." Dad's voice sounds kinder, mostly sad. You imagine his beard shaking back and forth regretfully. "That color of brown is a sure sign of faulty genetics. And his feet? I saw those shoes in the hallway and I thought they belonged to you, Linds. You can't trust a man with feet that small,

I've always said that."

If only you could walk down there and defend yourself. But Lindsi will stand up for you. She has such a temper; she's probably fuming, ready to—

"I should have listened, Dad." Her sigh heaves up the stairs into your room. "I should have known the first time we went out and he passed on the steak for—" her voice breaks a little. "*The fish special.*"

You hear a collective gasp. Oh, for fuck's sake, that place is renowned for its seafood!

You hear footsteps nearing your door. Maybe this person can help! Or at least bring you water—you have to fortify your vocal cords to shout loudly enough for the Judases to hear you.

"Who's there?" you call.

Lindsi's brother Lars sticks his head around the door.

"Lars! Perfect. Would you mind bringing me some water, or something to eat? I just need a little food to help my body—"

You stop short. His sneer is so vicious it's literally left you speechless. Shaking his head, he slams the door. You hear his heavy, manly feet tramping down the hallway, but you're powerless to follow.

The End.

198

If you don't go through with it, Mom will never forgive you. She called ahead, after all, and you're already up against such virulent disgust on that front.

How different can dog spines really be?

"Let's get started," you say, trying to keep the fear out of your voice.

"Great!" You hear him approach the couch.

"Should I be on a table, or…"

"No, this is fine. I'll just compensate for the sag in the springs…"

"Maybe I should remove my sweater." Your voice is getting nervously high. "So you can see my spine?"

"I know about where it is."

You feel a heavy hand on the lower part of your back, and another one gripping around your neck. Oh, Jesus, you'll never walk again.

"Do you think this is a good idea? I've had some serious—"

You can't finish the sentence because suddenly he's ripping you in two.

You feel something pop deep in your back, then a series of crackles all along your vertebrae, then your muscles tearing away from your bones.

"AHHHHHHHHHHHHHHH!" You shriek in pain.

"Good, that's good. That's how it should be," he says.

You're still screaming a minute after he's let go of you.

"Well, uh…" He sounds slightly abashed. "I guess…go home now."

You're physically unable to stand. Instead, you crawl on all fours out the door. Maybe *now* he'd be able to find your spine.

Turn to page 226.

WHATEVER IT IS, IT'S MORE THAN YOU WANT TO FIND OUT.

"I'm just going to dress this," you say, backing away slowly, like you would from a rabid animal. "Upstairs."

She nods, her face supremely calm.

Back pain totally forgotten between the aching, pulsing inferno that was your hand and the fear creeping up from your stomach, you head upstairs. You run cold water over your hand and wrap it in gauze from the medicine cabinet, then pack your things as best you can one-handed.

"I just got a call from my mom," you say as you walk through the kitchen, looking at no one. "My dad has had a health emergency. I have to go home."

You glance over at Mom, but she's still weirdly calm, like a partially sedated frog enjoying a day off. Before she—or anyone else—can change your mind, you run out the door.

• • •

Why are you feeling like this?

The pain in your hand makes sense. And the loneliness of the empty city at Christmas explains the melancholy. But this is more than that. It's almost a hollowness. Like everything you've done before, even the big things—family weddings, the time you got that promotion at work, games of croquet with your college roommates—was empty. Meaningless.

Your phone buzzes on the bedside table. You don't recognize the number, but the grisly picture of an oozing, puffy hand can only have come from one person. You scroll to the message.

I've absorbed you into me. Now you'll always be a part of the VanWhittington family line.

You should be horrified—how did she even get your number? But strangely, that's not how you feel at all. No, you feel comforted. Gratified.

Before you can think better of it, you've snapped a picture of your own destroyed hand. It's grisly, what with the missing skin and the raspberry-jelly-like section on the palm, but there's something fiercely beautiful about it, too.

You think you see a spot where a pale piece of skin is still clinging to the raw pink flesh below, a lake of oozing yellow encircling them both.

You hold up your other hand for comparison. Yes, your first inkling was right: it's far too pale to have come from you. It must be Mom's skin. VanWhittington skin. Grafted into you by fire, never to be removed.

You gaze at the picture.

You shouldn't send it, should you?

No, you should. You definitely should. And you do.

The End.

YOU LOOK AROUND, SMILING CONTENTEDLY.

A storybook Christmas dinner spreads across the dining room table, the turkey golden and succulent, the stuffing dotted with dried fruits and moist with drippings from the bird, the mashed potatoes fluffy and creamy and drenched with melting butter.

Best of all, the entire family is treating you like the guest of honor. Dad has just given you some prime dark meat, Lars keeps topping off your wineglass with "the good stuff," and Mom has just been quietly beaming at you throughout the meal.

And Lindsi is actually spoon-feeding you. Your hand is useless under all the swaddling, after all, and for some reason, none of the family members seem to find it off-putting or unmanly for you to be fed like an infant.

Man, families are *so weird*.

But really, is your family any less strange? Sure, you don't have "provings" that, according to Lindsi, usually involve crossbow hunting but are sometimes swapped for "endurance of extraordinary pain" instead—wait, were you paying attention? She must have said something less weird than that, right?

Even if she didn't, though, who are you to judge? Your mom's cousin once spent an entire Christmas dinner explaining how to get rid of a tapeworm orally. Your Aunt Edna has that entire room filled with taxidermied squirrels in traditional German dress. And didn't Uncle Kenny once open his kindergarten-aged son's Fritos before school, stuff a desiccated pig's trotter inside, and reseal the bag with his "as seen on TV" thing? The school had the FDA on the line before they realized it was a joke. The worst fucking joke ever, played on a kindergartener.

So really, even if there is a stronger emphasis on hand-to-hand combat and pain tolerance than you're used to, who's to say the VanWhittingtons are strange? They're just…different. There's nothing wrong with different.

"Oooh, sweetie, it looks like you're almost out of squash soufflé. But there's none left. Do you want mine?" Lindsi actually looks pained for you.

"No, I'll just make another." Mom gets up swiftly, smiling at you. She waves her bandaged hand in the air. "I'm more used to working around one of these than you are. And you deserve a treat after all your hard work."

Okay, deliberately burning yourself isn't exactly hard work…

…but Lindsi's lifting a perfectly layered bite of turkey, stuffing, and gravy into your mouth. Forget all your ridiculous concerns about borderline psychosis; you could get *used* to this.

The End.

"SORRY." YOU LAUGH AS NORMALLY AS YOU CAN MANAGE. IS THERE a normal "you just accidentally discovered your son's ejaculate" laugh? "I told Jimmy I'd help out with this."

"Why would you do that?" Luanne is looking at you with laserlike intensity. At least you're not the only person in this family who thinks it's weird for you to be sleeping with a teenaged boy.

"Honestly? I remember how mortifying it was when this sort of thing happened. Your—I mean, 'Mom' already had me bunking with Jimmy, so I offered to help him out. He seemed convinced you'd be angry with him or something if you knew."

You laugh theatrically. If you play this right, you can probably shame her into being cool. After all, she can't *actually* be mad at her son for having a wet dream.

"I told him that was ridiculous, but you know how it is at that age, the idea of your parents knowing you have a sex drive is just…" You shake your head and roll your eyes dramatically.

She shudders, then seems to gather herself.

"Yes, of course. Thank you for helping out." She's still looking at you funny, but then, you *are* cleaning a pile of jizz laundry. It's not a comfortable situation for anyone. Finally, frowning slightly, she leaves.

The rest of the day, no one mentions the unfortunate incident. Phew. For once, you managed to get yourself off the hook.

Turn to page 227.

"I'm sorry, I shouldn't have been so…" Correct? "Forward. I'm just saying the chances are extremely high that there's a reasonable explanation for this. One that is perhaps… uncomfortable, but totally normal, especially for a teenage boy."

Everyone is still staring at you, though Mom has swapped her gape for a sneer.

"I mean, I still deal with that occasionally and I'm past thirty, right?" You look at Lindsi's brother Lars, whose eyes fill with pity, then at Luanne's husband, who shakes his head and looks away.

"Well." Luanne coughs loudly. "I suppose that explains that. Let's not talk about it again. Ever."

You finish the meal in complete silence.

• • •

The next morning everyone seems a little easier. Lars pats you on the back and asks, "How'd you sleep?" when you walk in, winking luridly at Jimmy. Luanne smiles tightly at you, as though to signal "no harm done." Even Mom refrains from the death stare when she brings in coffee for everyone.

You settle in around the tree and start handing out presents.

"Jimmy, why don't you go first," Mom says, smiling at him indulgently. Oh sure, blame the messenger, not the actor. "I know you're all grown up now, but you're still my little grandbaby."

"Technically I have not been a baby in over a decade, no matter how liberal you are with the term 'toddler,'" Jimmy says flatly, reaching for the present.

He opens it. It's a pair of boxer briefs. Ooooh, that's a little awkward.

"I just thought," Lars coughs awkwardly, "you know, since you're growing up now. Time to move past the tightie…whities."

Everyone forces a smile while Lindsi reaches for another box.

"Ooh, Jimmy, this one's from Aunt Josephine, out in California." She laughs too loudly, trying to smooth things over. "She always sends the funniest stuff, she's such a hippie." Mom shudders at the word.

"A book," he says, setting it in the center of the room.

…where it's perfectly placed for everyone to notice the title: *Your Changing Body and How to Love Yourself.*

Luanne represses a horrified squeal.

"Here," Lindsi sounds desperate. "Grandma Pearl—er, I mean, your great-grandma—sent you something. How nice! Probably she still thinks you're about five years old, though."

"This water gun's shape is ludicrous. Propulsion would certainly be compromised," Jimmy says, tossing the dick-and-balls-shaped Super Soaker off to the side.

Everyone clears their throats awkwardly.

You just have to pray they overlook your gift at the back.

Why in god's name had you thought it would be funny to give the teenager the old "just in case" condoms you found at the bottom of your luggage?

The End.

206

FUCK IF YOU'RE GOING TO APOLOGIZE FOR BEING THE ONLY SANE person in the room. You just let it hang there, ignoring Lindsi's dagger stare, letting the silence thicken like a salty, milky, disgusting Jell-O.

Finally, Mom sighs heavily. Everyone turns to her.

"I suppose there's only one option," she says, looking into each pair of eyes in turn. They all nod one by one. Unsure what else to do, you nod when she reaches you. You're starting to think that "we all just let this go" isn't the option she's going for.

"Then we're agreed. It's time for the purification ritual."

"The purification...what?" you say.

But she's already pushing back from the table, her air of finality seeming to infect the rest of the family. There's nothing to do but follow.

· · ·

"Let him absorb the blandness," Mom says, staring at the ceiling as she grabs a handful of unflavored Cream of Wheat straight from the pot and smears it on Jimmy's chest, on top of the layers of skim milk and the unscented, unlabeled lotion. You suppose the order of the layers is so the pasta cooked in saltless water will adhere?

Once she's done, she moves to one side, where Luanne and her husband are waiting. She nods at...you.

Fuck, are you really expected to do this? This is nothing like your family's holidays.

She nods again, eyes bugging out expectantly.

Sighing, you grab a handful of spaghetti and push it onto Jimmy's chest.

"The blandness," you say, rubbing until a few strands stick.

You've slept with a teenager, he ejaculated profusely, and you discussed it over dinner with his entire family, and yet you've never felt more perverse than you do right now.

The End.

YOU WAKE UP THE NEXT MORNING AND HEAD DOWNSTAIRS.

"Merry Christmas," you say as cheerily as you can manage.

Lindsi rushes out of the room, blushing furiously. No one else makes eye contact.

No, that's not quite true. Lindsi's mom is staring at you like you just slaughtered the baby Jesus on the kitchen island.

You all troop into the living room to open presents.

"Here's one for you," Lindsi says, smiling too hard. "It's from Lars."

You open it. It's a pair of boxer briefs, with a model on the cover who's all bulge.

"I just thought every guy can use socks and boxers at Christmas, right?" He coughs awkwardly and turns away from you.

A few minutes later Lindsi hands you another.

"From Luanne and Michael," she says, nodding to her sister and brother-in-law.

"We should just say, Lindsi said you were into food and, you know, hipster things…" Luanne frowns.

You unwrap a book about pickling. Dozens of long, plump cucumbers spread across on the cover, a few bulbous onions behind them.

"Thanks," you mumble.

Cousin Jimmy comes over with a long, narrow box.

"This is for you. According to the tag it is from Lindsi." He hands it over, then sits down abruptly. Jimmy's kind of strange. Robotic, even.

Lindsi is fawning over a gift from her mom, so you start opening it without her.

You pull out…a huge dildo?

"Wow, okay, so that's a massager. For your *neck*." Even Lindsi's earlobes are red, she's blushing so hard. "You said you were stressed at work. It's supposed to be a good model, I just…" She shakes her head and looks at the floor.

Jesus. This can't possibly get any more awkward.

"Did you realize all your gifts share a phallic influence?"

Jimmy says, voice utterly inflectionless. "This one is for covering your genitals, and this picture looks like genitals, and this object…"

He continues droning on. You can't hear him anymore over the roar of blood rushing through your ears.

The End.

"Oh, um, about these…" You wait for him to say you don't need to explain. He doesn't. "I was having some serious stomach issues during the service and…well, I made a mess of my underwear." You hope he doesn't make you explain sharts. "I thought I should make sure I don't ruin my pants, too."

"I'm so sorry to hear that. Are you okay?" He looks sympathetic, smiling at you with genuine parental worry.

"I'm fine. More embarrassed than anything."

"There's nothing to be embarrassed about. I've known plenty of strong men with weak sphincters."

You're not sure how to respond to that, so you just smile, finish up TP-ing yourself, put on your pants, and head out with Lindsi's dad's arm around your shoulders.

• • •

It's amazing what a good night's rest can do for your insides. You come downstairs feeling fine—chipper, even.

"Merry Christmas, VanWhittingtons!" you say cheerily. "Mrs. VanWhittington, could I trouble you for a cup of coffee?"

Lindsi's mom turns to you with a frosty stare, then glances at her husband and seems to relent.

"Of course. And call me Mom. Everyone does. He's Dad."

"Thanks, Mom," you say.

You follow them into the dining room, where a spread's already laid out. You reach for a muffin.

"Oh, no, no," Dad says, lightly tapping your hand. Maybe they're for the kids?

You reach for some fruitcake instead. You've always loved fruitcake.

"Not that either," Dad says, shaking his head. "It's filled with prunes. *And* fiber."

You frown, then reach tentatively toward the Crock-Pot of oatmeal.

"What are you thinking?" Dad chuckles, but he looks

deadly serious.

Are you not allowed to eat? "I'm sorry, I'm confused about what's going on."

"All those foods are too fibrous," Dad says behind a hand.

"Too fibrous?"

Everyone stares as he leans over and stage-whispers.

"*You* know." You're still not getting it. He frowns. "They'll exacerbate your *bowel control issues.*"

The End.

WHAT COULD POSSIBLY EXPLAIN THE FACT THAT YOU'RE MAKING underwears out of church toilet paper?

"I'm sorry you had to see me this way. It's just that money's really tight right now."

Really? That's the best you can come up with?

"So you've...run out of underwear?"

"No, I just try to...save on...washing costs. When I have a chance. I flip socks inside out, too. It's partly monetary, but also environmentally motivated." That makes it sound slightly less disgusting, right? "I didn't want to go to the laundromat until I had a full load of clothing."

"Ahh, I see. You've got that Depression-era mindset. You know my mom used to save on stockings, too. She'd draw a line up the back of her leg with a stick she'd rubbed in soot so it would look like a seam. Pretty clever idea."

You frown.

"Not that you want to look like you're wearing ladies' stockings." He coughs awkwardly. "You know, if things are tight, I could help out."

"That's not necessary," you say, shaking your head. The motion causes the toilet paper around your midsection to loosen. You grab at it hastily to prevent your dick from falling out. He frowns deeply.

"Please. I have...fifty dollars in my wallet. I'll take you to the store as soon as we drop off the family. I hate thinking my little girl might find you in pretend underwear."

If you have no choice but to take the money, turn to page 235.
If you feel obligated to refuse, turn to page 237.

YOU JUST MET THESE GUYS; IT WOULDN'T BE WISE TO RUFFLE feathers. Plus, Eyelashless looks like the kind of DM who would punish you for ruining his plans, even if it is just a Christmas module.

"I'll play lawful good."

"Your backstory?" Vampire looks at you expectantly. Like you came with a character backstory thought out on the off chance you'd run into a D&E game?

"I was kidnapped from my people—a wood elf clan who live mostly through gleaning and elemental magic—and taken by a rigid set of clerics at the tender age of thirty. Under their extremely strict training, any thought of rebelling against law, or rule, has been stamped out of me, though I still yearn, sometimes, for the wild ways of the forests I grew up in."

Apparently you *did* have a backstory on hand.

"Kinda thin, but whatever." Schlub snorts. Looks like someone's vying for King of the Nerds.

You start playing...but every time you try to do something interesting, even just turn water into wine to stretch the party's supplies, Vampire is on you.

"That's not in accordance with your alignment."

"Not strictly, but..."

"You can't do it; your character wouldn't do it."

Then he starts breathing heavily through his nostrils in a way that makes you so uncomfortable you just give in.

Which makes the game almost unbearably boring. You used to love this, even the dumb stuff, like chatting "in-character" with tavern wenches. But seeing the other grown men getting so into it makes you feel...itchy. Like you hope no one is near enough to hear any of you. Like you'd rather be anywhere else.

You used to love this game so much. You thought being a barely reformed geek was a defining part of your character. But this feels hollow, empty...embarrassing. Not because it's too geeky; because you feel like there's something deeply desperate about needing to get away from your real life this badly.

The DM puts you up against a cave troll.

You roll a fifteen, but manage to nudge it to a one before anyone notices.

"Oh, man. Critical failure."

"I'm sorry," Eyelashless says, blinking at you. "He crushes your skull. A lot."

"Oh well, guess I'll get going." You start to walk away.

"I have a healer's kit, I can…"

You pretend you can't hear Vampire's wails.

On the walk home, you feel strange. Adrift on a sea of personalitylessness. Who are you, if not the person you always believed yourself to be? What have you become since this went out of your life?

What's the point of it all? What's the point of anything?

The End.

Fᴜᴄᴋ ᴛʜᴀᴛ, ʟᴀᴡꜰᴜʟ ɢᴏᴏᴅ ɪs *ᴇᴠᴇʀʏ ᴅᴀʏ ᴏꜰ ʏᴏᴜʀ ʟɪꜰᴇ.*

"I'm playing him chaotic evil."

Vampire makes a sound of choking rage. You grin mischievously.

"But you can't *do* that. You're a cleric." Vampire is turning red, like he overate at his Christmas blood feast.

"Of course I can. Look at the entire history of the church— clerics can absolutely be evil."

"But *chaotic* evil? Your class is defined by ORDER." Vampire's spitting, he's so angry.

"Fine, neutral evil."

"But lawful evil would—"

"Nope, I'm out for me no matter what. Your laws mean nothing. I have *magics*." Schlub snorts appreciatively. Vampire looks like someone's punched him in the Adam's apple.

"Okay, if we're ready to begin," Eyelashless says, turning to his printout of the module. "Imagine yourself in the tiny hamlet of—"

"NO, we are NOT READY!" Vampire is shrieking. People at the party turn to stare.

"Dude, you don't get to decide my alignment. Sorry, that's not how it works," you say quietly. Fuck this guy; the whole point of this game is to be someone else. Someone interesting. Someone *you* choose.

"You need to balance the party. I won't be subjected to another—"

"Buddy, it's just a fucking *game.*"

"AHHHHHH!!!!!" He shrieks and flies at you, slapping at your face. His hands are bony, and it hurts like hell.

"Get a hold of yourself," you say, trying to get a grip on his flailing hands. They're so flimsy they're impossible to control.

"TAKE IT BACK."

"Seriously, you need to—"

"TAKE IT BACK!"

He dives into you, which is so unexpected that you immediately topple to the floor. Schlub pulls him off and you stand up, brushing at your clothes.

"I'm gonna go."

"I think that would be wise," Eyelashless says.

Well, *that* was awkward. At least pretty much nobody here knows you. Now it's time to make a quick retreat.

• • •

The next morning you wake up to fifty-three notifications on your Facebook.

What the fuck?

You open it up. The top thing in the feed is a video from your former coworker, Brad, titled "My xmas party was awesomer than yours (NERD. FIGHT.)"

There you are, getting slapped by an Edward Gorey illustration.

And of course Brad's tagged you in it. So much for keeping your D&E history secret from Lindsi.

The End.

"I SHOULDN'T," YOU SAY VAGUELY. "I HAVE TO GET BACK TO my sister's."

"Oh, okay," Wayne says, obviously disappointed. Jesus, you didn't even know each other in high school. Smiling awkwardly, you grab a few cartons of stupidly expensive eggnog and head back to your sister's.

"Late again," Lauren says the second you walk in the door.

You did exactly what she asked and nothing more. But at this point, you don't even bother mounting a defense.

Your utter lack of fight seems to appease Lauren slightly. Dinner actually goes relatively smoothly.

"Let's leave a few dishes for the morning; I'm exhausted," she says afterward.

You check your watch. It's not even seven thirty.

"Let me give you a hand with those," you say. "Then if you don't mind, I think I'll read on the couch for a bit."

Lauren raises an eyebrow. "Looks like we have a regular night owl on our hands, Gregory."

They both chuckle. You repress a snort of disbelief.

After scrubbing a few pots and pans, you pour yourself some of the expensive bourbon you bought earlier and sit on the couch, grabbing a paper off the coffee table. It's an old copy of *Der Spiegel*, and even if it were in English, you can tell it would bore you to tears.

You decide to peek under the tree. Maybe if you push your gifts underneath some that Lauren wrapped, they'll look less like paper abortions.

That's weird. The Harry Potter set you got for Harrison seems lighter than you remember...

You peel back a corner of the paper.

Fuck, it's the Super Soaker. You must have accidentally donated the books to Toys for Tots.

If you want head back to Toys for Tots to trade out the gift, turn to page 239.
If you want to claim one of Lauren's gifts as "from you," turn to page 240.

YOU FOLLOW WAYNE TO A NEARBY BAR.

"So, what are you doing for work these days?" you ask.

"I'm in newspaper sales."

That's still a thing? You wrack your brain for a follow-up question.

"Ummmm.…ABC, right?"

"What?"

"Always Be Closing. Isn't that what you sales guys say?" You hope so. It's literally the only thing you can think of to add to this conversation.

"Actually, it's more complicated than that. We look at each market…"

Wayne drones on. It's Christmas Eve and you're having drinks with a guy you barely knew, even back in high school. Why did you agree to this in the first place?

After twenty minutes of forced conversation, you decide it's time to bail.

"Well, on that note, I should probably head back. I don't want the eggnog to spoil."

"Oh, okay. I thought it was my round, though?"

"Maybe next time," you say, knowing full well there will never be a next time.

You head back to Lauren's. She's waiting at the door in pajamas and slippers, looking annoyed.

"You missed dinner *and* stayed out late on Christmas Eve?"

You look at your phone. It's seven fifteen.

"I'm going to put a few presents under the tree. Sleep well," you say.

"Don't bother," she hisses. "I didn't know if you were even coming home tonight so I had Gregory do it."

"You didn't have to do that."

"Yes I did. It's the only way to ensure my sons wouldn't have to face Christmas without a gift from their thoughtless uncle." She stomps off.

218

You roll your eyes. Why even bother arguing? You'll be home soon enough.

Seven fifteen, huh? And already the house is totally silent...

If you want to force yourself to go to bed so you don't piss off Lauren more, turn to page 241.
If you want to try to make it up to her for missing dinner, turn to page 243.

YOU BUNDLE UP AND HEAD BACK OUT TO YOUR CAR.

You've had a few drinks, but it doesn't concern you. You know you're good to drive. You'll just stick to the back roads and drive slow to be extra-safe.

You pull out of the driveway and head toward the bar.

WHEEEEEEE-YOOOOOOO, WHEEEEEE-YOOOOOO.

Unfuckingbelievable. You're being pulled over.

A portly cop in his mid-forties waddles up.

You roll down your window.

"You're gonna have to step outta the car, sir," the officer says.

He produces a breathalyzer. You blow.

"Ho-ho," the cop says with a sadistic grin. "You're not gonna like this."

If you want to keep your mouth shut, turn to page 244.
If you want to try to bargain with the cop, turn to page 245.

YOU WAKE UP ON A STRETCHER OUTSIDE THE BAR. AN EMT IS preparing an oxygen mask.

"Where am I?"

"Oh, you're awake. Good. We're taking you to the hospital to make sure you're okay. Do you remember what happened?"

You're confused. Your throat hurts. What exactly *did* happen? The last thing you remember is screaming "rape."

You mumble weakly, "I was yelling 'rape'…because…"

"Rape? You mean someone raped you during the fire? DEAR GOD."

What? No. That's not it at all. You struggle to get your thoughts straight.

"Joe!" screams the EMT. "Grab the ass-swabbing kit, STAT!"

The End.

IT'S CHRISTMAS MORNING AND YOUR NEPHEWS ARE UNWRAPPING THE presents you bought them. You can't wait to see the excitement in their eyes.

"A junior geologist's kit?" Harrison says, obviously disappointed.

Wait, what?

"I didn't..."

Lauren hisses at you.

"I know who bought this," Harrison says, pointing at Lauren. "Because it *sucks*." He tosses it on the ground and stomps on it. "I HATE you! You always ruin everything!"

Lauren looks horrified, but she can't have any idea that you started this fire.

"Geology kits are boring, mom! Take the stick out of your ass."

"Excuse me?!" Lauren yells.

Harrison looks at you for moral support. You turn away, smiling awkwardly at your sister and shrugging.

You've created a monster. Thank god it's not your problem in a week.

The End.

It's Christmas morning and the entire family's gathered around the tree for a picture.

"Should we sing a few verses from '*Stille Nacht*'?" Gregory asks, setting up the camera. Jesus, just call it "Silent Night" already, like every other English-speaking person in the world.

He sets the timer and the multiple picture option and walks over to the group, throwing his arm around you as he softly croons to himself.

"*Stille nacht, heil'ge nacht…*"

Once it's over, you grab the camera and start scrolling through the photos.

In every one Harrison looks like he's been mauled by a pack of angry raccoons. His entire lip is swollen and raw, sticking out at a weird, drooly angle.

Woof.

Lauren peeks over your shoulder.

"Hideous."

She glares at you with even more hatred than usual.

Ahhh, the Christmas spirit.

The End.

YOU WAKE UP EARLY, FEELING GREAT. AND WHY WOULDN'T YOU? After all, you're the fun uncle!

It's still super early. Everyone's asleep.

What would be the funnest thing you could do right now?

Get donuts, obviously! The kind with chocolate frosting and neon sprinkles. Yeah, that's such a fun-uncle thing to do.

You get dressed and run to the local bakery to grab two dozen. Why not be generous? It's Christmas, after all.

When you get back, the kids are downstairs, poking at their presents under the tree.

You put a finger over your lips conspiratorially and present the donuts.

"Take an extra for later," you whisper.

They instantly devour two donuts apiece.

"You're the best uncle in the whole wide world!" Otto screams.

Aw, that's sweet.

He sprints away, Harrison close behind, making weird, wheezing sounds. You hear Lauren stirring.

"Did you give them refined sugar?" she calls from the top of the stairs.

"I bought donuts! Want some?"

Lauren looks pissed. Even more so than usual.

"You've completely spiked their glycemic index!" she shrieks. "Their systems aren't equipped to process simple carbohydrates this early in the morning."

"I'm sorry. I was trying to be fun…"

"Fun? You call setting my kids on a road that leads straight to diabetes *fun*?"

Otto runs up to you and vomits all over your slippers. He sprints off, wheezing even harder than before.

Your sister runs after him, obviously livid.

All of a sudden, you hear the Christmas tree in the living room crash to the floor.

"HAHAHAHAHAHA!" cackles Harrison manically.

Then he pukes.

Oops…

The End.

YOU HAVE TO TELL LAUREN. IF THE SHOE WERE ON THE OTHER FOOT, you'd want her to tell you.

You corner her in the kitchen before Otto and Harrison wake up.

"Want some coffee?" she asks.

"Sure. After I tell you something."

"What is it?"

You urgently whisper in her ear. "Psst...right on the taint... psst...the old Jelly Roll Morton..."

Lauren pulls back, clearly shocked.

"How dare you! My marriage is none of your business."

That wasn't even close to the response you were expecting.

"I'm trying to save you from being the last to know about Greg cheating!"

"For your information, we have an open marriage. Parties are in the safe zone. Just last month I filmed Gregory and Sarah's husband—"

"OKAY! OKAY! Please don't finish that sentence. I get it."

"Then back the fuck off," she hisses. "I don't need your judgment."

"Sorry. I just wanted to help."

You feel a tap on the back of your leg.

It's little Otto. How long has he been standing there?

"What's an open mawwiage?"

Apparently long enough.

"Since you felt the need to discuss it on CHRISTMAS MORNING, you tell him," Lauren says, storming out of the room.

The End.

It almost physically pains you, but you have to keep your mouth shut. Saying something will ruin Christmas for everyone.

You sit on the couch, scooting your feet away from the slippers Gregory lent you. They make your feet feel sleazy. You watch listlessly as the kids tear through their gifts. They look so happy.

Not for long…

You look around the living room.

The plastic Christmas tree is a lie.

Those stockings aren't real.

Your sister's marriage is *totally* fake.

Even this holiday is one big fucking lie. Didn't some scholar figure out Jesus would have been born in April?

Everything in life is a lie. Only death is real.

You watch the boys open gift after gift, jumping around the room with joy every time.

They should cherish this now. Who knows how soon it will all come crashing down?

"Here you go, Harrison." You pass him your gift.

"Whoa, Moon Boots! You're the BEST."

Ahh, innocence. You muster a weak smile.

"Can I please see you in the kitchen?" Lauren hisses. "I need help…brewing the coffee."

You know that's also a lie, but you go. It's probably for the best. Your nephews should see as little arguing as possible right now.

"You had to know Moon Boots were off-limits!" she scolds you in a hushed voice. "I need you to tell Harrison you made a mistake and you're taking them back to the store."

Fine, you'll ruin it for him. Everything is already ruined anyway. Turn to page 246.
No. You can't tell your sister about the cheating, but dammit, you'll preserve this child's joy a little while longer! Turn to page 247.

"Oh, that's not good."

The specialist looking at your X-ray is frowning deeply. At least, you think he's frowning; you can't fully see his face because you still can't completely straighten your back, even though it's been ten days since the "chiropractor" incident. You couldn't get an appointment sooner.

"What's going on?"

"Well, you've ruptured at least two disks." The doctor screws up his face, confused. "And somehow you've pinched several nerves between the others. I've never seen anything like it. Frankly, I'm shocked you were even able to get yourself to the appointment."

See! At least *someone* understands fighting brutal back pain is its own form of manliness. If only Lindsi were here to hear that.

"You're looking at major surgery. Possibly more than one. And of course you'll be confined to a wheelchair for at least six months. Let me clear out my schedule. If you don't get this done soon, well…" The doctor actually shudders. "Let me clear out my schedule."

On the way home, you text Lindsi the news. Surely now she'll stop being so distant and disapproving. It's like she doesn't even believe your back issues are real! But she'll have to understand when a noted specialist said that—

Her response rattles the phone against your hip, making your back scream in renewed pain.

Wincing, you look at it.

Lindsi: *That sucks, and I totally pity cripples, for real, but I can't risk tainting my line with inferior stock. Sorry.*

What the fuck does that even—

Lindsi: *Sorry if that wasn't clear. I'm breaking up with you.*

Dammit. Now who's gonna drive you home from surgery?

The End.

"WON'T YOU HELP US?" KERMIT SAYS. "IF WE DON'T FIND THE MAGIC biggening stone, we'll all be this size forever!" The rest of the Muppet Babies nod eagerly, desperate for you to save them.

Just then, however, the door to the nursery swings open, and two tree-sized pillars of striped sock walk in.

"Hello? Children?" Nanny's soothing voice echoes down from above, like some sort of celestial childcare worker. Even though you can't see her face, you can tell from that voice, from those sinuous calves, that she's a total fox when the nursery's closed for…

"MERRY CHRISTMAS!" Luanne's cheery voice wakes you from your recurring dream. Why always the Muppet Babies? Why does Nanny still get you so horny now, past the age of thirty? She was a cartoon. A cartoon that was *only socks*.

Luanne steps across the room and kisses Jimmy on the forehead. Fortunately, you're curled up on the complete opposite side of the bed. She can't think that you two…

She whips the covers down.

"Get up, sleepyheads, the rest of the family is—oh."

You grimace, feeling her stare on the raging morning wood that your flannel pants are helpless to conceal. You stand hastily, grabbing a T-shirt from your bag and holding it at your waist.

"Oh. Oh god."

You turn around.

Jimmy's had another wet dream. And from the size and stiffness of that crusty sheet tent, it was a doozy.

Man, and you *just* washed these sheets.

The End.

THERE'S NO WAY YOU CAN CARRY ON LIKE THIS. YOU'VE NEVER HAD the experience before, but you have a gut feeling that if you peed right now, it'd come out bloody.

As soon as you get back to the house you pull Lindsi aside.

"I think I really hurt myself cutting down the tree," you whisper. "Don't make a big deal of it, but I have to lie down."

"Were you a big strong *man?*" She hooks a fingertip into your front pants pocket. You look around, immediately nervous, but her family is busy setting up the tree.

"Well…" Can you spin this so you *sound* like a big strong man? Clearly she's used to Lars and his freakish giant strength. "I haven't swung an axe in so long, I didn't realize how hard I was throwing it. I really nailed my back with the axe head."

"You're too strong for your own good." She makes a pouting duckface and leads you up the stairs by your waistband. You're extremely uncomfortable—there are so many people in this house, and none of them particularly like you—but you don't run into anyone. The minute you reach her bed, you fall into a deep, dreamless sleep.

• • •

Why is there hair in your mouth?

You slap at your face, trying to brush it away.

"Ow!" Lindsi squeals, sitting up. She's straddling you, already tugging at the button on your pants.

"What are you doing?" You push at her futilely, but she grabs your wrists and pins you with her entire weight.

"Shhhh." She releases you just long enough to pull off her shirt. "I want you."

"Lindsi, this is a bad idea."

"Don't worry, I can be quiet. I was all through high school and college."

"Lindsi, your entire family is, like, twenty feet away."

"That's why it's so *hot.*" She whips her bra off and leans

over, slapping her boob over your mouth and nose, like a fleshy gas mask.

"Linzzeee…" You can't speak around the boob. But you hear footsteps approaching. They're getting nearer. They're right outside the—

"OH!" Mom shrieks, dropping the stack of presents she'd been carrying. Since she's not sharing with anyone, Lindsi's room has been designated the wrapping room.

Lindsi pulls a shirt over her front and flips around to face her mother, lips pursed in defiance.

But Mom isn't looking at Lindsi; she's looking at you. And she looks even more monumentally disgusted than she usually does when she's looking at you.

If you want to apologize profusely, turn to page 248.
If you'd rather throw Lindsi under the bus, turn to page 250.

You grimace through the ride back to the house, "mmm"-ing anytime you're addressed.

Magically, it seems to work on Lindsi's family. By the time you pull into the driveway, they're cheery again. Lars is even calling you "Backswing," which you assume is a mostly affectionate nickname? Success!

Well, at least socially. When you're forced to get out of the car, you almost scream in pain. Your kidney hurts, you feel achy everywhere, you're having stomach cramps, and you can't fully unbend your back.

You stumble to the bathroom, leaving the seat down to pee; you're in too much pain to lift it.

Pee isn't supposed to be pink.

You bend to flush, terror rising from your stomach in waves of nausea—unless that's your kidneys, too—when you hear it.

POP.

It sounds like something out of a cartoon.

But it feels like someone stabbed you with a machete in the left kidney, then just swiped across your entire body, severing every nerve ending along the way.

You're in searing, almost blinding pain.

If you really have to go to the hospital, now, turn to page 252.
If you just want to push through to the end of the day in order to not be entirely emasculated, turn to page 254.

"Well, if it's really no trouble…"

Lars smiles broadly and helps you through the door. You lean heavily on his arm so he'll think you're still injured. That, and it's nice to lean on someone so strong.

After another hour, a doctor comes in, staring at a chart.

"You say you damaged your kidney?"

"I think so. I hit it with an axe. Hard. The pain is severe."

He palpates you briefly, then turns to his clipboard, looking supremely bored.

"Have you urinated yet?"

"Yes."

"Any blood?"

"Well, no, but the pain…"

"It's bruised. Go home and rest. You'll be fine."

You're losing all your Lars cred!

"Shouldn't you do an X-ray, or…"

"Bed rest. If you see blood in your urine, come back. They'll take your information at the exit for billing."

He whisks out the door. Apparently that's it.

You and Lars are about to leave when you hear a knock. Thank god, it must be the doctor back to tell you you're sicker than he thought.

It's not, though. It's a man in a Santa suit. He looks familiar…

"Oh, it's *you*."

You recognize that voice. It's the man from the gas station. This was where he was heading? To volunteer at a *hospital?* Suddenly your fears of front-seat axe murder seem a little unfounded.

"You must be mistaken." You try to push past. You don't want Lars knowing you were afraid of this Santa. Especially since it's now clear you have at least fifty pounds on him.

"No, I'm not. It was just last night that I saw you at the gas station. Why were you so rude? At Christmas, no less?"

He's coming toward you, spluttering. Out of the corner of

your eye, you see Lars's questioning look.

You have to end this. Now.

If you want to call security on the Santa, turn to page 255.
If you want to just admit to knowing him to make this
end sooner, turn to page 256.

"No, I'll be fine."

"You need someone there when you're hurt. Everyone needs someone to lean on."

You're stunned by how excited you are that he's insisting. You really want him there with you. The idea of going in alone is... actually, that's not even it, you just like being around Lars. He's so reassuring. So solid. So chiseled.

Wait, chiseled? That's weird. True, of course. His face is like something a Norse god hewed from purest marble, and you can tell that underneath that flannel, his abs would be rock hard, like something on the cover of...

Jesus, what is going on with you? It's Lars. Lindsi's brother. A *man*. You're not into men. Are you?

Are you into him?

The thought terrifies you. Could you have spent over thirty years on the planet and been so fundamentally wrong about yourself?

Or maybe he's the one who's into *you*.

"Please, Lars, they're just going to poke and prod me. They'll probably make me get naked, and I'm sure you don't want to see that." Does he? Do you want him to want to? *This is the most confused you have ever felt.*

"We're practically family, and family doesn't—"

"We are *not* family."

You're not sure if you're more upset about the idea of committing to Lindsi this soon, or about the idea that he sees you as a brother, nothing more.

"I know, but you and Lindsi—"

"...have barely been dating four months."

"Well you're here for Christmas. That has to mean something."

"It means I missed a flight."

"Oh, come on." He elbows you chummily. His touch sends electric shockwaves through your entire body. *What is going on?*

"It means NOTHING. My Tinder is still up, for fuck's sake! This probably won't even last until spring! I mean, *Lindsi*?"

Lars stares in stunned silence.

Oh…that might have been a little too far.

"I mean, things could work out, it's just…"

"I only wanted to help," Lars puts both hands up. "It's not like I like seeing other dudes naked."

A nurse yells your name again.

You walk over slowly, looking over your shoulder the entire time. Lars watches, but doesn't follow.

When you return forty-five minutes later, he's exactly where you left him, staring at the wall, eyes glazed. Fuck, what have you done?

If you want to apologize, turn to page 258.

If you want to just pretend nothing happened, turn to page 260.

"Oh, uh…" You've already told him you're too poor for underwear, or basic hygiene. What choice do you have? "Thanks. That would be great."

He nods, obviously relieved. Awesome. You can't wait to underwear shop with your girlfriend's dad.

• • •

The next morning you head downstairs to find the entire family already seated around the tree, opening presents.

"Guess I overslept, huh?"

Lindsi frowns at you, obviously confused. It's her dad who speaks up, though.

"We thought since this was a *family* event you wouldn't mind if we started." He glares, his gaze even icier than his wife's. That's strange. Just last night you were laughing over boxer briefs. He even urged you to buy some lumberjack-themed ones. What changed?

You manage to pull Lindsi aside a few minutes later.

"What's up with your dad?"

"What do you mean?"

You glance at him. He's staring at you, teeth slightly bared.

"Did he say anything? Maybe about last night?"

"No. I don't think so. He just asked what you do and whether you were out of work at the moment. But don't worry, I talked you up. Told him how well you were doing, and how you got that promotion."

She keeps blathering on, but you're not listening anymore.

Eventually the family heads to the dining room for a lavish breakfast.

"Yes, it's just something we do around here," Lindsi's dad says, throwing an arm around your shoulder. His eyes look dead. He speaks loudly enough for everyone to hear him. "Provide for the people we care about. Generously. We don't try to *sponge* off them. Or take from them. Or take from a house of worship."

You feel the curious stares of Lindsi's entire family.

You'd pull him aside to pay him back, but you don't have any cash. You just have to hope he doesn't get any more explicit before the day is over.

"Can you believe some people will just take from anyone? No shame whatsoever."

Not likely.

The End.

"No, no." You wave a hand in front of you, even though it brings your wrappings perilously close to tearing. "I couldn't. Like I said, it's an environmental thing. And…because I hadn't packed for this trip…"

"Please, I want to help." He looks at you earnestly. God, he's probably the one decent person in this family, and you've convinced him you're too poor for underwear.

"No, I'm fine. Thank you, though. I'll be out in a few minutes."

He nods and retreats, leaving you to finish your groin-mummying alone.

• • •

The next morning, everyone's in a great mood. Lindsi's brother Lars is slapping people on the back like a proud coach, Lindsi is teasing her nieces about stealing their presents, and even her mom smiles tightly and offers you coffee.

Thank god. If Lindsi's dad had said anything, you wouldn't be getting off this easily.

You head into the living room to open presents, mostly watching the kids go to it.

"This one's for you," Lars says toward the end, tossing a small box your way. The tag says *From Santa*. It must be from Lindsi; you should have picked up something for her on the way, but you didn't have the time. Oh well, she'll get her present once you're back in the city.

You open it, expecting a gift card to her favorite restaurant.

Your jaw drops.

It's a stack of hundred-dollar bills.

"What'd you get?" Lindsi asks, scooting nearer. You're so stunned you don't have time to tuck it away. "Holy fuck, there has to be…" she rifles through the box, "a thousand dollars in here."

Now the whole family's attention is on you.

"Wow, Santa must really like you," Lindsi's dad says, winking exaggeratedly.

You should have just taken the fifty dollars. How can you give this back? Without mentioning the whole toilet paper underwear thing again?

It's clear Lindsi's family knows where the money came from. You can't meet their eyes; the discomfort you're all sharing is too intense.

"There's something else in here." Lindsi reaches into the box again. "It's a picture of...underwear?" She turns to her dad, horrified.

And you thought it wasn't possible for things to get more awkward.

The End.

YOU GRAB YOUR COAT AND HEAD BACK TO THE TOYS FOR Tots dropoff.

You park and start rummaging in the bin, hoping to find the gift you mistakenly donated.

You're about to concede defeat when you see it. Only Lauren could have that paper with German lyrics to "*O Tannenbaum*" on it.

You pull it out, doing a little fist pump of triumph.

"Khughhh."

You turn, surprised by the strange wheezing sound behind you. You didn't think anyone else was around.

It's an obviously ill child and her mother. The girl's barely able to hold up her present, which looks like a rubber ball. Oh, Jesus.

"Why are you taking presents…khughhh…that are meant for the…khughhh…kids in need?"

A single tear runs down her thin, pale cheek.

"You've got it all wrong."

The girl's mother stares at you with burning intensity.

"The only thing she wanted to do this Christmas was give back to others. She didn't even ask Santa to get better. This was the one thing she was still holding onto: her belief that people are fundamentally decent. And then she has to find you here, stealing from needy children. You should be ashamed."

"No. It's not like that. You're jumping to the wrong conclusion."

"Really? Are you or are you not taking presents from the donation bin?"

"Welll…yes, but—"

"You're a monster," she hisses.

The mom hands a tissue to her daughter. The little girl cries harder. "If people are this bad even on Christmas, is there any good in the world?"

"There, there," says the mom. "Let's get you back to bed."

If you want to go home empty-handed, turn to page 262.
If you might as well make the swap now that those two are gone, turn to page 263.

YOU'LL JUST HAVE TO CLAIM ONE OF LAUREN'S PRESENTS AND EXPLAIN it to her later.

You grab a box and open it, tossing the wrapping paper to the floor. You at least need to know what "you're" giving, right?

A French mime costume? That's literally the worst present you've ever seen. Giving Harrison that would be like gifting him perpetual social outcastdom.

Now what?

If you want to suck it up and slap your name on the mime costume, turn to page 264.
If you want to try another present, turn to page 265.

You head up to your room, lie down, and stare at the ceiling.

God, you're bored. How does any adult go to bed at dinnertime?

Eventually, though, the depth of your boredom allows you to doze off.

• • •

You wake up raring to go.

You check your phone. It's 4 A.M.

Incapable of falling back asleep, you head outside to shovel the snow. When you're done with that, you brew a pot of coffee for the family. Man, you're the best brother around! Probably in the running for best uncle, too.

You manage to slide a tray of chestnuts into the oven just before the kids begin to open their gifts. Nailing it.

"A SUPER SOAKER!" Harrison screams when he gets to yours.

Wait. That's not right.

Your sister looks like she just bit into a lemon. Apparently she and Gregory aren't on the same endocrine-disrupting page.

Harrison immediately starts pretending it's a submachine gun.

"BANG, BANG, BANG. DIE!"

"It was an honest mistake," you say, not sure what, exactly, went wrong.

"Then fix it," she says.

You consider standing up to her, but things are going so well. Plus, you know it's futile.

"Harrison, that toy isn't for you." You grab it away. "But don't worry, because I have something even better…which I'll give you tomorrow."

Tears start rolling down his cheek.

"I want the Super Soaker!"

"I'm sorry. You can't have it."

"I HATE YOU! You're the worst uncle EVER."

Harrison's scream sets off Otto.

"WAHHHHHHH."

You look at the clock on the wall. Great, it's not even 9 A.M. That's a hell of a lot of Christmas to go.

The End.

YOU THINK BACK TO WHEN YOU WERE A KID. EVERY YEAR YOUR DAD would dress up like Santa, climb on the roof, stomp around, and jingle a bunch of bells.

It's easily one of your favorite childhood memories. It felt so magical. If you did that for Otto and Harrison, there's no *way* Lauren could stay mad.

You rummage around the house in hopes of finding a Santa suit. No luck. Though you did see a doorknob with jingle bells on it. You could just do the reindeer bit, right?

You grab the bells and head outside, giddy with excitement. You know you saw a ladder around the side of the house…

There's a patch of nasty-looking ice near the roof's edge. Man, that looks pretty slippery. You carefully pick your way around it.

DING-A-LING! RING-A-LING! You shake the bells as hard as you can right over the boys' window.

From your perch atop the garage, you see two people approaching the front door. They're dressed all in black and they're peering in the darkened windows.

Oh god, now they're bending down, presumably looking for a key under the mat.

BURGLARS!

*If you want to be a superhero and leap off the roof
onto these Grinches, turn to page 266.
If you want to creep down the ladder and sneak up on
them from behind, turn to page 267.*

YOU SAY NOTHING. HE PUTS YOU IN THE BACK OF THE SQUAD CAR AND drives you to the station.

You make your one phone call to Lauren's house line. She *would* be the kind of person who puts her cell on "Do Not Disturb" after seven.

"Who is this?" Shit, that's Harrison's voice. "Hello?"

"Harrison, it's your uncle. Is your mom there?"

"It's late, where are you?"

"Nowhere. I'm...I just need to talk to her."

"Why didn't you use your cell phone? The caller ID says 'County Sheriff.' Where's that?"

"Uh, you know what? I'll call your mom later." You hang up, embarrassed.

"Belt, shoelaces, phone, and wallet," says the cop checking you in. She's clearly done this thousands of times before, which makes you feel mildly less shitty about yourself. "We're gonna put you in the drunk tank until you sober up," she adds.

You're pretty sure you're already sober, but what's the point of protesting? You walk into the cell. Luckily, it's empty.

A few hours pass.

"Okay, you can leave," says the officer as she opens the cell.

"Where can I pick up my car?" you ask.

"It's been impounded. You can pick it up in 24 hours."

You press your face into your hands. Fuck.

You grab your cell from the officer and dial Lauren.

Turn to page 268.

"LISTEN...OFFICER...ISN'T THERE ANYTHING I CAN DO? I'M BARELY over the limit."

Is that convincing? Probably not. You have to up your game.

"I need to get home...to my kids. One of them has a terrible flu."

He can't tell you're lying, can he?

"I've got a pair of little ones at home," he says. "Always getting sick, aren't they?"

Awesome! You nod somberly. "So very sick."

"Well, since it's Christmas, I suppose I *could* be nice and let you off with a warning."

"I'd *really* appreciate that," you say.

"That is, if you were willing to do something nice for me in return. You know, share the Christmas spirit?"

Fuck. This guy is totally going to force you into some weird sex act. Still, it's better than losing your license.

"Sure. Anything."

You brace yourself.

"I need you to make me look like a hero."

Well, that's not at all what you expected.

Turn to page 269.

You're too hungover and depressed to fight Lauren on this. Anyway, she'll have enough to deal with soon.

You trudge back into the living room.

"Sorry, bud. Those Moon Boots were meant for Toys for Tots."

"NOOOOOOO!" Harrison shrieks.

"I'm sorry, they gotta go."

"I HATE YOU!" Tears stream down his cheeks.

Lauren is standing aside, letting you take it. You do, impassively.

"WHY DID HE EVEN COME?"

Harrison's screams set off Otto.

"WAAAAAAHHHHH!"

Harrison throws the Moon Boots at your feet and storms out of the room.

And to think, this is probably the last good Christmas he'll have. It's only 9 A.M., but you desperately need some Christmas spirits.

The End.

THERE'S NO WAY YOU'RE RUINING CHRISTMAS FOR HARRISON. IT could be the last good one he has for a long time. It has to be perfect.

"I'm not returning the Moon Boots."

"It's not up for debate," Lauren snips. "Go in there and tell him it was a mistake."

"You're being ridiculous!" you yell. "You know what happens when you try to control everyone? They rebel and make stupid decisions!"

"What?"

"RECKLESS DECISIONS!"

"What are you talking about?"

"It's going to come back to bite you in the ass. Your whole family's ass!"

You're cut off by a shriek of pain from the living room.

"AHHHHHHHH!"

"Grab some ice!" Gregory screams into the kitchen. "This looks bad!"

Lauren stares daggers at you.

"AHHHHHHHH!"

"Keep your ankle still, *liebling*! *Nicht bewegen*!"

"AHHHHHHHH!"

Hmmmm…maybe you should have picked a different battle.

The End.

YOU STARE AT EACH OTHER FOR A MOMENT, BUT YOU CAN'T THINK OF anything to say. With a *hrumph* sound, Mom stomps off. Even her footsteps sound disgusted.

"Fuck."

"Yeah, you should definitely go apologize," Lindsi says, looking at you sideways. You try to glare at her face, not her boobs.

"Seriously? You're the one who—"

"Before she *really* gets angry."

Sighing, you hoist yourself out of bed and shuffle downstairs. At least the rest seems to have improved your kidney pain. Mom's in the kitchen, making disapproving noises to a pan on the stove.

"Umm, excuse me," you say to Mom's broad, chenille-sweatered back.

"Yes?" She doesn't turn, but you can imagine her shit-on-my-upper-lip look.

"I just wanted to apologize. For...for what you saw."

She sniffs.

"I didn't mean to disrespect your house rules—"

"But you did. Flagrantly."

You grit your teeth and keep going.

"It's just that Lindsi and I are still so new as a couple, I suppose our emotions got the better of us."

"You mean your animal lust."

"Yes, well, it takes two to tango."

Mom whips around, lasering you with her eyes.

"I'm sure it does. It only takes one to corrupt, however."

You exhale slowly. Don't punch an old woman.

"Anyway, I'm sorry. It won't happen again."

"I know it won't. I'll make sure of that."

You blink, unsure what else to say.

Fortunately, just then Lindsi walks in, smiling widely. Mom turns to her, also smiling. Seriously? Lindsi walks over to you and weaves a hand through your hair. "Hey, hon, do you want to go to the mall? I know you haven't had a chance to shop for presents yet."

Mom gives you a saccharine smile, but her eyes look like a reptile following prey. "That would be nice," she says, squinting at you. "I'm sure it's hard to be a houseguest and not have *any* small tokens with which to thank your generous hosts."

Turn to page 272.

MOM IS STARING AT YOU WITH SUCH UTTER CONTEMPT YOU BLURT IT out before thinking.

"I had nothing to do with this, I swear."

Now both Lindsi and Mom are staring you down, their faces nearly identical pictures of disgust. Shit, that's a peek into a grim future. There's nothing for it now but to plow ahead.

"I was in here sleeping, because of my injury, and when I woke up Lindsi was...like this." If eyes could laser off body parts, Lindsi's would do it to you now. You wonder what you'd lose first. Actually, you can probably guess.

You try to backtrack.

"I think both of us are still just so excited about this relationship, and where it's heading, that it's hard not to give in to some of the temptations of...uh, young...love."

You really wish you hadn't had to use that word. Though Lindsi's rage seems to have dialed down ever so slightly.

"Yes, well, she always was a disappointment to Reverend Mather," Mom snips.

"Oh my GOD, MOM," Lindsi twists around on top of you to stare daggers at her mother. The force of it causes her boobs— still free-flapping—to swing pendulously from side to side. "Why are you always such a fucking *prude?*"

"I didn't raise my daughter to be a sexually promiscuous—"

"It's not promiscuous to be with your BOYFRIEND, MOTHER." Lindsi is full-on screeching now. "It's always like this with you. You drove Steve away with your judgmental bullshit and you're doing it again. It's like you don't want me to find love."

"I just want you to act in a way that does the VanWhittington name—"

"You were a WAY bigger slut than I've ever been. Yeah, Uncle Warrington told me, *Mom*." Lindsi smirks triumphantly. "About your 'proving' of every dick in Wickachaw County." Proving? Is that like local slang for a beej? "Knocked off quite a few, huh, Mom? Too bad no one provides a haunch for someone who gives away her honey for—"

Mom strides across the room and slaps Lindsi across the face. Whoa. This is some daytime talk show shit.

"WE'RE LEAVING," Lindsi shrieks. "SEE IF WE COME BACK, YOU BITCH. I HATE YOU!" Mom narrows her eyes and strides out of the room, leaving only a red handprint behind.

Lindsi grabs her bra and jams an arm through a strap.

"You're ready, right?"

You'd really rather not go anywhere with her like this, but you're too terrified to disagree.

"Mmhmm," you whimper.

Turn to page 274.

You crawl out of the bathroom.

"Hospital," you whisper to the first feet you see. Judging from the timbre of the sniff overhead, they belong to Mom. Awesome.

Luckily, Lars can deadlift a full-grown man. He carries you to the car, and you head to the ER.

It takes approximately ten minutes in the waiting room to regret the decision. There's a person a row over clutching—and occasionally vomiting loudly into—a bucket. An impossibly old man has fallen asleep near the wall, a thin stream of drool trickling down his spotted chin and pooling on his dingy collar. Someone nearby—you're not certain who, but the blubbery guy in stained sweatpants seems likely—keeps farting. Unless he's shitting. You don't want to think about it too hard; it's making you nauseous.

After at least two hours hunched in your chair, your name is called. Without prompting, Lars cradle-carries you into the room, which should be embarrassing, but is actually an overwhelming relief.

The doctor asks some questions, draws blood, and shunts you off to get x-rayed. Another hour passes before a different doctor—who looks at least ten years younger than you—returns, frowning at a chart.

"When did the incident occur, mister…" She squints through styleless wire-framed glasses, then mispronounces your name. Come on, it's the twelfth most common surname in certain parts of the Midwest.

"Around ten?"

"That explains these levels." She starts talking in a slow sing-song, as though she's doctoring a kindergarten class. "You know when something hurts us, we need to go to the doctor right away!" She must think her smile is kind. You deeply hate her.

"It's been at least three hours since I got here."

"If you *had* come in right away, things would probably be fine," she says, ignoring you. "We would have recommended bed rest. But you seem to have done real damage. Of course we can't force you into procedures against your will—I want you to acknowledge that."

"Uh, yeah, I know."

"Good. Then you understand that I am *recommending*"—her eyes widen back to kindergarten teacher size—"very *strongly*, that you undergo emergency surgery to prevent renal necrosis."

"Necrosis?"

"Also, you should know rates for this surgery are 25 percent higher because of the holiday."

Turn to page 275.

You just have to grit your teeth and push through it.

Unfortunately, the VanWhittington family has dozens of Christmas Eve traditions. Like building gingerbread houses, complete with homemade gumdrops and "photorealistic" scenes in the poured-sugar windows.

Endless hours of hand-whipping frostings, bending over your piping bag, and forcing yourself to smile as you sample enough sugar to cause kidney death in a healthy horse, are really taking their toll. Even sitting upright pours waves of nauseating pain over your entire body. Except for that one bout of norovirus, you've never felt worse. And that wouldn't even compare if it hadn't hit in the hot tub with those friends of your boss's. Next time you go on a work retreat, you are *not* eating the shrimp.

You grab the bowl of blue sprinkles, bending to arrange them into individual snowflakes on the roof (Mom did *not* like it when you argued that was "hardly photorealistic").

You feel lightheaded. It's hard to distinguish the shapes of the snowflakes. Your whole body suddenly goes cold, and you can't feel your fingers or toes. The edges of your vision are going dark.

Oh god, you're going to faint.

As your head crashes to the table, you vaguely hear Mom yell, "I told you his bloodline was inferior."

You'd stick up for yourself, but it's too late. You're out cold.

Turn to page 276.

"LARS, CALL SECURITY," YOU SAY, HOBBLING AWAY FROM THE SANTA. "He's unstable."

"SECURITY!" Lars bellows. Seconds later, two men in uniform appear. Lars points. "He was threatening my friend."

That's not exactly true, but it sounds more impressive than "he might have revealed that you're a paranoiac pussy," so you let it slide.

They haul him away and you head home.

"What happened?" Mom's lips are pursed in preemptive disapproval.

"He's hurt pretty bad," Lars says. "But they said his constitution is remarkable. If he rests, he might avoid surgery."

Mom looks taken aback, then smiles and starts preparing a tray of snacks "for the strongman." Once she's finished, Lars carries you to bed, balancing the tray on his other hand. He leaves it on the bedside table.

"I'll have Lindsi check in once we get back from mass. And Jimmy can sleep in the basement tonight. This bedroom is just for you."

"Thank you." Lars might be your favorite person ever. As you drift off to sleep, you briefly wish you were with Lars, not Lindsi.

You think the funniest things when you're near sleep.

Turn to page 270.

This will end sooner if you own up. Plus, you're starting to feel guilty for being afraid of a guy who plays Santa for cancer kids.

"I'm sorry, I know I acted…strangely the other night. I just got nervous. I didn't know you, and you hear horrible stories with hitchhikers. I was rude, I admit, but I…well, I panicked."

Santa's look of outrage transforms into what you think is a smug sneer. It's hard to tell under the fake beard.

"I suppose I understand. Especially since you were at such a notorious cruising locale."

"Notorious…what?"

"You must have known. The signs were everywhere. If I were into that sort of thing I might have been nervous, too. Never know who might be a cop, right?"

"A cop? Is cruising illegal?"

He ignores you.

"Is that how you two met?" He turns to Lars with a sickly-sweet smile. "People have the strangest get-together stories these days."

"NO. No," you say. "This is my girlfriend's brother. He just brought me to the hospital."

"Instead of her? Interesting." Santa smirks and raises an eyebrow. "I should go. After all, these gifts won't make it to sick kids on their own. Especially since I arrived so *late*." He narrows his eyes accusingly and walks off, whistling "Holly Jolly Christmas."

You follow Lars to the car, too embarrassed to speak. Once the silence feels utterly oppressive, you blurt out, "It wasn't like that. He looked crazy. Actually insane. Did you notice how dead his eyes are? Like a turned-off robot? And I didn't know anything about cruising, obviously, I—"

Lars puts a meaty hand on your knee and gives you a knowing smile.

"Don't worry. You don't have to explain to *me* what happened at that rest stop. I wouldn't judge."

His hand inches up your thigh.

Wait, doesn't Lars have a wife?

Does this mean he thinks you're using Lindsi as a beard…and that he's okay with that?

If you want to make it clear to Lars that you're definitely straight, turn to page 278.
If you'd rather say nothing, since it seems to be getting you off the hook, turn to page 279.

"Lars, I just wanted to say…I'm sorry. I was acting like a jerk. I get so nervous around doctors, I think I overreacted."

He looks at you, his face transforming into a beaming smile. What a beautiful smile he has. You feel the light of it warming something deep inside you.

"That's okay, I understand." He stands, slapping you on the back. "Honestly, I even get your concerns. I've lived with Lindsi almost my whole life, you know?"

You laugh together. It feels so good to laugh with Lars again.

"And she probably slept with you on the first date, right?" Lars shakes his head. "Classic Lindsi. I mean, it's hard to want to commit to that, am I right?"

"Well…sure, yeah." How would he know that?

"She doesn't cheat, though. She's just up-front slutty."

"Oh. Cool." You're glad things are okay with Lars—you desperately wanted that—but this is getting a little uncomfortable. On several levels, actually.

"You know what we should do?" Lars says brightly.

"What?"

"Sneak in some guy time. To bond, you know?"

"Totally." It's so cool Lars wants to bond with you. You try not to smile too hard.

"Get away from the hens for awhile. They're so…well, men are just better, you know?"

"Absolutely."

"So, you in?"

"Yes. I can't wait."

• • •

You've been driving through the woods for so long now, you're not even certain you're still in the state. Finally, after miles of nothing but trees, you spot a tiny wooden shack.

"There it is," Lars says, smiling widely.

"There…what is?" Did you drive all this way for an outhouse?

"The sauna!"

"Ohhh." That makes more sense. Plus, he's not expecting you to do anything athletic, which is nice. You can tell just by looking at his muscled physique that Lars would beat you at any sport invented.

"Of course, there won't be any towels. Usually I keep some in the back of the car, but I didn't think I'd be able to get away today."

"That's all right."

"It's better! Nothing like being naked in the winter, am I right?" Lars hits you on the shoulder, like you're friends.

"Totally."

Turn to page 280.

WHATEVER YOU DID, IT'S TOO LATE NOW. DWELLING WILL ONLY MAKE it worse, right?

The two of you head out to the car, Lars's face getting darker with every step.

About a mile from the hospital he turns to you, frowning. Fuck, here it comes.

"I didn't want to see you naked. I just wanted to help."

You actually laugh in relief.

"What? What are you laughing at?"

You swallow. Lars is incredibly intimidating when he's yelling.

"I just…I thought you'd be mad about me saying it wasn't serious with Lindsi. Which, like I said, it's just new. It could become…" You trail off. Probably you shouldn't have reminded him why he should *actually* be angry.

"Oh. Well, yeah, that too," Lars mutters, frowning harder. "That's what I meant. I just thought you were being…weird."

You'd protest, but he's right. Part of you wanted Lars to want to see you. How is it that less than twenty-four hours with Lindsi's family has fucked with your head this much?

"Anyway, because of that, *all* that, I think you should do something. Something to prove you're serious about Lindsi." Lars looks at you fiercely, swerving the car. Luckily you haven't seen another car in miles. Which makes you wonder…shouldn't you be home by now?

"Umm, okay. I mean, no offense, Lars, but I'm not ready to go ring shopping."

"I didn't mean that. I meant the prov—" He stops mid-word, shaking his head. "In my family, all the men complete a sort of… ritual. A passage into manhood thing. We've been doing it since 1682, when we first settled here. Anyone who's serious about marrying a VanWhittington daughter does it, too. It's like a… test. To prove you're committed to this family. And that you can provide if things get tough."

The lack of buildings is suddenly starting to seem very unnerving.

"We call it the *proving*," Lars says, his face taking on a look of near-awe at the word. "And I want you to do it. To prove you're not just fucking around with Lindsi."

You might in fact be "just fucking around" with her. You're 74 percent certain of it. But alone in this car, miles from anything, with an angry blond giant, does *not* seem like the optimal time to mention that.

"Okay."

"Good. I have a crossbow and a Bowie knife in the trunk. The bow has a laser sight, which isn't regulation, but you didn't have time to prepare."

What the fuck?

"What am I supposed to do with those?"

"Kill a large animal, obviously." Lars rolls his eyes. "And skin it, and bring it back to civilization. You can call me, though, and I'll come pick you up when you're finished." His face softens. "I had three years of orienteering training before my proving; it's only fair you get a break."

"Kill a…with a…"

"Deer are easiest. They're slow. Used to backyards." Lars pulls over, staring at you until you feel you have no choice but to get out. He pops the trunk. You've barely gotten hold of the weapons when he whips the car around.

"GOOD LUCK," he yells out the window as he drives away.

You need to walk toward civilization as fast as humanly possible and make sure Lindsi knows Lars has gone off the deep end.

Though now that you think about it, Lindsi has mentioned her family's "hunting culture" more times than you'd expect in a four-month relationship. And she has a lot of curved, holstered knives for someone in PR.

You're pondering your next move when you see it, about twenty yards away, emerging from a sparse thicket.

It's a deer. A huge one, nibbling at the leaves. It clearly hasn't seen you. And you do have a laser sight…

What else can you do? Shoot it. Turn to page 282.
Uhh, anything else. Don't shoot it. Turn to page 283.

262

You go home, empty-handed and utterly ashamed.

You've barely finished opening presents the next morning when Lauren lays into you.

"You really are a piece of work, aren't you?"

"There was this sick-looking girl. I couldn't take back my gift with a clean conscience."

She shakes her head in utter disbelief.

"Let me get this straight. You were trying to *steal* from *Toys for Tots*?"

You roll your eyes.

"Yeah. That's it. You got me," you say sarcastically.

"Don't talk to me like that," she spits.

"Look, I donated the wrong present. I was swapping it out for the present I intended for Harrison, but this little girl and her mom got the wrong impression of what was going on."

Harrison walks into the living room. Your sister immediately turns off her bitchy face and beams at him.

"Why don't you go into the kitchen and help Daddy cook the *k*äsespätzle?"

"Okay." Harrison sprints down the hall, making weird ambulance noises to himself.

Lauren looks back at you, obviously unimpressed.

"I can't believe that you would use the illness of a child as an excuse for your own laziness and selfishness. Wait until Mom hears about this!"

You start to zone out, allowing her to berate you.

In truth, some part of you knows you deserve it.

The End.

YOU STAY THE COURSE AND MAKE THE SWAP. YOU'VE ALREADY endured the worst of it, after all.

That night, you lie awake in bed. The Super Soaker seems kind of paltry now. What kid would even want one in winter?

The next morning the boys rabidly tear through all their gifts.

"Those aren't even edited!" Lauren sputters as soon as she sees the Harry Potter novels.

Edited? Oh god. She's even worse than you thought.

The boys immediately forget the books, though—they have more presents. Dozens more. Each.

You can't help but imagine how overjoyed an underprivileged kid would be with those books right about now.

The toys start piling up in the corner.

"Give me that!" Harrison screams at his brother.

"No. It's mine," shoots back Otto, trying his best to defend his toy stockpile.

They're feral. Will they even read the books?

You feel worse than you did before.

Lauren hands you a cup of coffee and sits down beside you.

"Thanks a lot," she hisses. "Now I'm going to have to figure out how to print out substitute pages that look enough like the Harry Potter originals to fool the boys."

God, you hate this fucking holiday.

The End.

YOU REWRAP THE MIME COSTUME, SHITTILY, AND SCRIBBLE ON THE tag: *From Your Cool Uncle.*

• • •

Christmas morning.

Harrison is clearly disappointed in the mime costume, maybe because he's still too young to have been totally ruined by his parents. And Lauren's fuming, even more than usual.

"Your cologne is burning the inside of my nostrils," she snips, glaring at you accusingly.

You're not wearing cologne, but you don't want to argue. You should have known she'd punish you for lifting literally the worst present ever and claiming it as your own.

You hate your sister.

You hate this holiday.

This is exactly why you were supposed to be in a tropical country, basking in the sun, frolicking on a beach, drinking mojitos.

This was a huge mistake. You'll definitely never do it again.

"What a *perfekt* Christmas it's been," says Gregory. "We'll have to do it again next year at your place."

Both you and Lauren force smiles.

"Great," you say, gritting your teeth.

"Can't wait," Lauren mutters.

The End.

YOU TRY ANOTHER PRESENT.

Oh, come on, a helmet? That's even worse.

You're going to have to rewrap these ones anyway. You might as well find something that doesn't suck.

You spend the next thirty minutes tearing through gifts in search of that elusive unicorn.

"What are you doing?"

You jump. You didn't hear Harrison come into the room.

"Hey, buddy…"

"Why are you opening all the presents from Santa?" he asks.

"No, no, you have it all wrong. These aren't from Santa. They're from me and your parents."

Harrison bends down and looks at the tag.

"Look, it says, 'From Santa,'" he says, tapping the label. "This one's from Santa, too."

"Yes, well some of them are, but others…aren't…"

Harrison takes a step back. You can almost see the lightbulb going on over his head.

"I *knew* it! I *knew* Santa wasn't real."

"What? NO! Santa is real. Of course he's real!"

Harrison starts blubbering. "I knew it."

Your sister comes running in.

"You lied to me, Mom!" Harrison cries. "There's no such thing as Santa."

"What did you say to him? And why are all of these presents unwrapped?" Lauren looks absolutely livid.

"I can explain…"

"It's all lies," Harrison wails. "All lies…" He trudges up the stairs, sobbing loudly. As he gets to the top, he turns and faces your sister. "I should have known no one would pay you for old teeth! AND WHAT ABOUT EASTER?"

The End.

266

You have to do something. Didn't one of the guys at the bar mention a Santa serial killer? These two could totally be that. Just thinking of little Otto and Harrison being tied up, gagged, and forced to watch their parents' brutal murders is enough to make you leap off the roof with reckless abandon.

"YAAAAAAAA!"

You throw yourself straight at the intruders. Somehow, you land right on top of one—it's a Christmas miracle!

You feel your bones grinding against stabby shoulder blades. Your chin drives into the person's head, causing your teeth to clatter into each other. You may have bitten off part of your tongue—you can't tell, your brain is shaking too hard.

Both you and the intruder scream out in pain.

"FUUUUUUCKKKKKK!"

"OOOOOWWWWWWWW!"

You collapse. You can't feel your legs. Could you have broken your spine? Blood pours out of your nose and over the sidewalk. You stare straight ahead, unable to move your head.

Is that a cranberry nut loaf on the doormat? With a big Christmas tree-shaped note attached?

You black out from the pain.

Turn to page 285.

YOU TIPTOE ACROSS THE ROOF TOWARD THE LADDER. YOU DON'T remember the ice until you're just inches away.

Phew. Good thing you spotted that. You could have broken your neck on that.

You go down the ladder and sneak around the side of the house to the hedges near the front walkway.

What's going on? Are the burglars retreating? Have they even stolen anything yet? Maybe they're looking for another way to get in. Whatever—point is, you have to stop them.

You burst out of the bushes, fueled by pure adrenaline.

"AHHHHHHH!" you scream as you charge.

They jump back. One slips on a nearby patch of ice, falling to the ground hard.

"OWWWW, my HIP!" the fallen person cries.

Wow, that voice sounded really…old.

You squint, trying to make out faces in the dark. The one who fell is a woman who must be at least seventy-five. Her much-older husband is standing over her, shaking in terror.

You look back at the porch where they were standing. You see what looks like a homemade cranberry nut loaf sitting on the mat.

Fuuuuuuuck…

If you want to run off and hope they haven't gotten
a good look at you, turn to page 286.
If you want to offer assistance, turn to page 287.

BOTH LAUREN AND GREGORY COME TO PICK YOU UP.

"What have you done?!" she asks, her face contorting with anger.

"Go easy on him. You know, if this were Austria, where the incarceration system—"

"Not now, Gregory. Just get in the car and let's go home."

• • •

It's Christmas morning and the smell of frying bacon fills the air. Lauren can't be that mad about the late-night-jail thing if she's making bacon, can she?

You head downstairs and sidle up behind her.

"Finally, you've repaid the debt from that spring break in Tijuana," you say. "I'll cross it off your tab. We're now equal on jailhouse pickups."

Lauren smirks. "You're still not allowed to tell Gregory about that."

"Deal," you say, "but now you owe me one again."

She jabs you with the bacon fork. It hurts, but you let it slide. Who knew she was still capable of being cool? About anything?

"Can I open a present before we eat?" Harrison whines. "Pleeeeeeeeeease?"

"Okay," Lauren says. "One each."

Harrison runs for your gift and tears it open.

"Yes! Harry POTTER!!!"

Lauren gives you the stink-eye. Seriously? You just made her son's Christmas.

"Trust my degenerate brother to give him uncensored versions."

"Uncensored? What is there to—"

"What's a degenerate?" Harrison asks.

"Nothing," Lauren spits, stabbing the bacon furiously.

"Is that what it means when he calls late at night from the sheriff? That he's a degenerate?"

"Yes."

The End.

"How can I make you look like a hero?"

"Easy. Just jump in your car and follow me."

"Shouldn't I *not* drive?"

"Naw, you barely blew over," the officer says. "You're fine."

You set off down a dark and windy road. You're feeling uneasy; that sex act scenario still seems pretty likely.

The officer finally pulls over and steps out into the foggy night.

You're hesitant to follow, but you don't really see another choice.

"See that reindeer pen?" He points at an enclosure about twenty yards away.

Oh god, he's going to suggest something WAY worse than what you've been imagining.

"Get inside," he says.

"Listen, I know I said I'd help, but I support PETA and—"

"Wait three minutes, then call the police and say you're trapped. I'll be nearby so I'm sure to get the call," he says, stamping his feet for warmth. "I'll pull you out, be a Christmas hero, and the guys at the station will have to stop picking on me for accidentally arresting that dead guy."

"How do you arrest a dead guy?"

"Shut your mouth and get in the pen. Unless you want a DUI?"

You shake your head meekly.

The police officer nods once and heads off into the night.

If you want to get into the pen, turn to page 288.
If you want to just call as soon as he's out of sight
and then drive off, turn to page 290.

You wake up feeling a thousand times better. Better than you have in weeks! It's like the axe blow fixed your ongoing back pain. Huh!

You stumble downstairs. Mom, Dad, and Lindsi are at the kitchen table, sipping coffee and watching the local news.

"Here, sit." Mom pulls out a chair. "Let me get you some coffee. Are you okay? Lars said you needed rest."

"No, I'm okay." You try to sound mildly pained. "I'd rather tough it out. I'm not one for wasting away in bed."

Mom nods approvingly. Nailed it.

A blonde reporter standing in front of a hospital flashes onscreen. Wait, isn't that where you—

"Dozens of sick children are suffering a lonely Christmas after a local Santa was ejected from the hospital yesterday afternoon. Witnesses say this do-gooder was falsely accused."

Oh god, don't let it be…

They show a picture of your Santa.

"Terrible," Mom mutters.

"A patient alleged he was threatened, and the volunteer was promptly removed to the county jail. Unfortunately, this Good Samaritan didn't have enough money for bail, since he'd spent it all on gifts for sick children."

"That poor man," Lindsi whispers.

"The patient couldn't be reached for comment, but hospital workers agree the Santa must have been falsely accused."

God, let this be over. There has to be a cat dressed like a reindeer somewhere, right?

"But this story has a happy ending. After learning what had happened to this longtime volunteer, hospital workers took up a donation. Not only is this Santa getting the gift of freedom this Christmas, but he'll have thousands left over to make the season bright."

The man comes on, still wearing his Santa suit. You *weren't* wrong; that smile is too wide. Creepy. Skin-suit-makery.

"I'm just grateful people I care about know I never would

have done this. And grateful that I'll have even more money with which to brighten the days of the sick and the needy."

It's almost over. Soon you'll be able to breathe easy—

Lars walks in.

"Hey, isn't that the guy you had me call security on yesterday?"

Mom, Dad, and Lindsi turn to you, mouths dropping open in horror.

"Umm…maybe?"

The End.

"I'M *SO* SORRY ABOUT MY MOM," LINDSI SAYS FOR THE FIFTH TIME, swinging into a spot at the far end of the mall parking lot. You know you ought to be happy to get a little exercise over the holidays, but fuck that—why even *have* holidays if you're going to ruin them with walking?

"It's fine," you say. The more you think about it, the less you care what Lindsi's mom thinks. You'll only be here another couple days. If things work out with Lindsi, you might just insist on holidays with your folks...forever.

You head inside. The mall is absolutely glutted with people. You try to move as little as possible, deep breathing to calm yourself, while Lindsi flits around picking things out.

"Oooh! Lars loves this cologne. Bear Hunter. It's so manly." She heads over to a stack of sweaters. "And Dad loves plaids. Oooh!" She dashes to a display of gaudy costume jewelry. "You wouldn't believe it to look at her, but Mom *loves* glitzing it up."

"Okay." You grab the rhinestone-studded bracelet to look at the price.

Woof.

"That's really nice, but I hadn't planned on spending quite so—"

"Spending? No, don't worry about it, I've got these. Just put your name on them."

"Lindsi, there's no need to—"

"Please. I'm the one who asked you to come for Christmas— you should be on a beach somewhere! Besides, I feel bad that they're being such jerks. I want you to knock their socks off with the presents. It's on me."

"Well..." You suppose you should feel emasculated by your girlfriend picking up the tab, but you don't. Not even a little. It's awesome living in more gender-equal times.

Lindsi pays and you head out into the main section of the mall.

"OOOOH!!"

She's jumping up and down and pointing over the crowd.

Oh, shit. At the mall Santa Claus.

"Can we, sweetie?" She leans against your shoulder, looking up at you with big, pleading eyes. "I *love* Santas."

She *has* been acting nice, buying all these gifts for her family.

But it's a fucking mall Santa. On Christmas Eve. How much can she ask of you?

If you want to suck it up as a thank-you to Lindsi, turn to page 294.
If part of your totally progressive gender stance is not being able to stomach full-grown women sitting on "Santa's" lap, turn to page 296.

274

LINDSI WHIPS INTO THE MALL PARKING LOT, IGNORING THE HONKS OF cars she nearly collided with.

"Fucking pussies," she mutters under her breath.

"Yeah, learn how to drive, right?"

Lindsi sneers at you, shaking her head dismissively.

So much for solidarity.

You putter through the parking lot in stony silence. Every space is full—of course, it's Christmas Eve. The idea of heading into a mall any day of the year makes you cringe. The idea of dealing with it today, with Lindsi like this…woof. Just woof.

Were there signs before now that she was this volatile? Or should you give her a pass because it's family? Whatever—either way, it sucks to be around her. If you enter the mall together, one of you is leaving minus an eye, and you have a sneaking suspicion it'll be you.

What else can you do, though? How can you divert Lindsi's hatred away from you?

If you want to come on to her, so she'll feel less weird about earlier, turn to page 298.
If you want to offer to get a drink—or ten thousand— somewhere, turn to page 299.

Your eyes flutter open to fluorescent tube lighting and a stained drop ceiling. Where…

"There's our little patient awake!"

You turn your head slowly—it feels like someone has replaced the interior of your skull with wet sand—and see a fat nurse smiling aggressively as she checks some IVs.

"You did great. And don't worry, you didn't even say anything embarrassing!" She chuckles. It's more soothing than it should be.

"How long do I get to stay?" You're not sure what drugs you're on, but they make you feel warm and soft, like your body is made of down comforters.

"Oh, a coupla days." She plumps your pillow. "We'll take real good care of you. It's Christmas, after all. Oh, that reminds me—I have a little something for you."

She reaches into her pocket. Is it a present? What kind of presents do they give in hospitals, painkillers? That would put this in the running for best Christmas ever.

"Here you go. Ring if you need me, okay?"

She places a folded paper on the table attached to your hospital bed. Maybe it's a prescription *for* the pain pills?

No, it's a bill. An astronomically high bill. Three hundred and eighteen dollars for latex gloves? How many pairs did they use?

A note's attached. Cheery, loopy writing reads, *Your insurance might cover some of this—make sure to call them after New Year's! Merry Xmas, Doris.*

Aww, that was nice of Doris. It could be the morphine talking, but this isn't the worst Christmas you've had. Room service on call, no expectations from friends or family, limitless Jell-O. Depending on how your insurance shakes out, it might wind up being one of the best.

The End.

Your eyes flutter open. The fluorescent tube buzzing overhead is garishly bright, searing an oblong bar into your retinas. Where are you?

"You're awake."

Lindsi sounds pissed. Did you get too drunk and make out with someone? No, that doesn't make sense. The last thing you remember is making gingerbread. Then…

"What happened?"

"You passed out. It completely ruined the gingerbread houses. Which are basically *the* most important element of VanWhittington Christmas." She sighs exaggeratedly. You think she's rolling her eyes; it's hard to tell with the Geordi La Forge bar of sightlessness.

"So I'm…in the hospital?" That explains the IV. They must have you on some pretty serious meds for you not to have guessed this already.

"Yeah. They had to do emergency surgery on your kidney. Apparently it was 'beyond repair.' So now you're not only passing out at the drop of a hat, you're a one-kidney. Which is just…" Lindsi shakes her head, mouth pursed. You think you hear her mutter "inferior."

"Wait, I only have…they took my…" Holy shit, you must have hit it *hard*. What will happen now? Will your pee come out half as fast? Your vision blurs; the horrible possibilities are fucking with your blood pressure.

"Anyway, call when you're better, if that's not *weeks* from now." Lindsi stands.

"Wait, you're leaving?"

"Uh, yeah." She tilts her chin down, aggressively. "My family is upset enough over how much time I've already wast—spent here. They'd never forgive me if I let your…*weakness* completely wreck Christmas."

"But you'll come by later?"

She's already out the door.

A few seconds later you hear a tentative knock. Thank god;

for a minute you thought Lindsi had been serious with the you-*losing-a-fucking-kidney*-is-pissing-me-off act.

A man in a Santa suit peeks in, a stuffed velvet bag in hand.

"Ho, ho, ho, Merry—oh, it's *you*." He narrows his eyes. Shit, it's the guy from the gas station. He was coming to Little Hampshireton to volunteer at a *hospital*? You really thought he was looking for people to turn into furniture.

He stomps over and slams something on your bedside table.

"There. Exactly what you deserve."

It's a lump of coal.

A few minutes later you hear another knock. Maybe he's relented? He's supposed to be charitable, right?

"I heard you're awake." A fat nurse steps inside, cheeks rosy pink and soft-looking. At least she'll be nice. "I thought I'd drop this off so you can start studying up. Now that you're down to one kidney, you need to be more careful." She drops a stack of papers on your bedside table and waddles out, whistling.

It's a list titled "Things to avoid."

• Excessive drinking

That was expected. Still, disappointing.

• Beach volleyball

Huh. That's specific. Maybe sports in general are going to be off-limits from now on?

• Clams under 3 oz. in size
• Flavorful cheese
• Amateur improv troupes

You flip through the list.

There are twelve more single-spaced pages.

Well, at least you have a lot of alone time to start reading up on this…

The End.

"Oh, whoa, I think you have the wrong idea."

"Do I?" His eyebrows waggle mischievously.

"I wasn't there to cruise. That guy was just bitter because of the hitchhiking thing. Which doesn't seem very Christian. But yeah, I'm straight. Like, exclusively."

Lars pulls his hand back, frowning.

"So you panicked over a guy who was trying to give sick children Christmas presents?"

"You have to understand, it was dark, and I was tired…"

"He is literally the least threatening person I've ever seen."

"Sure, in a Santa suit, but he was wearing a very…brightly colored button-down, and…"

Lars wrinkles his nose in disgust.

"Point is, it was a misunderstanding. But don't worry, I won't tell anyone you're gay, I swear."

"Who the fuck said anything about me being gay? Last I checked you're the pussy that can't even swing an axe." You've never heard Lars swear before, or seen him look so…big. Which is saying a lot, since he's always absolutely massive.

Luckily, he seems to have said his piece. You ride the rest of the way home in stony silence.

The doctor ordered bed rest, so you don't have to go to mass with the family. You're nervous about what Lars is saying in your absence, but the longer you lie there, cozy under the comforter, the harder it is to care. What could he say without implicating himself?

You drift off to sleep, certain everything will look better on Christmas morning.

Turn to page 292.

You know what? Doesn't matter. Better to have Lars on your side; the rest of the family dislikes you enough without him saying you hate cancer kids or whatever.

Eventually, he pulls his hand away, but the entire evening, he's friendlier than normal. After you tell a lame joke about "elves with benefits," he laughs uproariously, slapping you on the back like you're a comic genius. Whenever you look up at dinner, you catch him staring at you intently, until he blushes and looks away. He even asks if you want to chop wood with him, which you can tell drives his brother-in-law Michael insane, like it's that exciting to swing an axe *again*.

The weirdest thing is…you like it.

It's like you have some special in-joke, an exciting secret no one else understands. There's something exhilarating about it. Something thrilling. Something…sexy.

It makes you wonder: *are* you gay? It hasn't occurred to you before, but they say sexuality is a sliding scale, right? What if you've been gay all along and just never encountered the right person? Or what if you're not *gay*-gay; you're just gay for Lars? That could be a thing, right? Maybe you were so closeted that it took someone as perceptive as Lars to see it. Which is weird, since you always thought your college roommate knew you pretty well.

Should you go after Lars?

Is *he* even gay?

You've never felt so confused in your life.

The next night at dinner, you're seated across from Lars. The candles in the center of the table throw soft light onto his chiseled features. Being with someone so manly would make *you* manlier. But he'd be tender, you can tell. He's probably got the most amazing abs under that flannel shirt.

You keep staring, fascinated by the prospect of Lars. You're unsure what you want from him, whether you want *anything* from him, or whether you're imagining the whole thing.

One thing you do know, though: you're going to have to stay with Lindsi until you can sort this out…or find a way to get closer to her brother.

The End.

280

You strip and head into the sauna.

Lars bends over you to stoke the coals, junk swinging remarkably near your face.

Apparently he's pretty at ease being naked. You resist the impulse to cover yourself with your hands. A guy who *had* played sports wouldn't care if another guy saw him naked, right? Plus, Lars must know his dick is way above average. If you had that dick you'd swing it too.

He sits on the pine bench, spreading his legs wide until his knee touches yours. The space is pretty small.

Is he looking at your...you must be imagining it. Or maybe he likes to size himself up, too. That's reassuring, the idea that a man as obviously gifted by nature as Lars has to compare himself. It makes you like him even more, something you hadn't thought possible.

"This is nice," you say.

"Very nice." You feel more of his thigh pressing against yours. Okay, you're definitely not imagining it. He's staring straight at your dick. Is he...smiling?

"Thanks for bringing me here." You try to sound casual, like you haven't noticed.

"It's something I like to do with people I...care about," Lars says, voice rougher.

He's moved so close you can feel your ass cheek touching his. In the steam, his body is glistening like some kind of oiled god's.

"Oooh, looks like someone's...excited."

Fuck, when did you get an erection? Why is it getting harder at the sound of his voice? Are you...

"Can I...touch it?" he asks.

"Yes. Please." Wow. That was unexpected. Have you been gay this entire time? Are you gay for Lars? What is happening to you? You feel Lars's strong grip and moan with pleasure.

"What about with my mouth?"

"Yeeeeess," you groan. Lars grins greedily and gets to his knees, his blond head disappearing in the steam of the sauna.

• • •

Lars walks up behind you at the breakfast table and pats your shoulder…then rubs his hand down your back—one swift, soft motion—to your tailbone.

Now that you've slept on it, you're certain you're not gay.

Actually, you were pretty sure the moment Lars came on your leg and you almost screamed out, "GROSS." You're usually not that testy right after cumming yourself.

Once everyone else has filed out, he draws his chair closer, near enough that you feel his breath when he whispers in your ear.

"I understand if you want to keep Lindsi around. It's easier— why do you think I'm married? Besides, it's a good excuse to keep coming back for visits." He flicks his tongue around the inside of your ear. It arouses you slightly. Dammit, you'd been so sure about this.

"Oh, uh, okay," you mumble, not quite managing to keep the fear out of your voice.

"I like it better that way," Lars pants. "Being each other's secret."

"Yeah, secret is good," you say. Your upper lip is sweating.

"Anyway, I'll make sure Jimmy sleeps downstairs tonight. Then I'll give you a special Christmas present."

In spite of yourself, you're intrigued. Maybe you were right the first time, in the sauna. In that you'd been wrong about yourself your entire life, that is.

"Oh?"

"I like to call it…*Turkish delight*."

You simultaneously shudder and shiver. You're 80 percent certain you'll lock the bedroom door. Well, maybe more like 60 percent…

The End.

HANDS SHAKING SLIGHTLY, YOU TRAIN THE SIGHT ON WHERE YOU assume the deer's heart must be. Would a head shot be better? Can arrows even pierce a skull?

Wait, what are you thinking, you can't kill a…

You sneeze powerfully. You've always been a cold-weather sneezer. You look up, expecting to find that the animal has been startled away.

Nope.

The deer has collapsed in the snow, bright red spurting up into the air over its head from a spot in its neck. You must have hit the jugular.

It bellows in pain. It's literally the worst sound you've ever heard. Its legs twitch. You have to at least put it out of its misery. You run over, reloading the crossbow with one hand as you whisper to yourself, "Mercy killing. Mercy killing."

As you near the animal, it thrashes in fear, spraying your face and body with a huge stream of blood. You try to aim for its head, but can't get a grip on the crossbow. Your hands are too slippery.

It bellows again.

Jesus Christ, you have to kill this fucking animal to end its fucking dying.

You toss the crossbow aside and grab the knife. Closing your eyes, you slice across its throat. It feels like cutting an especially gristly steak.

You open your eyes.

Now what?

You've already killed the thing; you might as well win Lars's stupid game. Weeping openly, you scoot around in the bloody snow. With another swift slice of the knife, you open the deer's abdomen.

Viscera spills out in front of you, steaming in the snow.

You immediately vomit all over it.

This is too fucking much, man, you just have to get
out of here. Turn to page 301.
No, fuck that. You're in way too deep to give up now.
FINISH IT. Turn to page 303.

YOU RAISE THE CROSSBOW, STARING AT THE DEER. IT'S SO BEAUTIFUL. So majestic. So...alive.

No, no way. You absolutely cannot shoot this stunning creature. If that means Lindsi's family never accepts you, fuck 'em. That shit's barbaric.

You head to the road, walking back in the direction you came from. After about forty-five minutes, a car pulls up. Normally, you wouldn't hitchhike—only crazies are willing to offer a stranger a ride—but you're in the middle of nowhere and your phone is dead from searching for a signal. There's no other option. Besides slowly freezing to death, that is.

The driver drops you at a gas station.

"Can I use your phone?" you ask the teenaged boy behind the counter.

"Yeah, sure, whatever you want," he says, leaning away dramatically. "Here." He pushes it across the counter and ducks behind a display of cigarettes. Only when you go to reach for it do you realize you're still holding a crossbow in one hand and a Bowie knife in the other. Right.

You dial Lindsi's cell, ridiculously proud of yourself for having memorized it.

"Hello?"

"Hey, Lindsi? It's me. I'm at a gas station."

"So you have the deer? Already? That was so fast." She sounds excited.

"No, I don't. I saw one, but...I mean, I couldn't do it, you know?"

"You couldn't do it." Her voice sounds flat.

"Yeah, it looked so beautiful, outlined against the snow. I couldn't imagine killing it." The clerk is peeking out at you, but squeaks and ducks away when you make eye contact.

"Oh."

"Is something wrong?" Maybe Lars is right next to her, all menacing and tall. It must be hard for Lindsi, with such a strange, aggressively gender-essentialist family. It actually explains a lot.

Gives you a lot more perspective on her. And on Lars.

"Honestly?"

"Yes, please be honest. You can always be honest with me." Maybe you should offer to set her up with a counselor. Think what that kind of upbringing must do to somebody.

"I hadn't planned to ask you to do a proving for at least another year, and I think Lars should have set expectations better, with more advance warning."

That sounds very…carefully worded.

"But knowing that you wouldn't even try is just…"

Appealing? Sexy?

"…disappointing."

"WHAT?"

"Frankly, it's hard to be attracted to someone who has *proven* he's at best a beta male. Maybe even, like, a zeta."

"Seriously? You would find me more attractive if I crossbowed a—"

"I don't think we should see each other anymore. In this family only people who can hunt get to eat."

"Lindsi, can we at least talk about—"

"I'll leave your car at the rest stop outside of town with the keys in the ignition." She sniffs derisively. "Hopefully you get there before someone more…*aggressive* finds it."

Click.

The End.

YOU WAKE UP IN A HOSPITAL BED ATTACHED TO ALL SORTS OF TUBES and wires.

There's a cast on your wrist, and another on your ankle, but otherwise you seem to have gotten off pretty lightly. Nothing else seems broken. Still, you can't seem to move your other hand....

...fuck, because it's handcuffed to the hospital bed!

You look around frantically. The motion makes your entire middle shriek with pain. Jesus, you really need to start seeing a chiropractor. Or at least a masseuse.

Gingerly, you turn your head to the side. There's another person in the room. Poor thing, she's got casts on almost every part of her. She must be in pretty rough—

Wait, that's Mrs. Cranberry Nut Loaf!

Jesus, is she gonna die because of you? Did you murder an old lady on Christmas?

Your sister walks in carrying a massive bouquet. She glances at you, lip curling in disgust, then leaves the flowers on Mrs. CNL's bedside table and kisses her lightly on the forehead.

She turns and walks out of the room, refusing to even look at you.

The End.

286

YOU JUMP OVER THE BUSHES AND RUN OFF INTO THE NIGHT.

It's cold outside, but you're too scared to go anywhere close to the house, in case that lovely old couple spots you.

Man, it sure would've been nice if you'd had the sense to put on a coat. You need shelter soon or else you could be in serious trouble.

You see a shed in a neighbor's back yard. You walk up to it. Luckily, it's unlocked.

You crawl inside.

You're still desperately cold, but at least the wind isn't ripping through your bones anymore. Before you even have a minute to consider the absurdity of your situation, you fall asleep.

Turn to page 305.

YOU RUSH TOWARD THE OLD WOMAN.

"Ma'am, please, let me help."

She looks absolutely terrified. You turn to her husband, hoping to explain yourself.

"I'm so sorry, I thought you two were——"

"ATTACKER!" she screams at the top of her lungs. "ATTACKER!"

She sprays an entire can of Mace straight at your eyes.

The lights inside the house go on.

The last thing you see before you totally lose your vision is Lauren, cupping her hands against the window, staring.

• • •

It's Christmas morning. Lauren's still on the phone with the elderly neighbors. It's been at least an hour now.

"No, of course he won't bring charges; you had every right to protect yourself."

Your eyes are still a mask of puffy red pain, and you can't breathe through your nose.

You take a cautious nibble of the cranberry nut bread Lauren grudgingly set in front of you earlier.

Are you gonna—yup, you're vomiting. Again.

"BLAHHHHHHHHHHHHHH!"

It splatters all over the island.

You still can't see, but your nephews' horrified shrieking and your sister's yell of rage tell you you'll be mopping it up yourself.

The End.

9-1-1.

You hit send, then hoist yourself onto the fence.

"Help me!" you scream into your phone. "I'm trapped in a reindeer pen!"

You hang up and look down.

It's a decent drop, and from what you can tell, there are no real places to grip on the inside. Good thing the cop's already on the way; you don't know how you'd get out otherwise.

You jump down, falling forward gracelessly into the muck of the pen. You stand and try to slap away the mud that's caked on your pants.

Your phone starts to make a whistling sound, which means someone's texting you. One of the reindeers perks up and starts toward you.

The phone whistles again. Clearly whoever it is has a whole story to tell.

The reindeer is closer now, circling you and sniffing at your clothes. Suddenly it rears onto its hind legs, exposing a massive, erect penis.

Oh, shit.

The reindeer jerks toward you, like a circus dog doing a terrifying, hoofed trick. It's clearly trying to mount you. You jump to one side, tumbling to the ground and just barely avoiding a hoof as the massive animal settles back to earth.

While the reindeer is regrouping, you grab a rock from the muck at your feet.

The reindeer comes closer. You try to back away, but the fence is hemming you in. You're trapped between the wall and a ragingly horny reindeer.

It rears up again.

You see a bright flash of light in the distance.

"We're here live on the scene," someone says.

"Stay back, ma'am, this could be dangerous." It's the cop's voice. Apparently he decided to go full *COPS* on this "rescue." How'd he get a news team here so—

No time to think, the deer is coming.

It leans into you, hooves smashed up against the wall, dick long enough to bang your leg. Frantic, you swing out with the rock, hoping to disorient it enough to be able to run to safety.

You connect with its head. No, scratch that, you've hit the reindeer squarely in the eye.

The eyeball explodes. Blood and gore bursts out everywhere.

"What the fuck are you doing?" screams the cop.

The reindeer falls to the ground, spasming.

A reporter leans over the pen with a camera. Behind her, you see the cop staring at you like you've just fucked his sister. In front of him. Clearly this is not the heroic moment he was hoping for. You stare into the camera, looking crazed and bloody.

"Merry Christmas?"

The End.

You wake up Christmas morning.

It's lucky you were able to sneak into bed last night without waking anyone. And get away from the reindeer pen without the cop catching you again. You're totally winning Christmas.

You head downstairs. Lauren's making breakfast. You flip on the local news.

"And now for a 'News of the Weird' story with a Christmas twist!" the anchor says cheerily. "This call came in last night, and the police station let us in on the action. But what happened next no one could predict!"

It cuts to the cop huddling outside the reindeer pen. He's whispering to the camera.

"This is a very dangerous situation. It seems our victim may have already been attacked; he won't respond to my voice."

Wow, looks like he really went full *COPS* on this one.

He tiptoes over to the pen, hoisting himself over the slats and smiling for the camera.

"Stay back. Don't want you to get into trou— AHHHHHHHH!!!"

A reindeer has jumped onto the cop's back. It's thrashing wildly.

"Help me! Help! It's trying to rape me!" he screams.

The reindeer starts humping harder.

The scene cuts back to the television studio. Both news anchors are doubled over laughing.

"Don't worry, the officer was uninjured. And the deer, as we can all see, had a great time."

You hear a loud knock on the front door.

"I'll get it."

You open the door. It's multiple cops.

"We're here about an outstanding DUI charge, as well as charges of assaulting an officer and fleeing the scene of a crime."

You gulp. How can you get out of *this*?

"Are you sure that was me? I hear there's a dead guy running around who looks *just* like me. Fooling officers all over town, apparently."

The officers laugh appreciatively. Could this work?
"Good one. But we're definitely still arresting you."

The End.

THE NEXT MORNING EVERYTHING IS GOING SMOOTHLY. MOM IS cordial, not even wincing when she offers coffee. Jimmy and the younger kids are opening presents excitedly. It's Norman Rockwell around here.

Except when you look at Lindsi. She's been glaring since the moment you woke up.

Fuck Lars. Why would he tell her that?

"Lindsi," you pull her aside as everyone troops in for breakfast. "I want to apologize. I can guess what Lars told you."

"Yeah?"

"Yes, and while I'm sure it was hard for you to hear, you have to know there's no truth to it."

"You're calling my brother a liar."

"No, not a liar, just…I think he's confused."

"I don't. He's met all my other boyfriends and he's never said something like this."

"Well, he probably never came on to them."

"Came…what?" Lindsi's frown deepens.

"I'm sure he's embarrassed, so he probably went a little overboard, but I promise, I had no idea that gas station——"

"Back up. You said…"

"Came on to me. Right. I think he's probably embarrassed about his sexuality. He's obviously not out."

"What are you talking about?" Lindsi looks confused. And pissed.

"Lars? I assume he told you I was cruising, but…"

"He didn't say that."

"What did he say?"

"That you're kind of an asshole."

"Oh." That was unexpected.

"Jesus, what are you, homophobic or something? You see everyone as gay and that bothers you, or——"

"No, Lindsi, I swear, in the car, Lars——"

"I don't want to hear it. Lars is *married*."

"But Lindsi——"

"You should go, before I make a scene. I couldn't be with someone so...backwards."

"Please, Lindsi, it's a misunder—"

"Also, *everyone* knows that gas station is a cruising spot."

The End.

"MOOOOOOOOMMM! IT'S! TOO! HOOOOOOOOOT!"

The child in front of you throws his hot cocoa—*hot*'s right there in the name, idiot—at the ground, spattering the legs of everyone in a six-foot radius.

Just ten more people between you and Santa. You will endure. You have to; the line behind you is too thick with snot-nosed children and obviously livid parents to brave.

Finally, after what feels like hours, you reach the front.

Lindsi walks up and plops herself on Santa's lap, crossing her legs exaggeratedly. You look away. It's fine; it's just a show. If she had a Santa fetish you'd know by now.

"Santa, there's some things I *want*," she purrs.

"Yeah? Have you been nice?"

"I've been *naughty*."

"I should've known. Va-va-va-VanWhittington always was a bad girl."

Lindsi frowns, then tugs the beard. "Oh my god, *STEVE?*"

He laughs, pulling her closer on his lap. You bite your lower lip.

Lindsi turns to you. "You won't believe this. It's my ex-boyfriend, Steve."

"From…high school?" You try to force an isn't-that-nice smile. It feels like lockjaw.

"Yeah, and college some. Really, off and on for ages."

You see his hand creeping around Lindsi's hip, stroking down her thigh.

"Steve, stop it!" She slaps him playfully. "This is my *boyfriend*."

"Hey, bro," the Santa says, putting his hand back.

Lindsi's cheeks look extra pink, her eyes too sparkly.

"Steve was big man on campus. Senior football star, homecoming king. And I was this little mousy freshman—"

"You were a *hot* freshman with friggin' amazing tits."

"Steeeeeve. Anyway, it was like, love at first sight." She turns to look in his eyes. How can she be so googly about a guy in a fake beard?

You grit your teeth.

"And now he's a mall Santa. What a small world. You ready to go, Linds?"

"Aww, don't go." Steve grabs her around the waist. "I have to find out what presents to get Va-va."

If you just want to let it happen—it will end sooner that way—turn to page 308.

If you want to body-slam the mall Santa, turn to page 310.

"I KNOW IT'S FUN AND EVERYTHING, BUT CAN WE…NOT?" YOU SMILE ruefully. Lindsi pulls away, frowning.

"But it's my favorite thing at Christmas." Her voice is a perfect toddler pout. It doesn't do anything to change your thoughts on the creepiness of grown women sitting on the laps of grown men, pretending to be children, begging for gifts.

"I know, it's fun, but that line's so long, and your mom's already mad at me; I don't want to ruin…church, too." Do they do church? You hope so; it will get you out of this. Though you also hope not—church is the worst.

Lindsi sighs heavily.

"You're right. Maybe next year."

"Thanks, sweetie. It's so nice of you to look out for me with your family." Lindsi smiles. Literally any compliment seems to work on her.

"I have one more thing to get." She turns to you, eyebrow raised. "But *you* can't be there." She sticks a finger in your chest playfully.

"Ooooooh, do I get a hint?" You hate yourself right now. But it's working.

"Not unless you want to be on my *naughty* list."

Ugh. That's sorta the same problem you have with the mall Santa thing, but worse, because it's actually making you kinda horny.

"Okay, I'll make myself scarce."

"Meet at the Macy's entrance in twenty minutes?"

"Sure."

Lindsi disappears into the mall crowds.

Now what?

You look around. You now have presents for Lindsi's family, but nothing for Lindsi herself; you guys planned to exchange gifts once you got back from vacation. Hers is sitting in your apartment: a rather lovely Scrabble set, if you do say so yourself. It wasn't cheap, but she'll love it. You can just imagine all those nights together, the two of you, wine, something on Netflix, and Scrabble. Perfection.

Of course, it couldn't hurt to butter Mom up a little more. Maybe with a belated hostess gift? Keeping Lindsi happy is great and all, but if you want to make it through the next few days, she's not the woman you *really* need to please.

If you want to pick up another gift for Lindsi, turn to page 311.
If you want to look for a hostess gift, turn to page 312.

You put a hand on Lindsi's thigh, deliberately lowering your voice a few notches.

"Listen, I know we got interrupted at your house"—you choose not to mention that you then threw her under the bus with her own mother—"but seeing you get so...passionate just made me want you more."

"Yeah?" Lindsi turns to you, eyes alight. That transition was terrifyingly rapid.

"I thought we could finish what you started. But somewhere different, you know?"

"Yes. Maybe one of the beds in the Macy's housewares department. Once in high school, my boyfriend and I—"

"Or somewhere less busy? I want us to be able to be..." What will appeal to your apparently nymphomaniacal girlfriend without getting you arrested? "...loud. As loud as we want."

"YES." Lindsi's practically drooling now. She grips your thigh so tightly you wince. "I know the perfect place."

"Is it far away from everyone? I don't want to get interrupted again." You try to keep the nerves out of your voice.

"No one will be there, I'm sure of it. It will be so hot. GOD, I'm going to ride you *so fucking hard*."

Lindsi whips out of the parking lot, obviously on a mission. You're nervous, but at least she's not pissed anymore. Plus, even if the sex is uncomfortable, there's something kind of hot about fucking in the back seat of a car, or in the woods. And when it's as cold as this, she can't blame you for finishing really fast.

Turn to page 306.

"WOW, THIS LOOKS LIKE A SHITSHOW," YOU SAY. LINDSI GROWLS threateningly. "Why don't we get a drink instead? To relax."

"That's a good idea," she says slowly.

"I'll buy," you say, eager to keep her in this slightly better mood. "It's the least I can do."

"That works. Or…" She turns to you, eyes bright. "One of my high school friends is having a house party this afternoon. An ugly sweaters thing—isn't that funny?" You nod like the idea is original. "I'd been planning to skip it once you said you'd be here, but if you don't mind…"

"Not at all!" Ugh, a house party full of strangers? Is there anything worse? "That sounds fun!"

But you can't back out now, especially since Lindsi is clearly into the idea.

"Great, I'll just run into the house and grab some sweaters— Mom has, like, a thousand ugly things—and we can wear those!"

"GREAT!" you squeak. At least it makes it harder to hear your dread.

• • •

"LINDSIIIIIII!"

The minute you walk through the door people start yelling. Man, Lindsi must have been popular in high school. A pudgy bottle blonde comes over with two shots, reluctantly offering one to you. You put a hand up—it looks like cream booze, possibly the worst thing you can imagine—and she eagerly turns to Lindsi.

"Three…two…one…DRANK."

Lindsi and the girl take the shot. Already someone's appeared with more. You refuse again—electric blue is like an alcohol warning sign—and she, Lindsi, and Blondie take another.

Within minutes Lindsi is housed. In fact, everyone around you is wasted, except you, of course.

That makes it *so* much easier to be at a party full of strangers.

Blondie turns and leans against you, snorting wetly.

"How Lindsi fie you ennyway," she slurs. "You're too HOT for her." She giggles.

"We met at a friend's wedding."

"Dih she tell you 'bout me?"

"I don't think I caught your name, actually…"

"She'z juz jealous. She'z all-ees been jealous uh me."

"Oh my gah, Vicki, ged off my boyfrien." Lindsi is stumbling over, lip curled in exaggerated disgust. "Yer such a *slut*."

"Fug you, Linzi." The girl pushes up off you. "Juz cuz Steve all-ees liked me better duzzin mean…"

"He NEVER LIKED YOU." Lindsi is looming over the girl like some drunk demon. Somehow she's even more terrifying than when she was yelling at her mom.

"Thazz not what he sed affer we *fugged*."

Oh shit, you'd better break this up NOW. Turn to page 313.
You know what? They'll work it out on their own. Turn to page 315.

DEAR GOD, WHAT HAVE YOU DONE? WHAT HAVE YOU BECOME? HAVE YOU LOST ALL YOUR HUMANITY?

No. Not yet. You leave the carcass in the snow. Maybe some other animal will eat because of your deed today. That's good, right? Helping the circle of life?

You'd vomit again, but you're too dead inside to bother.

You stumble to the road, hands and soul numbed. After a half hour of plodding along in the direction of town, you see a car. You flag it down. The middle-aged, permed woman driving gives you one look, smiles blandly, and starts chatting about the weather.

You're literally covered in gore, with a Bowie knife blood-glued to your right hand and a crossbow death-gripped in your left.

You're starting to believe this town might *actually* be hell.

Maybe it's your dead-eyed silence, or maybe it's the heavy, used weaponry, but the woman drives you all the way to the VanWhittington house.

The entire family is sitting at the kitchen table when you walk inside, talking in low, urgent voices. Lindsi sees you first.

"Oh! You're here and—" She glances at you, squeals delightedly, and throws her arms around your neck. Her hand sticks to something on your ear. "You did it! Oh, baby, I'm so proud of you. I knew you had it in you, but this is even more than I expected."

You stare at her, eyes narrowing slightly. Who is this strange person?

"Is the carcass outside, or…"

"There is no carcass. The animals have the carcass."

"Oh. Well, that's okay, though. Even without the body, I think we can all agree." She turns to her dad, widening her eyes meaningfully. He nods once and she grins. "You've succeeded. You can join the family. Mom, bring him the cup."

"Of course!" Mom is beaming. She pours what you recognize as an *extremely* expensive scotch into a golden…there's no other word for it than *chalice*, and walks toward you.

You feel bile rising in your throat again.

You turn to Lindsi.

"You're a disgusting person."

She frowns.

You look at the rest of them, your voice rising. "All of you are disgusting people. You should be ashamed." You look at Lindsi again. "I hope you're fucking barren. I pray to all the fucking gods in heaven and the hell world you actually live in that you never, ever reproduce any more of your sick, twisted kind."

Everyone stares at you, stunned. You walk to the bedroom, snow melting pinkly around every footstep, grab your bag, and leave, driving away without looking back.

You make it to the city in some kind of fugue state. You must have stopped and washed off the blood somewhere, but you don't remember it. You don't remember anything.

At least, not until your exhaustion overwhelms you and you fall asleep.

Rivers of blood, steaming, stinking guts spilling through your hands, the dying cry of a—

"AAAHHHHHHHHH!!!!!!! AAAAAAAAAAAAAAHHH-HHHHHHHHHHHHHH!!!"

The sound of your own shrieking wakes you.

Every time you try to sleep it starts again. Eventually, you just decide to stay awake.

You spend the entire Christmas vacation drinking so much caffeine that you're regularly vomiting pure acid—you're that terrified of sleeping.

But you'll get over it eventually, right? You'll have to.

Right?

The End.

IT'S TOO LATE TO TURN BACK NOW. THE ONLY WAY OUT OF THIS IS TO finish the deed; after all, you're alone in the middle of nowhere, and killing this deer is the prerequisite to ending that.

Plus, you already did the horrible part; you might as well get the credit.

You don't actually know how to skin a deer, and even holding the knife close to the animal again makes you gag heavily.

There's no option but to haul the entire thing back with you and hope they give you a bye. After all, you did brutally slaughter the thing.

At first you try dragging the deer by the legs, but watching the head lolling over to the side makes you want to cry, so you flip it upright-ish, the rest of the insides spilling out into the snow, and haul it up on your shoulders.

At least you managed that one belly slice. You probably cut out at least thirty pounds of weight!

You stumble back to the road, leaving a dripping trail of blood and gore behind you. You can feel the warm, wet blood soaking through your coat, dripping down your back, pooling in the waistband of your pants. This must be what war feels like.

After about a mile your phone picks up a weak signal.

You dial the number Lars typed in before he left.

"Lars? Lars, it's me. I did it."

"Really? Already?" He sounds skeptical.

"Yeah. I mean, I didn't skin it. I don't know how to skin a deer."

"But you killed it?"

"I shot it in the throat."

"Did you gut it?"

"Uhh...I think so? That's the intestines and stuff, right?"

"Yes."

"Okay, then yes." The last of that shit fell out about a mile back.

"Wow." Is that a note of awe you hear in Lars's voice? "You're a natural. I'm not sure we've ever had someone finish a proving so fast."

"Really?" In spite of yourself you feel a little glow of pride somewhere beneath your ribs. Though that could just be a side stitch from hauling an entire deer on your back.

"Nowhere close. I was out for two days during mine. Nine-year-olds take a while to figure things out. Even Dad took six hours. Although he *did* bag a lynx."

"Whoa."

"I'm impressed, man. I wasn't sure you had it in you, and you nailed it in under an hour." Lars laughs merrily.

You join in. Now that you think of it, that was a pretty impressive thing you just managed. You feel closer to Lars than ever before. In fact, you've never felt this close to anyone.

Turn to page 317.

YOU WAKE UP TO A HULKING, HATCHET-WIELDING SHADOW STANDING over you.

"WHAT ARE YOU DOING IN MY SHED?"

Sweet Jesus, it's a murder-lumberjack.

"Soooo cold," you manage to squeak out.

"What?"

"The elements. Had to…escape…the elements."

"Get out of my shed. NOW," he bellows.

You stumble back toward your sister's house, covered in spiderwebs and dust from the shed.

Harrison opens the door and instantly starts screaming. You didn't realize you looked *that* rough.

"Look who it is," Lauren says. "The idiot brother who gave my kid a Super Soaker. After I specifically told him about our no guns, no plastic policy."

You stumble inside, too weak and cold to argue.

You try to untie your shoes but your fingers won't cooperate. In fact, your hands look completely blue.

You definitely have frostbite.

On your entire hand.

If you lose it, will you get a prosthetic? Or a hook?

The End.

LINDSI THROWS THE CAR INTO PARK.

"We're here!" She grins wickedly and leans over the console to lick your ear.

"We're…in the parking lot of a church."

"Exactly."

"Where did you think—"

"The crèche, obviously."

You look through the window to where she's pointing. Right. You'd missed that nativity scene because you were *so fucking confused about your girlfriend wanting to fuck in a church parking lot.*

"Do you really think that's a good idea? It's kinda…"

Lindsi's eyebrows lower dangerously and her lips pinch so hard they go white.

"What? Are you trying to shame me for my healthy sex drive? I *hate* that."

"No, no." You shake your head rapidly. "This is great. It's, uh, kinky. In a good way."

"Good." Lindsi leans back, smiling brightly. "Then let's get going. Evening services are only a couple hours from now."

Unsure what else to do, you follow her inside the nativity, carefully picking your way around the life-sized mannequins dressed in actual clothes. All their eyes are dead. It feels like they're staring at you.

Still, the sun has gone down, so that's on your side. And it's kind of hard to see anything behind the crib. This could work, right?

• • •

"Why won't it *work?*" Lindsi exhales in frustration, then starts sawing away at your dick even faster. It stays stubbornly limp under the gazes of Jesus and Friends.

"I'm sorry. Maybe I could just do you, and then—"

"NO." Lindsi glares. "Both of us or nothing."

"Okay," you squeak.

Several minutes later, you manage to get just hard enough to stuff yourself into Lindsi.

Then you hear something. Something other than Lindsi.

"Lindsi, shhh."

"OOOoOOOOOoOOOOOHHHH." She's moaning louder than she ever has before. And you *know* this isn't the best you've ever been. You're about half a centimeter from utter, limp defeat.

There it is again. Voices. High-pitched voices.

"Lindsi, wait. I think someone's—"

"UH! UH! UH!" She's making little yips now. "HARDER! HARDER!"

Her head is thrown back, so she doesn't see when they start appearing around the corner, first just a couple of people, then a dozen more.

Everyone's in robes, the youngest boy maybe fourteen, the oldest man way past eighty. It's clearly some sort of choir, though they're not singing. They're staring, horrified.

Well, except for the fourteen-year-old. He looks pretty into it.

A priest comes up from behind.

"Ah. Lindsi VanWhittington," he says coldly.

Your dick falls out, completely dead.

Everyone stares at you, even Lindsi. Do they expect a speech?

"We just, uh, felt that the virgin birth was so...miraculous," you begin. Someone starts chuckling in the crowd. "Anyway, what kind of Christian would watch? That's a sin too, you know." You try to look defiant, but the priest's stare withers your resolve. And, somehow, even more of your dick.

"I'd still watch," the ancient man says, grinning widely to reveal mostly toothless gums. "Unless that makes things too...*hard* for you?"

The entire choir bursts into malicious laughter. God, you hope the family hadn't planned on going to services...

The End.

You turn away, tapping your foot in frustration. This has to end soon, right? There's a huge line of kids.

Steve whispers something in Lindsi's ear and she giggles, slapping his cheek playfully. Thank god you don't know anyone in this town. It would be too embarrassing if…

Fuck, is that Lindsi's brother Lars?

It has to be—perfectly formed blond giants can't be that common, especially in the middle-of-nowhere town Lindsi grew up in.

Maybe he won't look over? Or if he does, he might not recognize you. It's pretty chaotic around the Santa.

Lars's massive head turns slowly on his thick, muscular neck.

He stares right at you, waves, and walks over. It's not until he's just feet away that he registers Lindsi on Steve's lap.

"C'mon, Linds, really?" Lars raises an eyebrow. "Let the kids have their fun."

"Oka-ay." Lindsi sticks her lip out in an exaggerated pout. "See you, Stevie."

"See you Va-va," he growls. His hand lingers as she stands, caressing her thigh and ass. Lars grimaces and turns to you.

"None of my business, but…man up."

The worst part is he just sounds sad. Like you're a puppy with cancer. A helpless, testicleless, inevitable failure.

Lars walks off, leaving you alone with Lindsi…and your boiling rage.

By the time you've made it to the car you can't hold it in anymore.

You snort loudly.

"Bless you," Lindsi says.

"Aren't you even the *slightest* bit embarrassed?"

She turns, obviously confused.

"About what?"

"About that little…display back there. You made an absolute idiot of yourself. It's bad enough you were acting like a Playboy Bunny, but letting him grope you in front of me? Do you respect me in the *slightest?*"

"Letting him…" Lindsi frowns. "Steve?"

"Yes, *Steve.*"

"He wasn't groping me." Lindsi's face is dripping scorn. "He has a *prosthetic hand.*"

"A prosthetic…?"

"He lost his hand in the war. 'Cause he was a soldier? But you're right, I should have definitely made a big deal about him not being fully aware of where his *fake hand* was sitting."

"Oh." You still feel pissed, but simultaneously ashamed. "Well, you were still being too flirty."

"Wow. Now who's an embarrassment?"

You ride home in impenetrably icy silence.

If you want to apologize, turn to page 325.
No, fuck that, she was being ridiculous. Let her stew. Turn to page 327.

JESUS, DO THEY EVEN CARE THAT YOU'RE HERE? DOES HE SERIOUSLY think it's okay to grope your girlfriend while you're three feet away?

"Hey," you say, voice tight. He looks up, eyebrow raised, lip curled in a sneer.

"You need something?" His hand drifts higher up Lindsi's leg.

You feel hot and red, like all your blood vessels have burst simultaneously. Letting out an inarticulate grunt, you rush forward, pulling Lindsi off the Santa's lap roughly.

"What the fuck?" she squeals.

But you can't really hear her, you have to focus on—

CRACK.

Your hand explodes in pain as you connect—hard—with his stupid fucking stubbly jaw. He falls over sideways, gripping his face as he hits the floor.

"SIR!" A fat mall security man with a buzz cut and a moustache wheezes over. "You need to calm down and come with me, or I'm going to have to use this." He holds up a can of Mace. You almost laugh—rent-a-cop bullshit weapons—but stop yourself. Mace sucks, after all.

Too stunned by what you've done to resist, you follow him to the mall security office where he calls the actual police. They arrive fifteen minutes later to take you to the county jail.

"I'll follow in the car," Lindsi says, her face riddled with worry.

"There's no need, I'm the idiot who lost my temper." You feel your face turning bright red.

"No, I want to," she purrs. Huh. That's a little unexpected.

Turn to page 319.

You're not going home with Mom after this week is over. And Lindsi would probably be annoyed if she didn't have something to open from you on Christmas morning, even knowing you have another gift waiting at home.

You squeeze by a harried-looking mother with a double-wide stroller, force your way past a large, sweatpants-wearing woman in the Auntie Anne's Pretzels line, and skirt around a crowd of a dozen teenagers simultaneously texting.

Think. What would Lindsi like?

Something expensive. You head into the department store.

You try to ignore the salesgirls screaming from the makeup counters, spritzing overpowering perfume on you, as you make your way to a display you saw on the way in.

Cashmere.

Every girl likes cashmere, right? Plus, the whole family would know you spent some serious—whoa, two hundred dollars for a sweater? You look around, hoping for something smaller—a scarf, maybe, or a 3″ × 3″ square for petting—but this is all that's left. And judging from the extremely limited size and color options, even this won't be here for long.

You know what? Fine. Lindsi will love that you spent a lot on her. The fact that the sweater is yellow, a color Lindsi regularly mentions "looks terrible on all white girls," doesn't matter—it's the thought that counts. Plus, you don't have time to look for anything else; you're supposed to meet her in two minutes.

You grab the sweater and head to the checkout.

You really hope this thought will count for at least a couple of blow jobs.

Turn to page 331.

Lindsi will understand her gift being at home. If you don't somehow reverse Mom's opinion of you within the next couple days, she'll probably look at you with that sour, who-just-farted face forever. It's gotta be another gift for the hosts.

Of course, you don't actually *know* anything about your hosts. You look around. What store would be best?

There's a Body Shop, a Yankee Candle, a Wet Seal...

Oh, "Fine Wines and Spirits." That's definitely the winner. Who doesn't like a nice bottle of booze? You'll pick something obviously expensive, buy the wrapping right at the counter, and totally redeem yourself with almost zero effort.

You beeline for the scotch. Lindsi always talks about how she comes from a "hunting family"—what's better after a hunt than scotch by the fire? Manly men drink scotch. It'll be perfect.

You nab a bottle sleeve, write up a card at the counter, and head out to meet Lindsi. You slip it under the tree when you get back.

Ta-da! You'll definitely score some big points with this one.

Turn to page 321.

"LADIES," YOU SAY IN YOUR BEST CALMING VOICE. IT COMES OUT incredibly patronizing. "No need to get nasty."

"Thiz bidch juz said she *slep* with my *BOYFRIEN*," Lindsi screams, lunging toward Vicki.

Unsure what else to do, you step between them, trying to restrain Lindsi with an outstretched arm.

She leaps. You lift your hand to get better leverage on her shoulders...

THWAP.

You feel your elbow connect with something hard. When you turn, Vicki's on the floor, clutching her face. Blood's pouring through her fingers. Oh, fuck, this is—

"YAAAAHHHHHH!"

You barely register the hulking, bearded man before your line of vision is full of his fist.

SMACK.

The last thing you see as you collapse to the floor is beard hair. So much beard hair.

• • •

You wake with a splitting headache. Something to your right is beeping steadily.

It's a heart monitor. Ahhh, the hospital. Wonderful. Depending how long you were out—you grab your phone from the bedside table. Yup. It's Christmas day.

You hear a gentle tap on the door. Maybe it's a doctor here to cheer you up with meds. Or Lindsi; she might have brought something to apologize for the party. Or Beard Guy—he must have been Vicki's boyfriend—bringing you a bottle of really nice scotch to make up.

You kind of hope it's the doctor.

A red hat pokes through the door, followed by a white beard. You repress a scream. It's not an *evil* beard, idiot, it's a Santa.

"Ho! Ho! Ho! Merry—oh. It's *you.*"

Why is Santa so disgusted? You squint at him…

"Recognize me? From the gas station?"

Fuck, it's the hitchhiker.

"I'm sorry about that. It was late, and I've had bad experiences with hitchhikers," you lie. You've only ever seen them in movies, but those movies are always *terrifying*. "I guess I panicked. You understand, right?"

"Oh, sure, I understand." He walks to the bed, slinging his bag to the floor. "You know who doesn't, though? The kids here, sick with terrible diseases, who almost missed Christmas because a *dog poop* like you wouldn't act like a Good Samaritan for just one day."

"Dog poop? That's pretty harsh."

He squints.

"You know what you need?" he asks.

"What?"

He bends over. Oh, are you going to get a present? He probably wants you to feel guilty, but you totally won't.

"A lesson!" he shrieks, flipping something over your head. You're immediately soaked with…you blink, wiping your eyes until you can see him holding…

Ah, a bedpan. Your bedpan.

Turn to page 323.

YOU'RE NOT GETTING IN THE MIDDLE OF *THAT*. YOU STEP BACK…

…which leaves a clear path for Vicki's drunken punch. It lands square on Lindsi's jaw, knocking her head sideways cartoonishly. Lindsi stares, dazed, too drunk to realize what's happened.

"Lindsi," you say cautiously, stepping toward her. You hear Vicki screeching as someone pulls her back through the crowd. "Let's go." You rest a hand on her shoulder.

A couple of tears blink through her lashes. She touches her jaw absently, then flinches, obviously confused.

"You give me the keys and we'll go home—won't that be nice?" You keep your voice calm. Level. It's like with toddlers—if you don't react when they fall, they don't realize they're supposed to be hurt, right?

"Okay," she says, reaching into her purse mechanically. "We'll go."

You lead her to the car and somehow manage to find your way back to the house.

It's empty when you arrive. Thank god; they must all be at services. Which means you also got to miss services.

You lead Lindsi upstairs, pull her clothes off—she doesn't resist; she's like a life-sized doll—and tuck her into bed, leaving a glass of water on the table beside her.

That could have been worse, right?

You head into your room, tuck yourself in, and stare at the ceiling until you fall asleep.

• • •

"MERRY CHRISTMAS!"

The entire family shouts it in unison as you shuffle into the living room. You can't help but smile. They might be strange, and judgy, and in some cases overtly rude, but at least they sincerely love the holiday.

"Is Lindsi up yet?" Mom asks, handing you a cup of coffee.

"Oh, I assumed she'd be down already."

You hear the stairs creak.

"That must be her. Good, we can get started on pres—"

Mom's mouth drops open.

You turn. It's just Lindsi in her pajamas, what's—oh. A massive, purple-black bruise covers the entire right side of Lindsi's face.

You look around. Everyone's staring at you.

"Listen, this isn't what it looks like." Lindsi blinks. Winks, actually—her right eye is swollen shut. "We were at a party, and Lindsi got too drunk…"

Lars frowns.

"I just wanted to get her out of there; it…"

Dad shakes his head and looks away.

"It's not her fault, it's mine; I should have…"

You gulp. Even you hear how wife-beatery that sounds.

"I'm just gonna get Lindsi some coffee," you squeak, running out to the kitchen.

You hear a cough from the doorway.

Mom is there, and she looks…happy?

She sidles up.

"See this?"

She pulls down the neck of her flannel nightgown. A livid bruise circles her throat.

"Jesus, are you okay?"

"Of course." She grins conspiratorially. "Sometimes I 'forget' the safe word too. On purpose." She chuckles. "Like mother, like daughter, I guess, huh?"

Oh god. You haven't actually done anything, but you feel like you should look into couples counseling *immediately*.

The End.

Six Years Later…

THERE'S NOTHING LIKE A VANWHITTINGTON CHRISTMAS. THERE'S Mom's fantastic turkey dinner—she always saves an entire leg for you, "her favorite killer-in-law!" There's days roaming the woods with Lars, getting sweaty and sore hunting game, then unwinding together with a manly sauna. And of course Lindsi, your wife, always going out of her way to make sure you're treated with love and respect. You truly look forward to her Christmas cookies. And her Christmas blow jobs.

"Wake up, it's Christmas!"

Mom's cheery voice rings along the hallway.

"Mommy, Daddy, wake up! WAKE UP!"

Oh, little Warrington, your pride and joy, the most adorable son who has ever walked the earth. Even though you're tired, and still foggy after last night's "bender" with Lars, you're happy to wake up for your son, the pride and joy of the entire VanWhittington clan. And you'd been worried Lindsi's kid would turn out like cousin Jimmy. You should have known she was from good stock. Jimmy must be from his dad's side. How…unfortunate.

You head down to the tree, sitting in your usual place on the loveseat with Lars, your wives at your feet, eager to hand out presents to the children.

"Honey," you say, rubbing Lindsi's shoulder absently. She turns to you, eager to please. After all, you *are* an excellent provider. Let's give little Warry his *special* present."

She smiles adoringly and hands the box to your son. He tears it open. When he sees what's inside, his face almost splits in two from joy.

"MY LITTLE CROSSBOW!" He jumps up and down, squealing, the child-sized weapon clutched between his pudgy fingers.

"Hmm," you say, looking at him sternly. "That's pretty exciting. But is that *everything*?"

Warrington's eyes go wide and he dives back into the box.

"AND A BIG BOY BOWIE!! THANK YOU, DADDY!"

"You're welcome, son." You pull him onto your lap, ruffling his white-blonde hair. "If you're good, we can practice today."

"For my proving?"

"The proving," Lindsi echoes absently as she stuffs the discarded wrapping into a plastic bag.

"Exactly. You have a lot to live up to, after all. And you can never get started too early."

Warrington bounces excitedly on your knee.

This. This is perfect happiness. Who needs their own family when they can be part of the VanWhittington bloodline, forever and ever? Hopefully your mother understands that, since contact is strictly forbidden.

You hope nothing about your life ever changes.

The End.

"I'M SORRY, IT'S REALLY JUST PAPERWORK, BUT WE'RE SO UNDER-staffed because of the holidays. Would you mind staying here while…I can't leave you unattended in the waiting area, and the records room is off-limits…" The weedy, ridiculously young cop who picked you up gulps awkwardly and gestures at the single jail cell.

"Sure. Whatever makes this easiest."

"Oh, thanks!" His voice actually breaks. "I really appreciate it."

You sit in the cell while he rushes off, muttering, "Intake form, intake form," under his breath.

A minute later Lindsi peeks her head down the hallway. You wave lazily.

"I just want to say, Lindsi, I'm sorry that I—"

"Shhh, shh." She steps into the cell, pressing your head against her chest. Since you're seated, it hits just below her belly button. "Don't apologize. You were right to hit him; he was over the line. I just wanted to make sure you're okay."

Wow, that was unexpected.

"Uh, yeah. I mean, I'll need some Neosporin for these"—you hold up your split knuckles—"but otherwise I'm fine." That's a lie; you're actually terrified your entire hand is broken, but Lindsi seems so cool with this that you don't want to wreck things.

She sits next to you on the bench, setting a hand on your leg.

"Thanks, by the way," she whispers.

"For what?"

"For defending my honor." Her hand slides up a few inches. "It's hot to see you get all…aggro." It moves up to cup your balls.

"Oh, uh, sure," you sputter. "I just hope we can sort this out soon."

"Not before I get what I want." Lindsi stands up quickly and pushes your shoulders against the wall. "I want to *fuck* you."

"Okay, well, he said it was just basic paperwork, so I'm sure—"

"NOW."

She sits down on you hard, slamming you fully into the wall. You'd push her off, but her weight has completely thrown out your back. You feel your kidney twinge painfully. You're helpless to stop Lindsi as she unbuttons your shirt, leaning down to lick a nipple. Jesus, are you going to get prison-raped by your girlfr—

"OH!"

You look past Lindsi.

Of course. Mom is there, hand over her mouth, the picture of horror.

"What's she doing here?" you hiss-whisper in Lindsi's ear.

"I called her. I thought she might be able to get you out faster—she knows the chief of police." Lindsi seems entirely unembarrassed by the appearance of her mother in the middle of her sex attack.

So it's just you that's mortified. Again.

This time you're tossing Lindsi right *under that bus. Turn to page 328.*
Just be cool. Mom must be used to this by now, right? Turn to page 329.

"MERRY CHRISTMAS!"

Mom's voice rings through the hallways as people bustle out of bed. You yawn, stretch, and pull a sweater over your pajamas. Time to make up some lost ground.

You troop downstairs with the rest of the family.

"That's strange," Lindsi says. "I can't even smell the *pannekoeken.*"

"What?" you ask.

"Our dad always gets up early on Christmas to light the fire and make his traditional *pannekoeken* breakfast," Lars says. "He only makes it on Christmas. Maybe he's behind schedule?" He shrugs and continues down the stairs.

"OH!"

Mom shrieks and claps a hand to her mouth. You run into the living room and edge around her, wondering what's going on.

Dad is half naked in the middle of the room, grinning stupidly at you all.

"Hey, shweedy," he slurs, swaying slightly. "Juz one secon, I haffa pee."

He turns, pulls his dick out, and starts pissing on a pile of presents.

"Oh, Jesus," Lars says, looking disgusted.

"Who brought alcohol into the house? WHO?" Mom turns to glare at all of you, eyes wild.

"I thought…we were all drinking wine last night at dinner," you say cautiously.

"Yes, wine and beer only. He's fine with those. For him to be like this…someone must have brought in liquor."

"Oh." You nod sagely, but say nothing. Maybe they won't realize it's from you?

But Michael, Lindsi's brother-in-law, is already picking up the bottle sleeve. Dammit, evidence in your own hand!

He points at you.

"How *could* you?" The look on Mom's face is so withering that you actually recoil.

"It was an honest mistake."

"He's been able to maintain his sobriety for over twenty years. And you ruin it with one *thoughtless* move." The whole sentence comes out like a hiss.

"Well…I mean…what kind of sober person can't even *see* a bottle of liquor without getting wasted?"

Now *everyone's* giving you that look.

Lindsi nods toward the kitchen. You're happy to follow, if only to get out of pee cleanup duty.

"I'm sorry, Linds," you say once you're out of earshot. "I really had no idea."

"I think you should probably leave," she says quietly.

"I just thought—"

"I know, it's not your fault, it's his, but you should go. Mom will get upset if you stay."

"Yeah." You laugh hollowly. "As though she could be more upset with me than she already is."

Lindsi frowns.

"You've never seen Mom upset," she says.

Oh, Jesus.

You sneak out of the house and drive home in silence.

What are you getting into if you stay with Lindsi? You thought your family could be difficult, but these people…and she clearly *likes* spending time with them. But how can you dump her now? When you've destroyed her dad's sobriety? And she helped you escape?

There's no good option.

At least you'll get some of those ridiculous rental car expenses back.

But when you pull up to the lot, the lights are off. A sign in the window tells you they're "closed for the holiday."

Awesome.

Where the fuck are you going to find parking in the city on Christmas Day?

The End.

YOU PRESS THE RED BUTTON ON YOUR BED THAT YOU ASSUME CALLS the nurse, then press it again several more times. A few seconds later a harried-looking middle-aged woman huffs through the door, shelf-of-boob heaving under peppermint-striped scrubs.

"What's…going on…here?"

"This man attacked me!" you yell, pointing at hitchhiker-Santa.

"Oh, my, no," he says. All the evil has drained from his voice, and his eyes are wide and imploring. The nurse looks back and forth between you, frowning.

"He threw a bedpan at my face! It was full; he…"

"Oh no, no. I would *never*. Though I'll admit, clumsy me, I *did* knock over his bedpan when I set down my sack of toys for the *sick children*."

"Oh, Freddy, when are you going to learn to buy smaller gifts?" She smiles indulgently at the evil Santa. Dammit, she's chosen team Freddy.

"I feel just terrible. Here, let me help." He leans over, dabbing at your face with a towel. His eyes look so sincere; you almost start to wonder whether it *was* an accident.

"It's fine. If you could just help me to the shower, nurse." You push the Santa away. He stumbles back exaggeratedly, like you shoved hard. The nurse glares. Oh fine, blame the victim.

"Freddy wouldn't hurt a fly," she whispers in your ear as she helps you up. You feel your own urine drip down your spine. Jesus, gross.

"But I'm certain I saw him…"

"We have you on a lot of medication, hon. I'm sure it seemed like that, but I promise, it was a mistake. You were confused, is all."

"Oh." You frown. Looking at Freddy now, smiling at the pair of you, it's hard to believe he would do that. And he *is* spending Christmas volunteering for sick kids.

Maybe you were wrong?

"Well, I should go," Freddy says. "Ho! Ho! Ho!" You look at him. He's staring at you. "MERRRRRRRYYY Christmas." He winks leeringly, sticking up a middle finger.

"Oh, COME ON!"

But the nurse didn't see. He disappears out the door.

You *knew* you were right about hitchhikers.

The End.

You're not wrong—she, at least, was being wildly inappropriate—but it's not worth spending the rest of an already incredibly stressful holiday fighting with the one person in the house that likes you. Sometimes.

"I'm sorry," you say between gritted teeth. "I didn't mean to overreact. I just get so…" What would Lindsi accept as an excuse? "…jealous when I see you with another guy."

Her look of icy scorn immediately melts. She actually looks kinda horny.

"I get that. I'm sorry I made you jealous. You know me, I don't even *think* about that stuff. I'm friendly with everybody."

"Totally." If by "everybody," Lindsi means everyone with a dick, it's a pretty fair assessment.

"So now that we're made up, Steve has nowhere to be for Christmas, and I really hoped we could invite him over."

"Oh."

"I won't if you have a problem," she says. "But I thought since you're being so understanding, you'd get it. He's alone, and his parents don't even cook; he needs somewhere to go. Especially since…you know, his hand."

Well, fuck, how can you argue with a prosthetic hand?

"Okay, sure," you say.

"Thanks, sweetie." Lindsi leans across to kiss your cheek. "You're the *best*."

• • •

The family has barely made it downstairs Christmas morning when the doorbell rings. Before anyone can answer, Steve sticks his head inside.

Of course he's in full Santa regalia.

"Ho! Ho! Ho! MERRRRRRYY Christmas!" he bellows. Lindsi's nieces shriek in excitement. Even Jimmy almost-smiles. Mom's beaming.

"Steve! This is the best Christmas gift I can think of,"

Dad shouts.

Lars walks over and hugs him.

"Hey, bro. We've missed you around here," he says.

"I've missed you too. Especially you, Mrs. VanWhittington."
He smiles coyly as he pulls off his Santa gloves.

"Oh, Steve," Lindsi's mom giggles. Actually *giggles*. "You
always were a charmer."

The day wears on, but Steve's welcome never seems to wear
off. No one can get enough of his inane stories about when he
was on the high school football team, like that wasn't *over a decade
ago*. He's patting Dad on the back, twirling Mom in dance steps,
pinching Lindsi's cheeks…

All with his right hand. The "prosthetic" one.

It looks pretty damn realistic to you. With full range of
motion. Especially when you see it sneak around the chairs at
Christmas dinner to grab Lindsi's ass.

She turns to Steve with a secret smile.

Goddammit, you should have never apologized.

The End. Possibly of a lot of things.

FUCK IF YOU'RE APOLOGIZING. SHE WAS THE ONE ALL OVER A *mall Santa.*

"Just so you know," Lindsi says as she pulls into the driveway. "I don't think you should come tonight." She doesn't look at you. Her lips are white, they're so pursed.

"To what?"

"To caroling. And mass. Our family traditions."

"Come on, Linds." You follow her into the kitchen. "Your family will think it's rude if I don't come. Don't overreact even more."

She turns to you, eyes bugging so wide it looks like someone burned off the lids with a laser. Over her shoulder you see Mom enter the room. Lindsi turns at the sound of her footsteps, then looks back at you, a tight, triumphant smile curling her lips.

"It would be hypocritical for you to come to church with us, since you're an *atheist.*"

Mom squeaks in what sounds like actual shock and bustles away, hand over her mouth. Lindsi's grin gets even more shit eating.

"You know I don't really care if your family knows I'm an atheist, right? That's just true. If it's a problem for anyone, it's not going to be me."

"Yeah, well…that's just…*SAD,*" Lindsi sputters. "Enjoy your Christmas Eve alone. Jesus *won't* be praying for you." She storms out, hair twitching behind her like an epileptic fit.

Getting out of church is a bonus, but you're too pissed at Lindsi for the mall, and for trying to fuck you over with her family, to focus on that.

If you want to pour yourself a drink right this second, turn to page 335.
If you'd rather go out to a bar, so you don't have to stay in this place one fucking second longer, turn to page 337.

THIS IS TOO MUCH. YOU CAN'T KEEP TAKING THE BLAME FOR LINDSI'S frankly ridiculously inappropriate sex drive.

"Can I just say, I had nothing to do with this."

Mom sniffs.

"I was waiting to get processed—because all we're talking about is a fine—and Lindsi came and basically attacked me." You turn to Lindsi. "I think you need to set better boundaries, Linds. This is getting to be a problem."

She slaps you across the face and wrenches herself off your lap, throwing your back out a little further. A parting "fuck you."

Now both Lindsi and her mom are wearing the same look of disgust. Sort of like someone smeared dog shit on their upper lips and the scent's just hit. They turn and walk out together, leaving you alone in the cell.

"Lindsi, wait," you call after her retreating form. "I'm sorry, I didn't mean to upset you, I—"

"Good luck with the drunk tank," she yells down the hallway.

What could she possibly mean by that?

Turn to page 333.

JUST PLAY IT COOL.

"Oh, Lindsi thought she could provide some moral support. That's why she was…massaging my back. Because of the injury."

Mom sniffs in elaborate disdain.

"Her weight keeps me from hyperextending the muscle while she works the knot." Jesus, are those even words?

Luckily, Mom is too disgusted to wait around for more of your elaborately flimsy story. She walks away in a huff, and you and Lindsi follow.

• • •

You wake up in the middle of the night to someone attacking you.

"Ahhh, no," you whimper, flailing around. The attacker pins your wrists down.

"It's *me*," Lindsi hisses. "Shut up, Mom will hear."

You blink, confused. Forget Mom; you're sharing this room with cousin Jimmy.

"I thought we could finish what we started at the police station." Lindsi leans in to nibble your ear. Despite Jimmy lying mere feet away, you feel yourself start to get hard.

"No, you have to go."

Lindsi starts pulling your pajama bottoms off with her teeth. "Seems like you want me here."

"My back. It's spasming. And someone could come by. They could catch us *again*."

"Don't be a wimp," Lindsi says.

"No, really." You're getting desperate. You think you hear creaking down the hall. Someone could be coming. You cannot lie for Lindsi again. Think. THINK! "I think the uh, punch, really messed something up. I hit him pretty hard, threw my whole body behind it. I can't do this; I'll do serious damage."

"Uhhhhh," Lindsi moans, caressing your chest with her hair. Fuck, you've said the one thing guaranteed to make her *more horny*.

But then she pushes back off you.

"I'll just have to wait, then. Prepare yourself. It's gonna be *nasty*."

She tiptoes out of the room, stopping at the door to growl at you. Jesus.

Seconds later you see Mom's silhouette in the doorway. You can't make out her face in the dimness, but you're certain she's sneering.

Whatever, she has no evidence. You silently congratulate yourself on the narrow escape as she plods back down the hall.

But you can still hear something. It's quiet, but insistent.

Fap-fap-fap. Fap. FAPFAPFAPFAPFAP.

Oh Jesus.

It's Jimmy. Masturbating. And moaning.

You pull your pillow over your ears and try to go to sleep.

Turn to page 339.

"MERRY CHRISTMAS!"

Mom's voice rings through the hallways as people bustle out of bed. You yawn, stretch, and pull a sweater over your pajamas. You actually feel mildly cheery. After all, you found that great gift for Lindsi, and she let you put your name on all those things she bought. This won't be so bad. Everyone's happy on Christmas.

You head to the living room and find a spot on the floor next to Lindsi. After the kids open a few presents, you pass yours to her.

"I got you something," you whisper.

"Oh, you didn't have to do that." She nuzzles her head into your shoulder. Mom looks at you...indulgently. Awesome. This plan is working perfectly.

"Let's just hope it's not a sweater," Mom says with a laugh.

"Oh my god, *right?*" Lindsi giggles as she pulls the ribbon. You frown at Lars.

"One year Lindsi brought home a boyfriend and he got her this hideous cashmere sweater," he says, grinning.

"It was *terrible,*" Lindsi rips through the paper. It's too late to stop her. "It's like he'd never even met..."

She pulls the sweater out of the box. In this light, it looks especially pucey.

"Oh. Thank you," she says mechanically.

"There's a gift receipt...somewhere," you mumble. No one is making eye contact with you anymore. You never should have tried to be nice.

"There is another present," Jimmy says, voice like a hospital monitor flatlining. "It is addressed to you," he says, depositing it in your lap. "From Lindsi."

Lindsi frowns, but you don't notice it. You're too eager to distract from the massive failure of your gift.

"That's so nice of you, sweetie. I know we were planning on exchanging our *real* gifts at home, but I should've known you'd go out of your way to make me feel like part of the—"

You pull out a set of leather straps, frowning.

"OH!"

Mom seems to have made the connection before you have.

Now that you're looking more closely, though, you see it: a leather bondage suit, the crisscrossing straps clearly too flimsy to cover anything meaningful. And there's a massive black dildo attached to the crotch.

Huh. Lindsi never told you she was into pegging.

If you want to fall on your sword to make it up to Lindsi, turn to page 341.

If Lindsi's going to have to take the fall for this one—because seriously, fetish gear at family Christmas?—turn to page 343.

A FEW MINUTES LATER, THE SCRAWNY DEPUTY COMES IN. AN AMPLE-bellied, impressively moustached man in late middle age is behind him. He's wearing a flat-brimmed tan hat and aviators, even though you're inside, in the winter.

"I'll take it from here," he says, grabbing the papers from the deputy. The deputy nods nervously and scurries away.

"Follow me, son."

"Where are we going?"

"To the holding pen. This cell we gotta keep open in case of major crimes."

"Major…? Wait, why am I…I was told I'd pay a fine and—"

"You need to stop interrupting me, son, or you'll be in a world of pain."

He glares at you over mirrored lenses. You gulp back your words.

"I spoke to my friend Mrs. VanWhittington just now, and once I heard what happened down at the mall, I agreed with her. You need to cool off. Lindsi's safety is at stake."

"Lindsi's…wait a second, it wasn't like that. Lindsi—"

"Here we are. Enjoy the night." He pushes you into what's clearly the drunk tank, laughing as he locks the door.

It's still early evening, but already a few alcoholics are sharing the space with you.

The entire room smells vaguely of stale piss. A guy with a red clown nose and wilting antlers is vomiting all around the tin toilet in the corner, mostly missing the bowl with his creamy-looking splatter. In the corner, a skinny man with a totally disproportionate gut has pulled his pants off entirely to sleep, limp dick rattling with every snore.

You sit down gingerly on a bench near the cell entrance, hoping against hope you're not in a puddle of anything. Hours pass, and eventually you slip into a nervous half-sleep.

This is easily the third-worst Christmas you've ever had.

• • •

You wake up to the sound of violent vomiting.

At least it's a different guy this time; Rudolph seems to have passed out next to Free Willy in the corner.

You rattle the bars until someone comes over.

"Am I free to go now?"

"Name?"

You give it.

"Uh, yeah," the woman on the other side says, frowning deeply. "You weren't even supposed to be in overnight."

Awesome.

You head to the front desk to check out. The same weedy deputy is there.

"Before you go, someone left this for you," he says, producing a small, beautifully wrapped box. The tag on top tells you it's from Lindsi.

Thank god. At least you won't have to deal with her still being angry when you get back.

"She said you should open it here," the deputy squeaks. You comply.

Inside is a rock with a rubber band around it. No, wait…it's a lump of coal. Where did she get an actual lump of coal?

The rubber band is holding a note in place. You pull it off.

"My Christmas present to myself is dumping you. Merry merry! <3, Lindsi."

You close your eyes against this new indignity.

The deputy leans over to look at your gift.

"Oooh," he says, voice cracking as he laughs. "Burned."

You'd tell him to fuck himself, but that could mean another night in the drunk tank.

The End.

As soon as everyone leaves for caroling, you head to the fridge. All they have is beer and wine, but you're not picky. You grab an IPA and head to the couch.

You turn on the TV, flipping through channels, hoping to find something you recognize. One of the local stations is showing the old Grinch cartoon. You loved that as a kid. You still love it. You settle back and turn up the volume.

Half an hour later the show finishes, but they follow with *Home Alone*. This station is *nailing* it. With no one around, the house is actually pretty pleasant. Relaxing. This is the kind of Christmas you wanted. If it were always like this, you wouldn't even make plans to escape.

The family dog, Toodles, comes up and nudges your knee with his graying muzzle. You've always liked golden retrievers. They're so easy. They don't get bitchy, or flirt with their exes publicly, or try to fuck you over with their moms. No, golden retrievers are the perfect…

Wait, what's that coming out of Toodles's mouth? It looks like foam.

Fuck, did Toodles catch rabies? *Et tu*, Toodles?

You back up on the couch as Toodles starts to convulse. Soon he's rolled over on the floor, his whole body twitching. You hear a choking sound. Rabies doesn't make dogs seize and choke, does it?

How do you save a choking dog?

The only first aid training you've received was back in sixth grade, when your mom made you take that babysitter's safety class in order to stay home with your sister. Are you supposed to…sweep the mouth, maybe? For foreign objects?

You kneel next to Toodles, preparing to sweep his throat clear, but his jaws gnash closed during a convulsion and you back away. Nope. Not doing that. It *could* still be rabies.

After a few seconds, Toodles stops moving.

And breathing.

You can't have killed their dog.

You lean in, putting your mouth to the dog's, pushing all

336

the air out of your lungs and into his. You see his chest rise with your breath. This could work. It could actually work! Then you inhale—oh, fuck, that's *foul*. You back away, gagging heavily. By the time you've gotten control of your breathing, the dog looks even deader.

With a trembling finger, you move his tongue out from the back of his throat. At least it will look like you *tried*.

If you want to call Lindsi and tell her what happened, turn to page 345.
If you want to go upstairs and pretend you were sleeping, turn to page 347.

YOU HAVE TO GET OUT OF THIS FUCKING HOUSE, IF ONLY FOR fifteen minutes.

You stamp out to your car—hopefully Lindsi hears how pissed you are—and Google the nearest bar. It's ten miles away. Jesus, why does anyone live in this godforsaken town?

You get to the bar and walk in. It's mostly empty—it's Christmas Eve, after all—except for one guy about your age sitting at the far corner of the—

Oh, FUCK that. It's Steve, the mall Santa.

You take a seat as far away as possible.

He gets up the minute your beer arrives and walks around to sit next to you. "Hey, don't I know you?"

"Yeah." You glare. "I'm Lindsi's boyfriend."

"Oh. Ohhhh." He looks away, sheepish. His hands are folded in his lap. "Sorry about earlier. Lindsi can be…flirty. I shouldn't have played along. I didn't realize she was seeing anybody."

"That's okay," you say grudgingly. He's right, after all. Lindsi can be more than flirty. You were only at the mall because of her sex attack.

"Here, let me buy you a beer to make up for it." Steve motions the bartender over with his left hand.

You can't argue with that.

After a couple of rounds, you're warming up to Steve. He has hilarious stories about his time in the army, but even better, stories about Lindsi in high school. You're cracking each other up over her sleep farts—you never thought you'd find someone to talk about that with. And frankly, being on the moral high ground—forgiving the veteran with one hand, because you're a bigger person—makes you feel pretty good about yourself. Pitying someone a little is always a good way to start a friendship.

You get up to go the bathroom. On the way, the bar door opens.

"BRO!" Steve yells at the guy entering. They man-hug, then start a complicated handshake…with their right hands.

Wait a second, isn't that one supposed to be prosthetic?

They're wiggling fingers, bumping fists—Steve's is definitely fully closed—even holding fake spectacles to their eyes.

If that's a prosthetic it is fucking top of the line.

Why would Lindsi lie about that?

Why would she let him grope her *right in front of you*?

You stare into the urinal, your thoughts getting darker and darker. She had to know he was the mall Santa all along—why else would a grown woman want to sit on a Santa's lap? Usually they're creepy old men with beer guts and beard-induced acne. If she knew, that means they must have been in contact. Recently.

Knowing Lindsi, they probably fucked before you showed up for Christmas. Steve really seemed to have strong memories of those sleep farts.

You head back to the bar, relieved that Steve is talking to his friend more than you.

You can only stay here so long, then you'll have to go back. For Christmas. With your cheating girlfriend who hates you.

You hold up your hand to the bartender, then point at your pint.

"And a shot, please."

The End.

WHEN YOU COME DOWNSTAIRS THE NEXT MORNING, IT'S CLEAR FROM the looks on everyone's faces that Mom has shared what happened.

Awesome. Now everyone thinks you're a sex perv because of your possibly clinical girlfriend.

You sit on the couch, forcing a smile as Mom hands presents around. Lindsi scoots in next to you, resting her hand on your thigh…then moving it higher.

Just pretend nothing's happening.

The longer you sit there, the more overt Lindsi's advances get. At one point she leans over to whisper, "I wish you would fuck me in my childhood bedroom," then licks your ear.

Jimmy's watching the pair of you hungrily, hand at the ready in his sweatpants pocket, like some sort of proverbial Christmas mouse waiting around for you to drop a proverbial Christmas sex crumb.

Mom coughs, trying to draw Lindsi's attention away from rubbing your pecs.

"Lindsi." She looks over, but doesn't stop rubbing. "Would you like to give your gift to…" Mom stares at you, lips drawn back in deep disgust. She can't even bring herself to say your name.

"Sure. We can exchange gifts."

Your real present for Lindsi is back in your apartment, but you figured she'd want something more, since you're spending Christmas with her family.

She opens the envelope you stuck under the tree. Inside is a handwritten "gift certificate" for "dinner on me." Whatever, your mom always loved those good-kid coupon books.

"Ohh, how *romantic*." She caresses the side of your head, drawing her finger down your neck. You're simultaneously aroused and terrified. "Now open mine!"

You unwrap the small box she's laid in your hand. Inside is a watch—scratch that, a fucking *Rolex*.

"Lindsi, this…this is too much."

"Not for *you*," she purrs. "Anyway, I need you to look fancy on our trip."

"Our...what?"

"To Jamaica! I booked us at an all-inclusive Kingston resort the last week in January. Don't worry, I called your boss to get you the time off."

"Oh. That's great. Wow." You try not to let the fear show in your eyes.

A week ago you would have said this relationship was on the right track, but now you're mildly terrified. You've been together, what, four months? And she's spending thousands on you? Where does she even get the money? PR isn't *that* lucrative.

Lindsi leans in as the family watches Dad open a present.

"Listen, I thought since your plans got canceled, you could stay here through New Year's."

"Oh, I'm not sure—"

"Don't worry, babe, Jimmy is leaving tomorrow, so we'll have your bedroom all to ourselves. I'll try not to scream *too* loud."

She said that *very* loud. Everyone's staring, horrified.

Same here, VanWhittingtons.

The End.

MAN, LINDSI IS GOING TO OWE YOU *HUGE* AFTER THIS WEEKEND. EVEN with the terrible sweater, you've earned a holiday beej... actually, several.

"Oh, haha," you laugh unconvincingly. "Thanks, hon, this is perfect...for that...play I'm in."

Lindsi frowns. Her face is beet red.

"Maybe Lindsi didn't tell you, but I do some amateur theater." Lars raises an eyebrow, obviously stifling a laugh. Lindsi's sister Luanne won't even look at you. "We're putting on a production of...the Marquis de Sade's...stuff. It's kind of a mashup."

You can't actually remember any of his books, just that he's a famous perv.

"It's a story of young love..." Mom coughs awkwardly. "And, uh...coming of age?" Why would coming of age involve dungeon pegging? Fuck, think fast. "And you know, it's very experimental. Pushes the envelope."

"What are you playing?"

Dad is staring at you, mouth in a tight line, as though trying his best to swallow your bullshit, despite his body's revolt against it.

"I'm sorry?" Does he want to hear about your sex play with his daughter, or...

"In the show. Your character."

"Oh. I'm, um...the...inquisitor? It's loosely set during the Spanish Inquisition."

Mom gets up and walks out of the room. No one else will look at you.

"Anyway, thanks, sweetie." You drop the dildo-suit into the box. "It'll be perfect."

• • •

The rest of the day is filled with awkward moments of quickly removed eye contact, a general refusal to sit next to you, and what you have to assume is a now-permanent look of disgust pinching Mom's features.

This is a baker's dozen beej day.

But at least the day is over. That's something. You head to the bedroom you're sharing with Jimmy, exhausted beyond comprehension.

Just as you're drifting off to sleep, you hear him roll over.

"Do you like my outfit?"

"What?"

"My outfit. Do you like it?"

You blink awake. Jimmy is wearing a near-identical straps-and-dildo contraption over a pair of tightie-whities. You'd swear it was the same one—that he'd just stolen it out of the box in the living room no one wants to go near anymore—but his has studs along the chest. Lindsi's had oh-so-ladylike heart cutouts in the leather.

"It's, um…" How can you possibly respond to this in a way that's not felonious? How do you respond to something like this, full stop?

"I thought I was the only one," Jimmy says.

"That was actually a woman's outfit."

"This will be our secret," Jimmy whispers, rolling over.

Oh Jesus, you really never wanted to hear those words out of a minor's mouth.

The End.

Jesus *CHRIST*. You have spent this entire holiday—which has only been one fucking day so far—covering for Lindsi, and now she just bends you over again and expects you to take it? Literally?

Fuck this.

"Wow, Lindsi, I have no idea why you would have bought this. Is this some kind of sick joke?"

Her eyes widen, like a trapped animal. It almost makes you pity her…then you look at the dildo contraption you're holding up in front of her entire family and forget that.

"You trying to force your perverse tastes on me is *not* appreciated."

Her sister, Luanne, gives a strangled sound of agreement.

"Beyond that, I'm shocked at the lack of boundaries. How did you think it would make me feel to open a fetish outfit in front of your father? Seriously, Lindsi, you need help. Professional help."

She glares, obviously livid, but says nothing. What can she say? She gifted a fucking dildo suit.

"Ahem. If I might interject." Mom's voice is even icier than usual. You suppose it's only fair she'd side with the one she actually carried in her uterus, even if she *is* patently in the wrong.

"Please." You're all benevolence. You're maintaining the moral high ground, dammit.

"I believe I made a mistake."

Lindsi nods vigorously.

"I'm sorry?" Your stomach drops. You really put all your eggs in the throw-Lindsi-under-the-bus basket. This doesn't sound good.

"On Christmas, I usually wake the kids," Mom says, smiling at Lars, Luanne, and Lindsi in turn. "When I went into Lindsi's room, I noticed a box with a tag on top indicating it was for you. It wasn't wrapped, and I just assumed she hadn't had time. I thought it would be nice if I wrapped it and snuck it under the tree. I see now she had no intention of giving it to you publicly. It's my mistake."

Mom's lip curls triumphantly.

"Now that we've cleared that up, who wants *pannekoeken?*" Dad sputters. Everyone shuffles out, clearly grateful to escape.

You follow a few paces behind, head down, until Lindsi stops you with a hand to the shoulder.

"Where are you going?" Her eyes are so buggy you're afraid they might fall out of her head.

"Breakfast?"

"Uh, no, you should go. Like, home."

"Lindsi, I'm sorry, but look at it from my position." She's shaking her head, lips pinched so tight they're white. "I'll apologize to your mom. Though really, she shouldn't have been snooping in your room. What did she think she…"

"Go."

"Lindsi, it was an honest—"

"And lose my number. Permanently."

She stalks off into the kitchen, leaving you alone in the hall.

By the time she comes back to the city, she'll have cooled off, right?

You grab the fetish suit and stuff it in your duffel on the way out. Just in case you're right.

The End.

THE THIRD TIME YOU TRY HER PHONE, LINDSI PICKS UP, WHISPER-hissing at you.

"What do you want? We're at *church.*"

"I know, I wouldn't have called if it weren't an emergency but…your dog. I think he's…dead."

"What?"

"He had some kind of fit, just keeled over on the rug, and now he's not breathing." You opt not to mention the failed attempt at mouth-to-mouth.

"Are you fucking *kidding*? You don't even recognize canine epilepsy when you see it?"

"Dogs can have epilepsy?"

"This is totally preventable. You just grab the rod chew toy—we keep one in every room for exactly this reason—wedge it in the back third of his mouth, then lean on Toodles with your entire body weight while not restricting his breathing."

What the fuck?

"No one even told me Toodles had a condition. If I'd known—"

"Just…stop. We're coming home now. Try not to kill anything else I love."

Lindsi hangs up.

About twenty minutes later the family walks through the door, Lindsi weeping, unable to look at you without narrowing her eyes murderously. Eventually, she heads out with her father and Lars to dig a temporary "snow grave."

As soon as they've left, Mom pulls you aside.

"Well done." She's smiling conspiratorially.

"What?"

"How could you possibly know how to help an epileptic dog, right?" She gives you an exaggerated wink.

"Are you…happy about this?"

"No, how could I be happy to be rid of an animal who's unpredictably incontinent? One who's broken three heirloom vases just this year? One who sleeps in bed with us 'in case

something happens' and is then incontinent? No, I'm devastated."
Mom grins more widely.

That's unsettling.

Turn to page 349.

YOU DASH UPSTAIRS AND THROW ON YOUR PAJAMAS, LYING UNDER THE covers and waiting silently for the family to return. You can say you were tired—that would be plausible, right? And the fit wasn't *that* loud. They'll have to believe you slept through it.

Finally, you hear the sound of booted feet tramping inside.

Wait for it. Just a few…

"AHHHHHHHH! TOOOOOODLES!"

Lindsi's shriek bounces up the stairs. You run to the head of the stairs, then slow down and dramatically rub your eyes as you descend.

"What's going on?" You yawn. "Is everything okay?"

Lindsi rushes into your arms, bawling.

"It's Toodles. He's…he's DEAAAAAAAD!"

"What? Oh my god, what happened?"

"It appears he's been dead for some time." Jimmy pokes at the dog while Lindsi weeps. "His tongue may have been moved postmortem."

Luckily, Lindsi can't seem to hear him over her sobs.

"Here, honey, let me get you to bed." You pat Lindsi's head reassuringly. She clings to you. Who knew dead dogs ended fights so effectively? "It won't seem as bad in the morning."

"Oh…oh-kay," she chokes. You head up the stairs and tuck her in, like a child. She smiles gratefully as she drifts off to sleep.

You head down to offer help—hoping they take it as hollowly as you mean it—but only Mom is inside.

You frown, confused.

"They're digging a temporary snow grave," she says. "Thanks to *you*." She should be disgusted—she's always disgusted with you—but instead Mom winks exaggeratedly, grinning ear-to-ear.

"I don't know what you're talking about."

"Right, because you were in bed at seven thirty. And didn't finish your drink. And didn't hear the dog dying."

She's still smiling.

"Any idiot can tell when a tongue has been moved postmortem. So I must have you to thank."

"Thank? Are you…happy about this?"

"No." Mom shakes her head. "How could I be happy to be rid of an animal that I have to baby-bird feed? One that broke three Precious Moments figurines just this year? One whose incontinence is never conveniently timed? No, I'm devastated." She grins more widely.

That's unsettling.

"Don't worry, though, it's our little secret," she says, patting your shoulder. "We're the only ones who ever have to know."

Turn to page 351.

CHRISTMAS MORNING, THE FAMILY DECIDES THEY'RE TOO DEVASTATED by Toodles's death to celebrate.

"You can help," Lindsi says flatly around ten. You pray she's talking about breakfast. What's the etiquette on raiding someone's fridge if they haven't fed you? Is two hours fair? Should you push it until eleven? You still have a few leftover Combos from the drive up…

"Happy to help." You smile widely. Lindsi sneers. "What do you need?"

"You to build the website for the memorial fund."

"Memorial…"

"We'll be taking donations for retriever epilepsy. I'm sure anyone would be generous after such a tragedy. At Christmas."

You nod silently, sitting down at the laptop Lindsi has set up on the kitchen table.

"What will you be giving?"

Fuck. You were hoping "building the website" would be your donation.

"Maybe fifty…" Lindsi glares. "Or, you know, a hundred and fifty dollars?"

She snorts and walks out of the room.

"You coming?" Lars claps a hand on your shoulder.

"For what?"

"We're gonna need all of us to dig the real grave, what with the ground being frozen. Lindsi said you wouldn't want to help— actually, she used a few choice words," Lars blushes slightly. "And called Steve, her high school boyfriend, to help. But I thought you should be included."

"Thanks, Lars." You force another smile. Gee, fantastic. You get to dig frozen ground in order to not look like a pussy next to Lindsi's ex. "Won't Steve have trouble, though?"

"Why?"

"The prosthetic hand?"

"What the fuck are you talking about?"

You frown, and follow Lars outside.

As Lindsi and her sister Luanne look on, crying silently (and Mom barely represses her glee), you help the men dig the hole. It takes you about ten minutes to fully wedge the shovel into the ground. You chip out a cubic inch of icy soil.

Awesome.

Every time you look at Lindsi, her face contorts in disgust.

Even better.

And every time she looks at Steve—who's really making some progress, whatever his hand's made of—she makes bedroom eyes.

Dammit, this is easily the fourth-worst Christmas you've ever had.

The End.

"Okay, and then put the seizure GIF here." Lindsi points to the laptop screen. You've been helping her set up a memorial fund for epileptic retrievers all morning. Hopefully a few people donate anonymously. Otherwise you're going to have to pay into this thing with more than just wasted hours of your life.

Oh, well. It's not exactly a typical Christmas, but it does seem like everyone's accepted your I-was-sleeping lie. Better than nothing.

After breakfast, Lars comes up and hangs a massive arm around your shoulder.

"We wanted to include you," he says, nodding toward the back yard. Through the door, you see Dad and Michael shoveling a small square.

"Include me?"

"We usually dig graves as a family."

"Oh, but…"

"He's right, you're family now." Mom smiles at you from the doorway. "Hopefully you'll get down to making it official sooner rather than later."

Jesus, yesterday you were the plague of the VanWhittingtons; today they're trying to turn you into a son-in-law. All because you murdered a dog. You're not sure if you're more relieved or horrified—both emotions are pretty strong.

You head out with Lars and begin digging the hole, each of you taking a turn with the shovel. No one even mentions the fact that your scoops of frozen earth are barely making a dent. They all seem to accept you—and your weak, human-sized arms—for what you are.

It would be reassuring if Mom weren't smiling at you over everyone's shoulders, pointing at the diamond ring on her finger, mouthing, *You can give it to Lindsi.*

On the one hand, it's nice to be included.

On the other hand, you're terrified to think what Mom will do to you if you tell her you saw this relationship as more of a casual thing…

The End.

Well, you've managed to make a complete hash of your fictional life. Are you proud of yourself?

But for all the endings in this book, this isn't the end for Choose Your Own Misery. Save up your booze money and keep your eyes peeled for the next installment in the Choose Your Own Misery series, coming soon to wherever books (and maybe booze) are sold.

In the meantime, keep mainlining misery straight into your eyeballs by following the authors online:

Follow Mike on Twitter **@theonald**
Follow Jilly on Twitter **@jillygagnon**

Get new, horrible adventures and updates sent straight to your inbox by signing up for the newsletter:
www.chooseyourownmisery.com

Like the Facebook page:
www.facebook.com/ChooseYourOwnMisery

And be sure to follow Diversion Books, which apparently decided that publishing this book was a good idea:

Follow on Twitter **@DiversionBooks**
Like the Facebook page:
www.facebook.com/DiversionBooks
Sign up for the Diversion newsletter:
www.diversionbooks.com/newsletter

Hope to do this all again real soon...

CPSIA information can be obtained
at www.ICGtesting.com
Printed in the USA
BVOW06s1041201216
471347BV00001B/1/P